A Lifetime of Afters

A Lifetime of Afters

Sage Ridge

Book 1

Devin Sloane

Table of Contents

Playlist

Leah Nobel - Not Ready to Say Goodbye

Dash Berlin – Better Half of Me

SVRCINA – Island

Freya Ridings – Blackout

NF - Paralyzed

Declan J Donovan - Numb

NF/Britt Nicole – Can You Hold Me

Elina - Here With Me

Dangerkids – Invincible Summer

Phil Wickham – It's Always Been You

Lady A - Ocean

Jasmine Thompson - Like I'm Gonna Lose You

James Arthur - Falling Like the Stars

Apollo - DNA

Caleb Hearn - It's Always Been You

https://open.spotify.com/playlist/1kCRl2pitJwbrTKOZa
Dsxq?si=9937e7ac29ba47a1

Sage Ridge

Hailey's Falls

Downtown Sage Ridge

Silver Lake

Wildflower Bluffs

The Beaver Dam

BAR

Little River

Crystal Beach

Carousel Island

Hope Harbour

Hawk's Place

Dedication

This one is for Crystal Kaiser and my entire ARC team who participated in this book like it was a Choose Your Own Adventure!

You're golden.

Chapter 1 - Goodbye

Camouflage eyes that reflected every color of the forest but hid his every thought locked steadily onto mine.

So.

This was it.

The sounds of the park that kept me company while I waited for him, the dogs barking, children squealing, parents and grandparents calling out encouragement interspersed with sharp warnings to be careful, receded into the background as I stared back at him.

Only yesterday I'd entertained the thought of bringing him home to meet my family.

No longer able to bear the weight of his scrutiny, I dropped my chin to focus on the rough wooden boards of the picnic table spanning the growing distance between us.

Out of the corner of my eye, I saw his big body momentarily shift toward me only to retreat abruptly. I watched as he stuffed his hands into his pockets. Hands that only yesterday would have reached out to hold me.

My heart recoiled as the sharp barb of loss pierced me. I sucked in a deep breath and pushed the pain back out. I didn't blame him. I couldn't. He didn't mean any more to me than I meant to him.

But I'd hoped we could be more.

"I understand," I uttered through wooden lips. "That special something that we should feel in our guts just isn't there."

Was that true?

The tension in his wide shoulders eased as his rumbly voice extended an olive branch. "We'll part as friends."

Pain twisted my guts, and my lips pressed together into a thin line. He was more than a friend. He was my companion. My lover. My *friend*. He was hope.

But he was not mine. He was never mine just as I was never his.

If you had given yourself to him, it could have been different.

I knew that, but I didn't think I was capable of giving myself to anyone.

Tears of disappointment prickled behind my eyes. I blinked them back quickly and offered him a small smile. "No, it's too late for that, but we don't part as enemies," I promised. "I'll remember you as the one who healed what was broken. And showed me how high to raise the bar."

For a moment I stared off into the trees as if they held the answers. *Why was I never the one? And, why, oh why, did it always come back to HIM?*

The wind picked up and tossed my long hair around as if it knew I needed to shake off those thoughts.

Turning back to Barrett, I took him in one last time, his severe features dear to me though perhaps not loved. Even so, my fingers ached to touch him one last time.

A goodbye.

I stood and circled the end of the table. With my palms cradling his wild beard, I pressed my dry lips to his immobile ones briefly before releasing him and stepping away.

"Good luck, Barrett. I sincerely hope you get what you deserve," I whispered, the only sound that could make it past the lump lodged in my throat.

The groove in his forehead deepened, and I could not help but laugh. "Don't think too hard, I'll rephrase. I hope you feel it in your gut next time and that she feels the same. I wish you every happiness." I paused to read his face. "Better?"

"Thank you." He gave me a rare grin. "You deserve nothing less. I hope you don't settle next time."

I felt my lips melt into the smile time spent with him never failed to elicit. "I have no regrets. You were exactly what I needed."

Walking away, the sounds of the park reentered my consciousness. Sundays at the park were always busy. I should have known something was up when he asked me to meet him here rather than our usual routine.

One fat, hot, tear stung my cheek. The only one I would allow.

As my long legs ate up the distance, carrying me away from him and bringing me steadily closer to my townhome, I did not look back.

I never looked back.

Chapter 2 – Infinite

I lay back on the couch, where I had a perfect view out the window, and I watched the near-naked branches of the trees dance and wave against a colorless sky.

Twelve weeks A.B. (After Barrett), I finally felt like myself again. A little too much like me.

As a child, I did not make friends easily. The situation worsened in my teens. For a brief spell in my twenties, I lived it up, but that was a knee-jerk reaction to the pain of rejection. And now I found myself almost completely alone for the first time in my life.

Five hours of driving separated me from my family and my best friend since childhood. My only friends here, if I could even call them that, were the few colleagues I occasionally had drinks with on a Thursday night.

No boyfriend.

No best friend.

No girl posse.

I'd been in Bridgewater for well over two years, so I'd had time to make connections and lay down some roots. But, just like the town before, and the town before that, I didn't.

Bruce kneaded his dainty paws into my thigh as if he could read my thoughts and blinked at me expectantly.

"I know I have you, my handsome little boy."

Bruce, a faded, scrappy, dilute calico of indeterminate age, joined my tiny household a little over a year ago. We'd been good for each other. Well, he'd been good for me, my catspeak needed improving.

I retrieved the faded satin ribbon I'd carried with me since I left home from beneath him, running the tips of my fingers over his tiny head to distract him as I rescued it. Frayed and faded from my twirling fingers, it would not hold up for long under his sharp claws.

My voice sounded loud in the quiet of the room. It struck me that I hadn't heard any voice other than mine since Friday afternoon. Okay, it was damp and cold outside, but even so, I'd reached a new level of isolation.

Bruce turned his little head and nuzzled into my palm, then unabashedly unsheathed his claws into the tender flesh of my thigh.

"Ouch!" I gasped.

He leaped off my lap and streaked across the floor like his butt caught fire.

"What is wrong with you?" I grumbled. "I'm showing you love! Affection!" I lifted my long skirt to check the damage. One solitary drop of blood beaded on my thigh. Only one this time.

"I suppose this is an improvement," I nodded to my thigh while I continued to address him where he sat watching from across the room. "I pulled you out of that dumpster. Remember? I got my *hands* dirty! A little respect is due at the very least, little man," I reprimanded.

He stared back at me from his one good eye, dropped his lid in a slow blink, then lifted his front paw to lick his patchy fur back into submission.

I crossed my arms over my knees and sighed. "You're a misfit just like me."

Bruce and I had a little too much in common lately. He'd been rejected and left out in the cold. By the time I found him, the infection had destroyed his eye. Which is how I met Barrett, a veterinarian who patched him up and fixed his eye the only way he could.

"You know I thought you were my good luck charm for a little while there," I mused, licking the tip of my finger and pressing it over the tiny cut.

Perhaps it was time to move on, I mused, weaving the long strip of silk between my fingers. Working in the hotel industry offered me countless opportunities to uproot pretty well any time I wanted.

Not that there was much to uproot. Looking around the kitchen and family room of my rental, there was not one thing that made it feel anything more than a temporary stop.

It was unfortunate in one sense because instead of waiting for a job opportunity that would allow me to move up into a higher-paying position, the constant moves at my request landed me in lateral positions over and over.

And I was bored.

I lay my head back on the couch.

Even the furniture came with the unit.

"If I give my notice now," I mused to Bruce, "we could be gone by Hallowe'en. What do you think?"

Memories of past Hallowe'ens crowded my brain. Usually, I didn't like to look back, but I felt my lips tipping up in a smile.

Our mothers trained us well. Since we were babies, they'd planned our costumes. The first year, there were only two of us. My brother Max and *him*. My mother turned their strollers into pumpkin patches and Lou turned them into pumpkins.

Every year thereafter the costumes became more complicated. Especially as the rest of us came along. Planning began in April most years. We did Scooby Doo, Narnia, and Harry Potter as our numbers allowed.

The year we did Angry Birds things turned violent and required a quick costume change. Hawkley and his younger brother Hunter had to be put on the same side, so they'd stop crashing into one another.

I laughed out loud as more memories tumbled in. The snow globe disaster. That costume lasted all of 30 minutes before we returned home demanding to change into the previous year's costumes.

Hawkley and Hunter's younger sister Harley, my best friend to this day, and I took over the planning in our teens. Our moms were pissed until we promised to let them help. My lips stretched into a wide, tremulous smile. Of course, they took over, but at least we got to choose the themes.

The sewing for Teenage Mutant Ninja Turtles kept them busy for months.

And of course, the boys argued over who got to be Shredder. Hawk's height secured it for him in the end.

The five of us were inseparable.

My smile faded.

Until we weren't.

I picked at the frayed edges of my ribbon. Looking back on good memories tended to resurrect the bad. The old sadness threatened to pull me under, but I swam under it and carried on.

Because memories of Sage Ridge were mostly sweet. The winters were brutal, but because of the Sage Ridge Resort, which Harley's family owned, we spent them skiing and snowboarding on the mountain or snowmobiling through the woods. Summers on Silver Lake, climbing the bluffs, and fishing in Little River were arguably better.

Four neighborhoods made up the town of Sage Ridge. Harley and her family lived in Hailey's Falls, within a few minutes walk to the resort they owned.

Like it was yesterday, I remembered going to the store with the boys to buy spray paint to change the i to an r on the sign, turning it into Harley's Falls. We caught hell for that stunt.

My eyes crinkled with happiness.

South of Hailey's Falls lay downtown. I hadn't been there in years. Anytime I visited my family, I stayed as close to home as possible. I never stayed long enough to shop anyways.

I missed those stores. Had they changed in the past ten years? Did Novel-Tea still host a book exchange? I missed meeting up with Harley at The Beanery. Did Anita still rule the roost at Mary Lou's candy shop? Mmm, Krippy's Chippy.

My mouth watered. I could go for some fish and chips.

South of downtown and divided by the river lay the neighborhoods of Little River and Crystal Beach, named for the river and beach they bordered.

I grew up in Crystal Beach. Crystal Beach and Wildflower Bluffs were my playgrounds, my running shoes filled with sand, my socks carting burrs. The footbridge that separated Crystal Beach from Hope Harbor led to Carousel Island. I could not begin to count the number of times I crossed over it after hours to sit on the painted ponies and dream.

Home.

I could go home again.

Where I was loved.

My mouth twisted wryly. Even if it wouldn't ever be by *him*.

Standing, I crossed to my furry frenemy and scooped him up. "Let's not be too hasty, hm? Might just be time to bite the bullet and grow up a bit. See if I can't shake things up a bit at work and get a promotion. Get back on dating apps. Join a," I swallowed then spat out the offensive word, "*club* of some sort."

Bruce's tiny paw batted a lock of my long hair.

I cuddled him close. "You're right. I'm not much of a joiner, but Mr. Willis, I need to do something."

Carrying him into my bedroom, I resolutely tucked the ribbon back into my jewelry box and climbed into bed. My furry frenemy curled into a ball on my chest. His nightly ploy to lull me into complacency. Sometime during the night, he'd move to my head, and I'd wake with a mouthful of cat tail.

I slowly pulled the covers up to my chin, careful not to provoke an attack, and drifted off to sleep with my newfound commitment to apply myself at work.

Morning arrived with a healthy slice of irony when I, along with a dozen other people, were laid off effective November 1st.

After the meeting, I sat at my desk twirling a long curl around my finger. My thoughts banged around in my head like drunken frat boys. I'd never lost a job before, but I wouldn't miss it. I should be excited. Usually, I reveled in packing up and moving on, but I did not feel that same sense of restlessness that usually spurred my moves.

April, one of the girls I ate lunch with, plopped down in the chair opposite my desk. My favorite of all of them. Always smiling, upbeat, and quirky...she played Pokemon Go for frig's sake!

She looked at me expectantly. "So?"

My eyes widened. I leaned toward her, searching her face for clues about what she wanted from me. "What?"

She scoffed. "What?" she mimicked then threw her hands wide impatiently. "What are you going to do?"

I shrugged and relaxed back in my chair. "I don't know."

She harrumphed loudly and sat back in her chair.

"What are you going to do?" I asked curiously.

She tilted her head and studied me. "You know that's the first time you've ever asked me something personal about myself or my plans?"

I drew back. "No... that's not possible."

She waved me away. "I'm not saying you're not caring. You are. When I was sick, you organized the casserole brigade. You brought me treats every morning when I was struggling with leaving the baby." She paused and stared into space before continuing softly. "You are infinitely caring, but you hold yourself back." Turning back to face me, she went on. "You're so very careful to not get personally involved. You never share anything personal. Not once in the past three years have you accepted an invitation to visit. Not from me, not from any of the girls."

I swallowed. The fear of having offended her clawed at my throat.

She stretched her hand across my desk and lay her palm over my madly twirling fingers. "I'm not criticizing you. I don't know what happened to you to make you draw into yourself the way you do, but I want to let you in on a little secret."

Stripped raw, my walls vapor, I stared back at her.

Her eyes watered. She squeezed my hand and whispered fiercely, "*You are infinite*. Your ability to give love and receive love, it is *infinite*. I hate to see you alone. You're far too beautiful, inside and out."

Closing my eyes, I momentarily shuttered my pain to gather myself. Twice I opened my mouth to respond.

Twice I snapped it shut.

My eyes were still closed when I felt the brush of her lips across my forehead. "I'll miss you, Noelle." Pressing her forehead to mine, she snickered. "Now you have to join Pokemon Go so we can still be friends."

I barked out a watery laugh.

She patted my hand and turned to leave before stopping abruptly. "In answer to your question, I'm going to stay home with my boys for a while. Maybe I'll finally enroll in that photography course I've always wanted to take." She smiled. "It's not a bad thing to revisit the dreams of the past now and then. Perhaps now is the right time."

Perhaps now is the right time.

November 1st.

I'd miss Hallowe'en but it might be better this way.

Less painful.

Looked like I was going home after al

Chapter 3 - Welcome Home

Unbelievable.

No matter which weather app I looked at, they all reported 8-10 inches of snow between now and tomorrow morning. My lips twisted wryly. In retrospect, saving one month's rent and moving out on October 31st did not represent my best planning.

I looked at my watch. If I left right now, I'd be home by 1:00 a.m. By the time the landlord came to pick up the keys, it would be closer to 2:00 a.m. I was getting off to a late start but at least I wouldn't be driving when the trick-or-treaters were out in full force.

8-10 inches before morning was a considerable amount of snow to drive through but it couldn't be helped. If I booked myself into a hotel, I'd have to smuggle Bruce in and risk getting kicked out. Also, I didn't fancy leaving all my worldly goods parked outside in my car overnight. Especially my beautiful shoes.

I leaned against the kitchen counter twirling my car keys around my finger. No one from home knew exactly when I planned to arrive. I'd done that on purpose, needing an out in case I changed my mind. I brightened. This worked in my favor. When my dad knew I was driving, he worried. No matter that I'd lived on my own for the past ten years. This way I could just call him from his driveway when I got there and tell him to open the door.

I paced back and forth checking my watch.

I'd already run out to the car and dug through my suitcases to exchange my artfully ripped jeans and funky sweater for cozy fleece. I'd been to the bathroom four times. Just in case. I'd checked the apartment from tip to toe.

It was sad really, how little space everything took up in my little car. Two suitcases, one of which was entirely shoes. My hiking boots. Laptop. A couple of boxes of books. The type I used to hide under the bed. A few framed pictures. My jewelry box which held precious little.

And Bruce's temporary lodgings.

There was nothing left for me to do but wait.

I could put the key on the counter and leave but I'd been burned before. One of my landlords tried to claim damages. I'd never left a key again after that.

Bruce wound around my legs.

"You ready for an adventure, buddy?" I rubbed the top of my foot against his furry chest.

He butted my arch with his little head, rubbed his scrawny body along the side of my foot, then turned and nipped my big toe.

"Ow! Shit! Bruce!" I snatched my foot away from him as he dashed off hell-bent for leather. "Why do you do that?" I exclaimed.

He winked at me slowly.

"You're so obnoxious," I grumbled. "I hope you like the set-up I made for you in the car, Mr. Willis. It won't be up to your usual standards, but it's the best I could do. It's going to be a long drive and I need you to behave."

One bright green eye studied me. "You'd totally eat me if I died, wouldn't you?" I scooped him up and scratched him under his chin. "Could you at least wait until I'm dead? Hm? No snacking beforehand?"

The doorbell interrupted my one-sided conversation. I never imagined I'd be a crazy cat lady, but I had to admit my conversations with Bruce bordered on the insane.

Leaving my townhome for the last time, I allowed myself a moment to remember the good times I'd shared there with Barrett. I missed him. I could admit that now. Then I got into my car and began my journey home.

Five hours later, I'd made it little more than halfway.

Twice I'd been forced to pull over. Once to wait out a particularly bad white-out and the other to clean Bruce's litter box. The first half of the car trip wreaked havoc with his tiny bowels. And my nose.

I peered at myself in the rearview mirror. Wadded-up tissue blocked both nostrils, my solution to his eye-watering farts. Zero visibility on the roads made driving horrendous but at least it hid my insane predicament. After I cleaned him and his litter box, I gave him the sedative and he slept. Right through his arse's regularly released, potently noxious, thought balloons.

Breathing through my mouth, the stress of driving under these conditions, and the blast of air from the heater dried out my throat.

Did farts have particles? Was I ingesting fart particles? Could a person get a lung disease from inhaling cat fart particles? Was that a thing?

I took a swig from my water bottle and crawled along, my knuckles white on the steering wheel. Ahead of me stretched a winding ribbon of flashing hazard lights. A sad parade.

I wondered who headed up of the line. Did they know where they were going? One thing was a certainty: If they went off the road, we were all going.

Every motel along the highway boasted no vacancy, and I thanked God, repeatedly, for the gas stations that peppered the route home. The pile on the passenger seat beside me grew with each stop. Emergency blankets, water, and snacks.

Lots of snacks.

I'd been so grateful for the first one. That coffee I downed in the first fifteen minutes ran through me like Niagara Falls. The bathroom left much to be desired, and I'd ended up peeing in that same coffee cup. Growing up in the country, we roamed the hills, and I learned I could precision pee into the neck of an apple juice bottle when need be.

The line drew to a stop. I let go of the wheel and shook out my hands, flexing the stiffness from my joints. Rolling my neck. Forcing my shoulders down from around my ears.

I would be sore tomorrow. Well, later today. At this rate, I wouldn't make it home until breakfast.

Needing sleep but knowing it wasn't an option, I continued on, the bright white of the snow, the reflection of the headlights, and lack of sleep doing a number on my eyes.

Finally, I reached the outskirts of town and pulled over. Somewhere, I'd read the statistic that most car accidents occurred within a mile of home.

It wouldn't be the first time.

My eyelids weighed heavily as I fought to keep them open. My head nodded forward, my chin nearly hitting my chest before it shot back up. I needed ten minutes, just ten minutes to close my eyes and then I could make it home. It's not like I could see even two feet in front of me anyway. At that last turnoff, me, myself, and I were the only ones going to Sage Ridge.

I blasted the heat while I pulled over. Just a few minutes and then I'd continue on.

Frantic shouting and aggressive banging on my window woke me from my stupor. Bruce lay curled up on my chest, my nose tissues shredded between his tiny paws. Oh, God, the smell. I blinked my bleary eyes. Where the hell was I?

A blanket of snow shrouded every window save the one Hawkley presently pounded on.

Was that Hawkley staring at me through my window? He looked furious. Did Max beat him at Mario Brothers again?

Was this a dream?

"Noelle, open the damn door for fuck's sake!"

No, not a dream. He never spoke to me like that in my dreams.

I rolled my window down. "Hawkley? What are you doing here?"

He gaped, then his eyebrows crashed down over his stormy eyes, and he scowled. "Me? What the fuck are you doing here?"

"I was heading home..." I trailed off. How did I get here?

The storm had ended, and the world lay blanketed in white. Silent. Sparkling.

New.

He leaned in the window toward me then recoiled, his mouth twisted into a grimace. "What the fuck? Did you shit yourself?"

"What? No!" I sucked in a deeply mortified breath, at which time the true extent of Bruce's unsavory condition made itself known to my olfactory system.

I gagged and covered my nose. "It's Bruce. The car ride didn't agree with him."

"That still doesn't explain what you're doing at the bottom of my driveway," he barked. If possible, his face darkened further with anger. "And who the fuck is Bruce?"

My lagging brain struggled to process information that seemed too fantastical to be real. These things only happened in romance novels.

Instead of answering him, I clarified, "This is your driveway?"

His mouth gaped open again. "You don't even know where you are?"

Beginning to fully wake, I took him in where he stood a safe three feet back from the fumes. Beanie pulled low over his ears, his beard wild, a thick, fleecy lumber jacket worn over jeans that did all kinds of good things for his long legs that drew my eyes steadily down to his sturdy work boots.

Combined with his angry scowl, he looked like a slightly feral mountain man and my neglected lady parts wanted to climb him.

I brought my eyes back to his to catch him staring at me incredulously. "Are you checking me out?"

That tiny shrapnel of humiliation supplied the brisk mental shake I required, and I snapped at him. "Close your mouth. You look like a mutant guppy."

His jaw slammed shut.

"I didn't know this was your driveway." My voice seemed to echo across the snow. "I've been driving all night. I needed a break, so I pulled over. I didn't think I'd sleep this long. So sorry to disturb you. Believe me when I tell you, I wish I'd picked another driveway. Any other driveway rather than yours."

He smirked. "The only other driveway on this stretch is Mrs. McGillivray's. You remember Mrs. McGillivray? She still makes homemade yogurt on the kitchen counter, the old-fashioned way. Can you even imagine the smell of sour milk mixed in with you and that fleabag?"

Half mad, half trying not to laugh, I opted for sass. "Probably still would have been preferable to you and your dramatics." I grasped the window crank to block him out and turned the key in the ignition.

Nothing happened.

He stepped back and crossed his arms over his wide chest, face smug. He never could hide his feelings.

I attempted to turn the engine over again only to hear the telltale click of a dead battery.

I dropped my head in defeat. I was tired. I smelled like shit. And I was cold. So damn cold. I slept far longer than I should have. The truth, which shook me, was that I was lucky he found me when he did.

I sighed. "Can you please give me a boost?"

"No." He turned and stomped away.

I screamed in frustration. "Are you fucking kidding me? You can't be serious?"

He spun around and stalked back, his finger in my face. "Potty mouth!"

I laughed. How many times his mother had reprimanded him the same way. "It's warranted!"

Instead of smiling back at me, his lips flattened grimly.

He really did not want me here.

I tipped my chin down, giving myself a private moment to absorb the pain before locating my purse and phoning my dad to come and get me.

His next words stopped me cold.

"I'm getting my truck to tow you up to the house. The roads are closed. You're not going anywhere," he stated grimly. "Welcome home, Noelle.

Chapter 4 – Impassable

I watched him walk away, grumbling, "That's not much of a welcome."

For years I'd successfully limited my contact with him to a mere few minutes here and there. Even that much only after his divorce. Most times I visited, I managed to avoid him altogether. Staying with him at his house, where he most definitely did not want me, stung more than I wanted to admit.

Would I ever be over this foolishness?

Bruce stood up on my chest, arching his back. His tail swished back and forth over my face. Something dry and crusty and decidedly smelly brushed across my cheek.

I gagged and grabbed new tissues to wipe my face and block my nose. The thought of ingesting cat fart particles through my mouth flitted through my mind but I dismissed it.

"If I die, I die," I stated resolutely. "Bruce, you have not lived up to your name during this journey and I feel you and I are not going to be friends today." I scooped him under his belly and spun him around to assess the damage.

Pleasantly surprised to find the mess contained to only one leg and his tail, I cleaned him up with a few wet wipes that had joined the supplies on my passenger seat somewhere around hour four. Pulling the larger turds away, I earned myself several indignant 'meows' and a bat of his tiny paw. No claws. Perhaps we'd be friends after all. I twisted around to see the damage in the back and screwed up my face.

Perhaps not.

A violent shiver raced down my spine just as Hawk's truck came into view. I hoped he had a big-ass fireplace up at his house. And I hoped it housed a roaring hot fire.

As he pulled to a stop, I moved to get out of my car.

"Nope," he held up a hand. "You and that cat are not getting into my truck until you smell better."

My mouth dropped open. "We don't smell bad! The car smells bad!"

He smirked, "Oh, I know." He drew an imaginary circle around his face. "I see your homemade filtration system. It's a good look on you. And believe me when I tell you, you smell like you've been marinating in shit."

The tissues. Ugh. I pulled them from my nose only to be assailed by the frozen air. "Mean!" I pointed at him.

He laughed and spread his hands wide. "What? You think you can sit in the car with him for all those hours and not have that smell in your clothes? *In your hair*?" he stressed.

I gasped. He knew my hair was my pride and joy. Long, lush, slightly wavy, the ends curved in the most arresting ways, lending my twitchy fingers the very best of fidgets.

My hands flew to my head. "No!"

He grimaced as he came closer and took a whiff. "Yes." Spinning he headed back to his truck, tossing orders over his shoulder, "Get in your car."

His broad shoulders rocked as he stalked away. Dark curls snuck out beneath his beanie. Worn jeans stretched across thick thighs.

He'd changed since the last time I'd seen him. Not all those changes were good, but physically, he was even more of a powerhouse.

My head tipped to the side.

What was it about the way men moved that so fascinated me? This particular man's walk made me want to spread my thighs. Filled me with the sudden urge to fall to my knees. A picture of us flashed in my brain. My palms braced against the hard length of his thighs, the hair crisp beneath my palms. His hands in my hair, hips flexing…

"Stop daydreaming, Noelle, and get in the damn car! It's freezing out here and no matter how bad you smell I've gotta get you up to the house and get you warm."

I snapped out of my lust-induced haze in time to see his back as he continued away from me. Gah! The man infuriated me. I dropped to my haunches and made three snowballs in quick succession. Back in the day, they called me 'the sniper'. It had been awhile, but I hoped I hadn't lost my touch.

The first struck him in the middle of his back.

He jerked to a stop, an actual growl reverberating from his chest.

I hummed with satisfaction.

The second hit the back of his neck. I stood with my arm cocked back, poised, ready.

He slowly turned around to face me.

I imagined him gathering his temper and laughed softly to myself in anticipation as I let go and hit him square in the face. "Bullseye," I whispered.

He roared as he swiped the snow from his cheeks and barreled toward me. "Noelle, what the hell do you think you're doing? I'm going to toss that round arse into the snow!"

Pressing my lips together primly, I forced a serene expression onto my face though I felt anything but. Fire raged and ice burned as a maelstrom of adrenalin ripped through me. Sadness, loneliness. The pain of rejection. The bittersweet of homecoming. People who should have still been there but weren't. Unrequited love.

I'd never felt so alive.

"Your mama's not here to correct your manners so I took matters into my own hands." I brushed the snow from my hands and held them up to illustrate my point.

Grabbing them in both of his, he yelled. "These hands, Noelle? These near frost-bitten hands? Fuck me, but is there a single, solitary thought left in your head?" Transferring both my hands to one of his, he unzipped his coat and shoved my fingers under his armpits.

I wiggled my fingers and laughed. "What are you doing?"

"You need to get into your goddamn car so I can get you up to the house," he growled.

With my hands locked under his arms, I searched his eyes. Eyes I'd known my entire life. Eyes that used to smile into mine. Eyes that filled with sorrow and regret as he turned me away.

Eyes that now sparked with fury and impatience.

Where was the Hawk I once knew? The one who would have tossed me over his shoulder before tossing me into the nearest snowbank?

Too many years had passed, and he was obviously not the same man. Another loss.

I sniffed, mortified to feel the icy kiss of a tear on my cheek, and attempted to tug my hands away.

His chest heaved with a sigh. "Noelle... I'm sorry... Seeing you out here asleep in your car in the freezing cold... it did a number on me."

Sudden and aching chagrin consumed me. Of course. "I'm so sorry, Hawk," I murmured.

He dropped his head to look at the ground. "Let's get you up to the house." He drew my hands out from under his arms and led me to his truck.

"I thought I wasn't allowed in the truck," I teased hesitantly.

He side-eyed me, a small smile threatening his beautiful mouth. "Don't remind me."

Retrieving Bruce, he carried him like a football and handed him to me so we could warm up in the truck while he hooked up the car. Up at the house, he ushered me inside before going back for my bags.

So caught up in the thrill of his proximity in the close confines of the cab, I'd barely taken a glance at the outside of his house. The inside, however, would not be ignored.

Rich wood, solid pine beams, a wall of windows along the back and one entire side overlooking miles and miles of open space.

Breathtaking.

Large couches and ample chairs the perfect size for his big body beckoned. And the fireplace. Gah! Wood-burning and still smoldering.

I headed straight for it and held my hands out to the heat. It stung as I flexed my fingers and shook them to dispel the discomfort.

Instead of feeling warmer, I began to shiver in earnest. The cold I'd barely noticed while the adrenalin pumped through me began to make itself known as it seeped into my bones.

The front door slammed shut but I ignored it, intent on getting as close to the heat as I could.

A heavy blanket dropped on my shoulders. "I'll build up the fire and then we'll get you into the bath to warm you up."

I nodded. Having lived up here most of my life, I knew the drill.

"Let me see your hands?"

"They're okay," I assured him.

"Noelle," he reprimanded. "I want to see for myself."

I opened my mouth to deny him when he continued, softer now, "I need to see for myself."

I gave him my hands. As the oldest of the five of us, well, the four of us now, he was well used to taking care of all of us.

And we were well used to following his lead.

He gently examined each finger. His beautiful face tipped down in concentration, his mouth pursed in disapproval. I could still read his expressions as easily as I knew my own.

"We can take care of this at home," he finally decided. "And good thing too because the roads are impassable. What were you thinking?"

Pushing me back toward the chair, he dropped to his knees and began to remove my boots.

I hissed in a breath, and he looked at me sharply, growling my name.

"I'm sure it's fine!" I quickly reassured him as he gave my feet and toes the same attention he gave my hands before stuffing them into his groin.

I froze, exclaiming, "What are you doing?"

His mouth quirked, the first hint of the boy I knew. "Not getting off on your icy toes, that's for sure."

Chapter 5 – Cold

I'm so cold.

Too cold to get out, too cold to stay in the now tepid water of the bath. The only thing that burned was the knowledge that this bathroom was designed with a woman in mind.

Deep, clawfoot tub. Rainfall shower. His and hers sinks.

The thought of her choosing all of this while planning a life with him poked at a wound that had never closed. Even the fact that they divorced years ago didn't change the fact that he chose her.

And rejected me.

My eyelids drifted shut. I braced my feet on the end of the tub to ensure I didn't slip under the water. My head was cold, but my hair smelled wonderful.

This is what he smells like. I closed my eyes, breathing deep, filling my lungs and my belly with him.

A sharp knock on the door elicited a scream from me and a chuckle from him. "Get out of the tub, lazy arse!"

"In a minute," I replied sluggishly.

"Noelle, if you're not out here in 30 seconds, I'm coming in," he warned. "You can't sleep in there."

"I know that!" Of course, I knew that. It didn't stop my eyes from closing again. My chin hit my chest.

"One, two..."

My head snapped up at the very idea of him bursting into the bathroom and seeing my naked body. It might help my cause. I smiled drowsily as I cupped my breasts, contemplating the possibilities. These babies were fantastic.

I held one leg up out of the water. Long and shapely. Nothing to sneeze at. The cool air forced it back under the water.

Nevertheless, they were not for him.

"Stop! You're being ridiculous!"

What crazy twist of fate led me to the bottom of his driveway? Any other driveway would have been better than this bittersweet torture.

"Six, seven..." He continued doggedly.

"For fuck's sake!" I roared pushing myself up to a sitting position.

"Potty mouth!" He laughed! "Nine, ten, eleven..."

So much of my childhood, indeed my life, intertwined with his. Shared memories, shared inside jokes, shared pain. I didn't need to cause him any more by having him worry.

I pushed up out of the water and stepped out. Immediately, I curled into myself as violent shudders wracked my body.

"Oh no, oh gosh…"

"What is it?" He rattled the doorknob.

"Just cold," I responded, my teeth clicking and chattering like an angry chipmunk.

"Open the door, Noelle," he cajoled softly. "Let me help you."

Now he wants to help me. I smirked. His mother would have his head and serve it to me on a silver platter if she witnessed his 'welcome'.

"Hang on." I quickly wrapped the bath towel around my torso, crossing the ends high over my breasts, unwilling to share even a peek. I flicked open the lock.

For a moment, I saw the Hawkley I knew, and loved, from my youth, but it was short-lived.

Fierce, dark brows lowered ominously as his eyes ran over my shaking form. "You're cold."

"Uh, yeah." I tried for sarcasm but had to settle for pathetic. I trembled from head to toe, and my teeth chattered so hard I imagined bits of enamel flying out of my mouth.

He stepped toward me abruptly and yanked me into his chest.

I froze at the contact, my eyes blowing wide.

"Fuck, Noelle," he whispered then took a deep breath and released me. "I'm going to get you a pair of my flannels and put you into bed."

Greedily, my eyes took in the master bedroom. Pure masculinity. Functional. Large. Warm. Comforting. The heavy wooden bedframe hosted a traditional buffalo plaid duvet so thick it threatened to swallow me whole.

How I imagined sleeping under something like that with him. Laughing and loving between the sheets. Someday adding children into the mix.

My chin fell to my chest. My walls wobbled. I mentally shook myself. I needed to get warm, get rest, and get the hell out of there.

I prayed his spare bed boasted a similar duvet. The bath had not eased the cold in my bones, and I didn't foresee ever being warm again. Turning to the door, I moved to seek out the guest room. I could forego the flannel if I could just get under the covers.

"Where are you going?" he asked sharply.

Irritation at his tone warred with fatigue and sorrow over my predicament.

Irritation won.

Looking over my shoulder, I pinned him with my gaze and replied tightly. "I'm going to the guest bedroom. After I get dressed, I'll get Bruce and bring him in with me and get us both out of your hair until we can go home tomorrow."

His breath came out in a sigh that deepened into a growl of my name. "Noelle. There are no guest bedrooms. Just empty bedrooms. You're sleeping in my bed. I'm sleeping on the couch. And I'll get your damn cat and settle him after you're warmed up."

With that, he tossed a pair of his pajamas on the bed and stalked out the door.

Pushing my arms into the long sleeves of his shirt enabled me to drop the damp towel. My shaking limbs barely managed to pull on the pants. The buttons on the shirt were well beyond the capabilities of my unsteady fingers.

There was no help for it but to climb into the bed. In any case, I wouldn't see him until morning.

Over and over, I assured myself I'd be warm soon. But as the minutes passed, the bed fairly vibrated with the quakes overtaking my body.

"You're still cold."

"I'll be okay. Just going to take time."

"You need skin-to-skin," he stated.

"I'm not stripping naked, Hawkley," I retorted.

I could hear the grin in his voice when he replied, "I've seen you naked plenty of times."

I peeked at him over the covers and snorted. "Not since I got breasts."

He grinned and held up a finger. "Once. Once, after you got breasts, I saw you naked."

"What? When?"

I had amazing breasts. In fact, on par with my hair, they were my best feature. If he'd seen my breasts and still had no interest, he'd never want me.

The reminder of his rejection, in addition to all I'd lost over the previous months, cracked the shell holding my tender heart together.

Silent tears.

Tired tears.

Hopeless tears.

I didn't even try to hide my face. The shame of his rejection, complete.

"Fuck." Hawk wrapped his arms around me and pulled me out from under the covers. Softly, his voice as sweet as it was commanding, he gruffed, "I'm sorry, Noelle. I'm an asshole. Please. Work with me here. Strip down and climb into bed. I promise not to speak. I'll just cuddle you until you stop shaking."

To be held. It had been months. But to be held by him? Could I take it? Knowing it was a one off?

How could I not?

"You can't make any faces either," I warned.

"You could maybe just not look at me?" he inquired hopefully.

I scowled and moved to pull away.

He chuckled and pulled me back to him, his large palm smoothing down the length of my spine. "I take it back. No faces."

Five minutes later, I lay naked and stiff as a board in his arms.

He crossed my arms over my breasts then wrapped his big arms around my torso. Aligning his body behind me, the hair on his thighs bristling against the back of mine, his wide chest sheltered me. The heat from his body began to leach into mine.

Shallow breaths kept my body still, unmoving. I shuddered in his arms, the hollow ache of the cold, the agony of his body, finally, next to mine, but for none of the right reasons.

Another tear squeezed past my tightly closed lids.

Jostling me lightly, he softly admonished, "Relax. It's just me. I've got you."

God, how I wished he had me.

He spoke to me softly, reminiscing about our shared childhood, carefully steering the conversation around the landmines that dotted our shared landscape.

Slowly, the quaking eased, and the warmth of his touch filled me to the marrow of my bones. My breathing grew deep and even.

Quiet now, only his thumb moved in a gentle caress over my arm.

Floating in that neverland between asleep and awake, I imagined his lips moved in my hair.

A whisper of a breath.

A dream of a dream.

"I've got you, Noelle. Sleep."

Chapter 6 - The Frivolity of Hope

Nothing could ever be better than waking with his beard tucked into my neck. His big palm kneaded my naked breast while his hips flexed against my ass, rocking his erection along my sensitive crevice.

Rosy light from the sunset warmed the room. We'd slept the whole day away.

I pressed my hips back into his groin, earning a big hand wrapped around my hip, dragging me further into him.

Soft lips trailed down the length of my neck. The first time they'd ever touched me. At the juncture of my shoulder, he latched on, teeth grazing, tongue laving.

"Hawk," I gasped out his name.

"Mm," he hummed against my neck, the vibration sending shockwaves straight to my clit.

His thumb strummed my aching nipple. I arched further and tucked my head back against his shoulder.

The hand at my hip circled around to my stomach and delved down, his long fingers seeking my core.

Lungs seizing, tummy quivering under his touch, I opened to allow him access to the heart of me, the heat of me.

His long fingers skimmed over my curls and covered my mound.

"Hawk," I breathed, unable to believe what was finally happening. Even knowing it might mean less than nothing to him, I found myself unable to resist.

"Noelle... so sweet..." he murmured, then froze.

All at once, his hands turned solid and unyielding against me. His entire body stiffened like a bow as he abruptly released me and tumbled from the bed.

"Fuck! Sorry, Noelle!"

Alarmed by the change, I rolled onto my back to find him standing over me, hands fisted in his unruly hair, eyes wide with horror. Even so, they seared a trail down my naked body.

"Oh, no, no, no, no, no," he spun away.

I swallowed my heart and rose from his bed, not bothering to hide my nakedness. I'd exposed my heart to him over and over. What did it matter if he saw my body?

"You know," I bit out as I glided past him with as much dignity as I could muster. "This is a new experience for me. I'm not sure I've ever garnered that reaction from a man."

"Noelle," he groaned, pained, his palms to his face, rubbing roughly. Even so his eyes skittered over my form before darting away and back again.

So, I wasn't completely repugnant to him.

At the door to the bathroom, I turned, leveled him with my gaze, and cocked my head. "It's been less than pleasant and not an experience I wish to repeat."

He raked a hand through his hair, his eyes bleak. He opened his mouth to speak but I held up a hand to hold him off.

"I'll be sure the next man knows exactly what he's getting before I take him into my bed."

His stormy eyes turned black while his chin dipped like a bull preparing to charge.

I lifted my chin. He would not cow me. "If you wouldn't mind getting my bag and leaving it outside the door, I'm going to grab another shower and get out of your life."

His shoulders slumped. "Noelle..."

Closing the door with barely a click, I held on until the sting of the shower on my face masked my tears. I didn't need another shower, but I couldn't go home with the smell and feel of his body imprinted on mine.

I cupped my hand around the breast he'd held and cried for the loss.

I washed the wet from between my thighs and wept for the frivolity of hope.

Sinking quietly to the floor, I wrapped my arms around my legs.

Wondered for the thousandth time if I had given myself fully to Barrett would I even now be happily ensconced in his strong arms? Arms that had held me, comforted me, loved me though he didn't love me. Could it have worked if

I had given myself over to him instead of waiting for that something that I'd felt only once?

With no way of knowing, but knowing well what happened when I didn't, I vowed to release my hold on impossible dreams.

And promised to not make the same mistake the next time life saw fit to gift me with a good man.

As asked, Hawk left my bag at the bathroom door. I took my time getting dressed, unsure how to face him after this most recent and humiliating rejection. I sat on the bed to plan my next move. I needed to get away from him. Once and for all.

Pulling the covers up around me again, I slipped my cell from my purse, dug deep, and pulled up my happy voice.

"Hi, Dad!"

"Noelle! Baby! When are you coming home?"

His obvious joy at the sound of my voice invited me to crawl into his lap and cry out my heartache.

I laughed instead. "I'm actually here! Well, sort of. I got as far as Hawk's place."

"Hawk's? How did that happen? I didn't even know you knew where he lived," Dad answered, dumbstruck.

"I didn't. It was pure, dumb luck that I happened to pull into his driveway." Emphasis on dumb, I added on silently. "My battery is dead. I'm going to get a boost from Hawk and then head over. I should be there within the hour."

"Honey, I don't think the roads are passable," he hesitantly responded.

I'd often wondered if he knew how I felt about Hawk. The tone of his voice gave indication that he did. "What do you mean? Surely the snowplows have been out by now?" Panic began to claw its way up into my throat.

"It's a mess out there, honey," he answered gently. "Dozens of trees are down, cars buried. We got twice as much snow as expected. It's going to take a few days to dig everybody out." He paused. "Are you going to be okay there?"

I swallowed. Hard. Then cleared my throat. "Yeah. Yeah, Dad. I'll be fine." I forced out another chuckle. "It's Hawkley you should be worried about."

He snorted. "If that boy had two brain cells they'd run away together."

I giggled. Both warmed and embarrassed that he knew the truth about my situation. "I'll be fine, Dad. Uh, can you not tell anyone I'm here yet?"

"My lips are zipped," he promised.

"Can't wait to see you," I admitted, not realizing until that moment how much I'd missed him.

He sighed into the phone. "Can't wait to see you either, baby. I'll come get you as soon as I can. Love you, Christmas."

For as long as I could remember, my dad had called me Christmas instead of Noelle. Mostly to taunt my mom. Since she'd been gone, the tease came far less frequently. I guess he only pulled it out now on special occasions. I grimaced at the fact he deemed this situation worthy of it.

"Careful, Dad," I teased back. "Not sure the boundary between heaven and earth is strong enough to hold her if she hears you."

"Would that it wasn't, Noelle. Would that it wasn't."

Now that. That was the kind of love I wanted. Needed.

Not some guy who dumps me after a year together without even trying. Not some guy who falls out of bed in horror after touching me.

But, I didn't think there were any guys like my dad left out there.

If there were, they obviously weren't for me.

An indignant meow sounded on the other side of the bedroom door. I sighed. Nothing to do but face the music.

Bruce darted inside as soon as the crack in the opening door allowed him. Weaving his way around my ankles, he stopped to sniff my toes and I jumped back. I'd learned that a sniff preceded a nibble. And though many of his teeth were missing, the ones he had left were razor sharp.

I scooped him up. "Good afternoon, Mr. Willis. I bet you're hungry," I cooed while scratching him under his tiny chin. "Should we go find you something to eat from the car?"

I didn't relish going back outside to the car. The cold alone was enough to deter me, never mind the mess.

I carried him down the darkened hallway to the family room, the view through the wall of windows stopping me in my tracks. I stood, rapt, until Bruce struggled to get down. I released him to dart under the couch. A temporary hiding place. Probably one of many he'd already scoped out.

My mouth watered as the smell of pancakes drifted from the kitchen and hit me in the face.

I stopped, pressed my lips together, and dipped my chin to my chest before taking a deep breath. "You'll be okay, Noelle. Just brave your way through it. Tuck away the pain. You've done it before and no doubt you'll do it again."

I headed into the kitchen.

Hawk stood with his back to me at the oversized stove, tension radiating from his large frame. Some of my anger dissipated. This couldn't be easy for him, either. It wasn't his fault he didn't want me. I needed to let it go. Didn't stop the mothertrucking sting though.

"I hope you made extra," I said brightly.

Hawk turned from the stove, a heavy frown marring his forehead, "Noelle…"

I swung my ass into one of his solid, hardwood chairs. It was surprisingly comfortable. "Yes or no, Hawk?" I replied sharply, indicating in no uncertain terms that I was not down for a discussion.

He frowned heavily before grabbing a plate and turning back to the stove. "You want syrup? Butter? Cool whip?"

"All of the above," I asserted.

He shook his head. "I don't know where you put it."

"Well, Hawkley," I retorted. "If you weren't such a prude, you would have seen exactly where I put it."

Spinning around, he jabbed a finger in the air. "Are we talking about this or not?" He threw his arms out to the sides and raised his eyebrows. "You don't get to make snide comments and not let me speak."

"Oh, I think you said enough," I snapped back. "I think it was to the tune of five no's, a fuck, and a sorry. But however ineloquent your words, your face expressed the rest." I turned my face to the side and slammed my eyes shut to block him out.

My resolution to let it go lasted all of thirty seconds.

I heard the fridge door open and shut. Wished I could fall through a crack in the floorboards. Prayed for him to leave me so I could find my tattered dignity and pull it up around me.

After a moment, he slid a plate down in front of me. I didn't lift my head until the last of his footsteps left the room.

Chapter 7 - Truce

Hawk disappeared in the time it took me to eat.

And I did eat. The first forkful proved tough to swallow, but I hadn't eaten anything of substance for more than twenty-four hours and they were the best pancakes I'd ever tasted.

Bruce had also disappeared again as was his routine in new places. For the first several days, he would hide, coming out periodically to touch base with me, eating and drinking at night. Usually by the time he got comfortable in his new surroundings, it was time to go.

Which made him an excellent houseguest.

Strangely, his process had accelerated at Hawk's house. Rather, his cabin. Because despite its sprawling size, it was designed like an old-fashioned log cabin.

Three bedrooms, including the master, lay along a hallway to the right of the front door with the living area to the left.

Only the cozy kitchen, situated at the front, boasted walls with two entrances, one off the front hall, one off the family room. The L-shaped great room began at the front of the house and swung around the kitchen to stretch luxuriously across the back.

Two adjacent walls of windows, broken only by the enormous brick fireplace, framed a breathtaking view. A view made more magnificent by the spectacle of great, fat snowflakes falling like gumdrops from a lavender sky.

My heart burst at the sweetness of the sight before my eyes.

Bruce stood on his hind legs on the back of the couch, his front paws braced against the window as squirrels attempted to rob the bird feeders. His tail swished back and forth like a metronome, his head on a swivel.

I cocked my head to the side. "We'll have to make sure we get you a birdhouse at our new place. What do you think, Mr. Willis? Would you like a birdhouse?"

Hawk's deep baritone startled me. "I thought his name was Bruce?"

I whipped around causing my hot coffee to slosh over the rim of my mug onto my hand. I sucked in a sharp breath, set the mug down on a side table, and shook the blistering hot liquid from my skin. "Mothertrucker, that hurt!"

Startled by my outburst, Bruce flew off the couch, his paws sliding across the floor as he torpedoed under the chair.

Hawk jumped back, his eyes wide, an unmanly cry erupting from his lips. "Fuck, he's weird!"

I fought not to laugh. My goal was distance from Hawk, not laughing together over the antics of my cat.

The sting on the back of my hand in combination with the vivid recall of my earlier mortification snuffed out the rest of my humor.

Two long strides brought Hawk to my side. He lifted my hand to examine the injury.

My mind spun stupidly with possibilities and contradictions. I snatched my hand back. "I've got it." Turning on my heel, I headed for the kitchen and stuck my hand under the faucet.

Unfortunately, I failed to test the water temperature and it was steaming. "Ah! Why is this so hot?" I demanded, swiveling to face Hawk.

"I was doing dishes," he winced and rubbed his hand over his face. "I'm sorry, Noelle. Here." He flipped the faucet to cold and tested it before drawing my hand beneath the cool stream.

With my attention centered completely on my hand, it took a moment before I noticed his proximity. His long fingers wrapped around my wrist. Holding me immobile. His wide chest barely brushing my back. His cheek at my temple.

I closed my eyes.

His breath in my hair.

Awareness flooded through me, and I edged away from him.

"Don't," he warned softly. "Don't freak out."

"I'm not," I retorted. "You've made it abundantly clear how you feel about me-"

His fingers tightened around my wrist and his other hand slapped down on the counter on the other side of my hip. His mouth to my ear, he pressed his chest against my back and whispered fiercely, "I haven't made *anything* clear. I can't even *think* clearly."

Releasing my wrist, he pushed off the counter with a growl and stomped out of the kitchen. Thirty seconds later, the front door slammed shut as he thundered out into the yard.

I stood, eyes wide, my insides quivering with shock and awareness. The hair on my arms stood up as the knowledge of what sizzled between us raced down my spine. Yearning spiraled low as my head fell back. "Oh, God..."

A sharp sting brought my attention back to my injured hand and I put it back under the water, twisting my neck to see him through the window as he escaped down the driveway in the rapidly failing light.

My chest expanded with a deep, shuddering breath. For the second time that day, I'd driven him from his kitchen.

I had to make it right.

I found his first aid kit tucked underneath the sink in the main bathroom. Stocked with all manner of bandages and gels, I quickly coated the burn with aloe vera and bandaged my hand. A latex glove protected it further.

Then I raided his refrigerator. Unsurprisingly, that, too, was stocked.

Traditionally, on November 1st, the fervor with which our mothers tackled Hallowe'en made way for a renewed mission to pursue healthy eating. Just as we celebrated Hallowe'en together, on November 1st we kicked off the

'Great Vegetarian Bake-off', a full month of vegetarian eating and meal-planning.

Meeting when Hawk and my older brother Max were babies, my mom and Lou recognized in one another a kindred spirit. A sister of the soul. And so began a lifelong friendship, their lives tightly intertwined, as they raised their families, built their marriages, celebrated their victories, and fought their battles. Together until my mother lost her battle. My mother's death seven years ago blew a crater-sized hole in both families.

My dad never fully recovered.

I'd wager Hawk's mom was the same.

I wiped a stray tear from my cheek and carried on making the soup my mother always made on this day.

I hated to cry, especially in front of people, but tears shed for my mother didn't count. I'd heard a Bible verse once that God collects our tears in a bottle. Those tears I shed for my mother were a kind of celestial email. I trusted God would give her the message that I loved her.

My heart rate quickened as the front door opened and Hawk's boots hit the floor. Chin up, facing the doorway, I waited for him.

Sock feet, white tee, flannel discarded, his worn jeans slung low at his hips, he rounded the corner with his hands in the air. "I want to call a truce."

Mothertrucker.

He looked delicious.

"Agreed," I nodded jerkily as I attempted to tuck my goggling eyes back in my head.

49

He jerked to a stop, seemingly unprepared for my answer. "Agreed?"

"Yes," I nodded firmly once again. *Change the subject. Change the subject!* "I'm making my mother's soup for dinner."

A wide smile chased the frown from his gorgeous face. "The smell hit me from outside. I couldn't quite put my finger on it." He breathed deep, then murmured low. "That brings back memories. All of them good."

I turned back to the stove and gave it another quick stir then turned off the burner. Cracking the oven door, the smell of fresh bread wafted out.

"You made my mom's cheesy bread?" he asked, his eyes closed as he breathed in the yeasty goodness.

"I did. I always make this meal the day after Hallowe'en," I admitted. "It makes me feel closer to both of them."

"I know you still talk to Harley. You two were always thick as thieves. But do you still talk to my mom?"

I raised my head in surprise. "Of course! At least once a month. Always have. I don't think I would have survived my mother's passing without your mom."

Passing me bowls and side plates, we set the table to eat. "She had a tough go of it for a while. She put on a good front, but she was lost without your mom for a long time."

I shrugged. "It makes sense. Their friendship lasted longer than most marriages. I'd be lost, too, if I ever lost Harley."

This was truth with a capital T. Harley, the youngest child and only girl in their family, was my best friend. It was, perhaps, weird at my age to think in terms of 'best friend', but there was no denying it.

Completely opposite to me in every way, Harley was the yin to my yang, the ping to my pong, the flip to my flop, and the tick to my tock. I could not imagine my life without her.

I cocked my head in thought. My brother Max and Hawkley had always been best buds. Harley and I were tight as a fist. Hunter, born smack dab in the middle between Hawk and Harley, hung with all of us. Yet, he was the only one of the five of us who enthusiastically sought out friends outside our families.

The social butterfly of our little group.

Full of life until the tragically premature end.

We sat down at the table, our food laid out in front of us. Hawk cleared his throat. "Does she know you're here?"

I looked down at my bowl and shook my head. "No." I cleared my throat. "I'd rather she didn't. When the roads clear, I'll just head home and call her from there."

The conversation skidded to a stop. The elephant in the room, one I could barely define, refused to be swept under the rug. The seconds ticked past, the strangely intimate sounds of eating the only thing interrupting the silence.

Anxiety gripped me by the throat.

"I need to, uh, go outside and clean out the mess in my car."

"It's done."

"You did it? Why?"

He shrugged. "Why wouldn't I? It was for you." He cleared his throat. "Where is stinky anyway?"

My mind raced. That sounded like I meant something to him.

"He's hiding. That's what cats do in new places." I'd lost my excuse to leave but I couldn't sit staring into space, the silence between us thick and uncomfortable. "You want to eat in front of the tv? Maybe put on a movie?"

Before I'd finished speaking, his ass cleared the chair. "I've got tv trays."

Within minutes, the sound of the horror movie we settled on filled the room. I sank with ease into one of his massive chairs and inhaled the rest of my food while he went back for seconds and thirds.

Curled up in leggings and an oversized flannel, I tucked my hands into the sleeves and half covered my eyes as the final gory moments unfolded.

Watching a horror movie in the dark upped the scare factor even with the kitschiest movies. Adrenalin pumped through my veins. With the tv off, the only light came from the fireplace.

The world beyond the glass shone silvery white as the moon's glow reflected off the snow. The beauty of the night seduced my senses, lulling me into a false sense of complacency, and it was then I made my mistake.

Chapter 8 - Kool-Aid

"Do you want a drink?"

I cocked my head to the side. It was almost like we were friends again. As much as I wanted to be more than that, I suddenly craved time with him in any manner I could get it. "Sure. You have any wine coolers?"

"Is Harley my sister?" he asked drily.

He stocked her favorites. I liked that. A lot.

I'd made a point of not asking Harley or Max about him over the years. I didn't know him the way I used to. After I threw myself at him and he came home with Diane, we separated like East and West.

Not a slow growing apart, but a deep fractured split.

When Harley brought him up in conversation, I squirreled away every tidbit of information. She worried about him, said he seemed fragile somehow. Brittle.

My heart ached for him. I would have gladly been there for him, but he didn't want me.

I listened, I asked questions, but I never started those conversations.

This, us being together like friends, felt both new and old. I wanted more of it.

"You want to play chess?"

He narrowed his eyes at me. "Backgammon. I seem to remember you were the chess champion at school."

"Well," I huffed, teasing him. "Not all of us could be popular jocks."

He snorted out a laugh. "It's not all it's cracked up to be. I was lucky. Most of the people in that circle peaked in grade twelve and it's been downhill for them ever since."

With the game board set up on the coffee table between us, the fire crackling beside us, and our drinks in front of us, we reverted back to the well-established patterns from our childhoods. Gentle teasing, fierce competition.

I won the first game tidily. The second proved to be more difficult. Probably due to Harley's wine coolers. Those things had always been a weakness of mine. They tasted like the Kool-Aid from my childhood and went down much the same way.

"Getting me inebriated and claiming a victory is morally repugnant," I groused.

Straight white teeth flashed in his beard a second before he threw his head back and laughed. "Morally repugnant?" he teased. "I offered you a drink. One. Any more are on you."

I held up the bottle and eyed the inch or so left in the bottom. "It's just that they taste so good. And the more I drink, the better they taste."

"Yes, well, I think I'm going to cut you off now." He stood and held his hand out for my bottle.

I tipped my head back and held his eyes while I drained it. Stormy eyes. As changeable as the Irish sea, as my mother used to say.

Passing him my empty bottle, I challenged, "Truth or dare?"

He laughed again, that raucous burst of joyful noise I didn't realize until that moment had been missing from my life. When he looked back down at me only to see a small smile on my face, he chuckled in surprise. "Oh, you're serious?"

"As a heart attack," I asserted.

"Okay," he replied carefully, placing my empty back down on the table before sitting back down.

Swinging my legs over the arm of the large chair I'd claimed, I lay back and watched him.

Sitting on the middle seat of his massive couch, he leaned forward, elbows resting on his spread knees, eyes to the floor. He tapped the tips of his long fingers together.

I waited. Unwilling to let him off the hook. After all this time, I deserved an answer. An explanation. Even if I didn't deserve it, I wanted it.

Finally, he leaned back and stretched his arms along the back of the couch. "Truth."

Excellent. "At one time, I thought you were interested in me. Was I wrong?"

"No."

I blinked at the baldness of his reply. '*No.*'

One word. A single syllable.

Two tiny letters.

My world shifted.

"Why didn't you pursue me?"

"You sure you want to know this?"

I nodded slowly, whispered, "Never been so sure."

If he could have been mine, I wanted to know what I'd done to lose him. I'd loved him for so long. And that love stood in the way of every relationship I'd had since I'd left home. Left him.

He did not delay. "Hunter loved you first. Before I'd even really noticed you in that way, to be honest. When he revealed his intentions for you and him, I was only beginning to wake up to the reality of you."

"Hunter loved me?" I laughed.

He didn't.

I stared back at him in shock. There'd never been the slightest clue that Hunter's feeling's for me were anything other than platonic. He certainly never hurt for female company and didn't hide the fact. The one arena Hunter lived up to his name was in the dating pool.

Hawk's lips pressed into a straight line, but he offered a tight nod. "He had a one-year plan. As soon as he got that promotion he'd been chasing, he intended to chase you." His mouth twisted. Bittersweet amusement. "His exact words."

"But..."

Hawk rubbed a harsh hand over his face and nodded as if he knew what I was about to say. "He dated other women at that time. Lots of other women. I thought perhaps he wasn't as serious as he let on. And despite my best efforts, you began to take up more and more space in my head. The day you told me you," he swallowed, "had feelings for me, was the day after he told me he was ready to go after you." He dropped his head. "He vowed to have you at the altar within the year. Asked me to be his best man."

"He never told me," I whispered. "He never pursued me."

Hawk met my eyes, his bleak. "The car accident happened two weeks later."

"Oh my God," I gasped.

What wicked twist of fate was this? I thought back to that terrible time. When the officer came to their door, I was there. Sitting on the front porch with Harley. My memory of that day boiled down to a mess of scattered impressions. Too many tears. Lou screaming, Harley asking questions, so many questions, and Dan's big body shaking as he wept.

And him.

Silent and withdrawn.

"The next time I saw you, you were with Diane."

"Yes. She was as good a replacement as any." He sighed. "I shouldn't have married her. I wasn't thinking straight. I wanted you but couldn't have you, then I could, but the *guilt*... I couldn't do it to him."

It wasn't my turn. That wasn't how the game worked, but I asked anyway. "Would you do things differently if you could go back and do it again?"

He hung his head. "No."

That stung. I allowed the nettle to work its way through me. I'd put myself out there, twice, and he rejected me. No matter how honorable he believed his actions to be, that fact remained.

If I asked my next question and got the answer I suspected, would I finally be able to move on?

A fragile hope broke through the winter of my heart's hibernation. What if he answered differently? What if this could be the beginning of my happily ever after? With him?

Pushing past my fear, I asked, "Do you still have feelings for me?"

His eyes met mine, the storm in them raging. "Never stopped having feelings for you."

"It's your turn," I whispered, feeling as though we stood on the precipice of either the best or worst decision we'd ever made in our lives.

Gruff, his voice full of gravel, he extended the age-old taunt, "Truth or dare?"

"Dare," I breathed.

He stared at me for too long, his fingers tapping. I saw the moment he began to retreat.

"It's been almost ten years," I whispered, reminding him of a fact I bet he knew too well.

Twice he parted his lips to speak.

Twice he changed his mind, then, rolling out the kinks in his neck, he leaned back and stretched his arms across the back of the couch before issuing his challenge.

"Kiss me."

I rose on shaky legs.

He watched me cross to him, his eyes trailing up from my feet to hold my gaze.

I swallowed. My lips parted. My fingers twirled madly in the ends of my hair before dropping back down to my thighs where they didn't seem to fit. Every step brought me closer to a tiny piece of heaven.

He didn't move when I reached him. Didn't take my hand or grasp my waist, he simply stared up at me. Waited. Challenge and warning in his eyes.

I met the challenge and ignored the warning by boldly slinging my knee over his thighs and settling myself astride his lap. Bracing my palms on his hard chest, I flexed my fingers into his hard muscles, watching first my fingers at play, then his eyes as I touched him. If this turned out to be one and done, I wanted to take my time.

His eyes flared to life like a fantasy come true.

Beneath me, his hips flexed, his body answering the question posed by mine. Gripping the back of the couch, he tipped back his chin. Through hooded lids, he studied me, my name a low warning on his lips as I reached for his beautiful face.

My trembling hands reverently cupped his bearded cheeks. My eyes greedily followed the path my thumbs traced along his sharp cheekbones before I closed them. Focused all my attention on the waking dream unfolding under my palms. The pleasure of touching him swelled and filled my chest as my fingers tentatively threaded through his dark curls.

Opening my eyes, I lifted my gaze to his as I recalled my vow to give of myself. If not now, when?

"I've waited a long time for this."

His Adam's apple bobbed in his throat.

I cocked my head to the side. My eyes blazed a path my lips yearned to follow. "Hawkley," I breathed. "Are you sure you want this?"

Are you sure you want me?

"At this point, I'm not sure I can live without it."

Eyelids heavy, his gaze dropped to my mouth and his lips parted in anticipation. "It's your dare, baby."

Would he regret me in the morning?

Would he tumble out of bed, turn his back, run?

Curving my hands around the back of his neck, I edged closer, watching the need build in his eyes.

Jaw tight, body taut, his hips flexed again, rocking me ever closer to the promised land without laying a single finger on me.

One man.

One woman.

One purpose.

I dipped my face closer, allowing my eyelids to drift shut as I took in the sweetness of his breath mixing with mine. A heady drug.

My body hummed in anticipation, the scent of my arousal easily detectable in the tiny space between us. If there were room for any other emotion, I'd have been embarrassed by my body's desperate plea to be under his.

Opening my eyes, my lips a whisper from his, I silently prayed, 'God, please, don't let this be over in the morning.'

Tunneling my fingers up through the back of his hair, I grasped the silky strands in my fists. I took a breath, knowing this moment marked the before in a lifetime of afters, and pressed my mouth to his.

Chapter 9 – Irrefutable Proof

The shock of first contact. A stuttered gasp. The soft rasp of his beard.

His sweet lips trembled under mine as I breathed him in and struggled to adjust to the overwhelming assault on my senses.

Heart thudding in my chest, I parted my lips, leaned in, and took my first nipping taste of his mouth.

Drunk on my love for him.

Dizzy with it.

His lips softened, parted, and invited me to explore.

I touched the tip of my tongue to his bottom lip then pulled it gently into my mouth.

My mind struggled to make sense of the unexpected bounty. I'd never tasted such sweetness and I feared I'd never get enough. Slightly bolder, I ran my tongue along the seam of his mouth, reveling in his sharply indrawn breath.

Suffused with the wonder of all that was him, I dropped a chain of gentle kisses along his perfect top lip, with each one a silent prayer and an unspoken declaration.

Other than the occasional flex of his thigh muscles, he didn't move, but he watched from beneath heavy lids as I continued with my gentle ministrations.

I needed more.

Sealing my open mouth over his, my tongue teased the tip of his, rolled along its velvety length, begged it to play with me. Pleaded with him to explore me back.

A single tear leaked from one of the cracks in my heart and rolled down my face as I learned his mouth, his taste, his *need.*

This close, there was no escape from the heat in his eyes, the fire barely contained, and I longed for the key to ignite and release the beast I sensed within.

Edging closer, I arched my back to press my breasts against his hard chest and tipped my chin back to offer him my mouth.

To offer him control.

His breath came out in a harsh exhale. His tongue snaked out and ran along his bottom lip as he studied me. Questions and possibilities swirling between us. I knew him now, but he did not yet know me.

I drew back, forcing my hands to relax their grip on his curls. Dragging my palms over his shoulders and down his chest to his abdomen, I skirted the edge of his jeans with the tips of my fingers. Then placed my hands, palms up, on my thighs.

His eyes dropped to my hands as he rolled his into fists on the back of the couch.

A heavy drumbeat of need pulsed between my legs. "Please," I rasped.

His head shot up. "You sure, Noelle?"

"I know what you are, Hawk," I sought to reassure him.

His eyes narrowed to angry slits as my meaning hit home in a way I never intended. His hands shot off the couch and wrapped around my hips. Yanking me forward onto his erection, he lifted his hips from the couch and dragged my core back and forth, forcing me to ride him.

"Don't speak," he snarled. "And give me your fucking mouth."

Without waiting, he pressed his mouth to the hollow at my collarbone then dragged up the length of my throat forcing my chin back before sealing his mouth over mine and delving inside.

I relaxed in his hold. Gave myself over to him.

To his way.

Where I was gentle, he was rough.

Where I tasted, he consumed.

Where I pleaded, he possessed.

Digging his fingers into my hips, he thrust against me, my soft leggings doing nothing to shield my tender flesh from that which he wished to give me. Not allowing me up for air, his mouth worked mine feverishly, his body straining to meet my need.

His hands, his strength, his want, his need, his body working under mine, taking what I so readily offered, giving back tenfold.

The first flutter hit, and I had a moment of panic. "Can I…"

One of his hands went to my lower back, the other wound into my hair and pulled my head back.

His mouth latched onto my neck as he rolled his hips harder into the cradle of my pelvis. "Fucking come, Noelle."

My body seized. I sobbed out my release as his hips slowed to ease me through it.

As the last tremors faded, his hands followed the length of my spine, rounded my hips, stroked my hair back from my flushed face then drew my head down to his chest as my bones turned to liquid.

One breath.

Another.

One tear. Another. Unbidden. Unwanted. Uncontrollable. I fisted my hands in his shirt.

Quietly retrieving my hands, he wound my arms up around his neck, then smoothed his palms from my wrists to my shoulders, along my ribs, back to my hips.

And still the tears flowed.

"Shh, baby," he soothed. "I've got you."

"I don't know why…"

He interrupted, "Don't speak, honey. Just lay here and let me see to you."

Slow, heavy hands traversed my back and hips. Talented fingers tunneled into the hair at the back of my head, rubbing gentle circles before sweeping back the hair at my temple only to begin all over again.

With my nose pressed to his chest and his heartbeat in my ear, my body melted against his, and my tears dried.

Pressing his lips to my forehead, he heaved in a deep breath. "I need you."

Three little words.

Not the ones I longed for, but I'd take them.

I lifted my head to find raw need etched into the lines of his face. My body immediately readied to receive him. "I'm here."

Pushing forward to the edge of the couch, he tucked his big hands underneath me where my butt met my thighs. With a jolt, he heaved me up his body and stood.

I wrapped my legs around his waist and cupped my hands to the back of his neck. Unable to bear up under the intensity of his stormy gaze, I closed my eyes and pressed my forehead to his.

Halfway to the bedroom he stopped. His voice gruff, he gave me one more out. "You sure?"

A truth I'd always known, for which I now had irrefutable proof, hit me anew. "I've never wanted to be anywhere else."

He tensed, his hold on me tightening momentarily.

Had I revealed too much? Would this be over before it began? Was this all I was to have?

My body and spirit ached at the thought.

"Shh," he soothed, brushing a kiss across my forehead.

I wrapped my arms around his shoulders and tucked my face into his neck. Inhaled his scent. Pressed my lips to the wonder of his skin. A miracle. A gift.

In his bedroom, he relaxed his hold and allowed my body to slowly slide down his until my feet hit the floor. Setting me back a step, his eyes held mine while his trembling fingers opened the first button of my flannel. His hands slipped under the open placket, spreading the sides wide. He bent and delivered a reverent kiss to my collarbone before attending to the next button.

With each released button, he spread my shirt wider and dropped sugar kisses to the newly exposed skin. Between my breasts, below the clasp of my bra, and down to my stomach which quivered beneath his seeking lips. His hands around my hips, he dropped to his knees and gave his tongue free rein along the waistband of my leggings.

Stopping, he gripped my hips hard and pressed his forehead to my womb. "Fuck, Noelle," he groaned. "I can smell you."

I gasped and closed my thighs tight.

His head whipped up with his demand, "Open."

I parted my legs, and he grunted his approval while his busy thumbs hooked into the waistband of my leggings and dragged them down along with my panties, leaving me standing before him in my bra and an open shirt.

Sitting back on his haunches, he dropped his hands and took me in. "Drop the flannel. Ditch the bra."

My hands shook as I complied, something undeniably sexy about a man, *this* man, fully dressed on his knees as I stood, trembling before him, a naked offering.

"Shirt," I blurted. I wanted it off. I wanted to see him.

Rising to his full height, his eyes on mine, he whipped his tee off then flicked open his jeans, letting them fall to the floor.

No boxers, he stood proud and ready to take me.

Walking toward me, I instinctively stepped back until the backs of my knees hit the bed forcing me to sit. With his knee braced on the bed beside me, he hauled me up the bed, opened my thighs with his other knee and slid deep.

My head flew back as the shock and the pleasure rolled through me.

Looming over me, he lowered to one elbow and sought my hand with his free one, linking our fingers and stretching my arm over my head. Kissing the corners of my mouth, my eyes, gentle brushes across my cheekbones, he gave me time to adjust to his presence.

My thighs relaxed. My body gave. My sex opened.

His mouth touched mine, and he rolled his hips.

"Hawk," I breathed.

I lifted my head to seek out his lips, but he snapped his hips, hard, sending my head back and exposing my throat. With my free hand, I circled around his back to clutch the muscles, reveling in his strength as he rhythmically fucked me.

Bowing his back, he tucked his face into my neck, his teeth grazing, lips nipping, tongue rasping.

A low moan parted my lips as I gave myself over to the symphony he flawlessly orchestrated. Body on fire, I drifted to that hazy space where rapture ruled, and inhibition fled.

"Come at will, Noelle," he murmured as he rolled his hips, grinding against my clit, seeking to reach every secret spot inside me.

At the first flutter, he sealed his mouth over mine and swallowed my cries, his hips flexing wildly until he stuttered to a stop, pulsing out his release deep inside me.

No condom.

Chapter 10 – Pussy Phobia

Mmm. Gentle kisses on my neck, warm chest at my back, strong arm around my waist, his deep voice at my ear.

"Good morning, Noelle," he murmured between kisses. "Your weird cyclops cat is on your head."

I blinked my eyes open slowly.

Weak, winter sunlight filtered through the blinds. Hawk's world, separated and surrounded by trees, held us in a silent cocoon. There was peace to be found here. Escape. A person could speak with the earth and worship the sky. Other than the birds outside, the only sound came from the man beside me.

And indeed, Bruce slept in his customary spot, wrapped around my head.

"Good morning, Hawk," I whispered, my voice not yet awake. "You're not going to fall out of bed again, are you?"

His arm tightened around me, and his deep chuckle vibrated along my throat.

I arched against the quiver skating down my spine, my bum nestling into his groin, his hard length seeking my heat.

"You can be punished for your sass, you know..."

I laughed. "Even when we were kids, you were always big on punishment."

He snorted. "I was a tattletale."

"You so totally were," I teased.

"Hey, as the oldest, there was a lot of pressure on me to keep all you guys safe."

"And Hunter didn't make it easy," I laughed at my understatement.

He did not laugh. "No. He did not."

I twisted back to look at him. "Hey," I called softly. "I'm sorry. Does it still hurt you to talk about him?"

For a moment, the veil over his eyes peeled back and offered a glimpse of the pain he carried inside.

"You feel responsible for him."

With a short nod, he affirmed, "I was responsible for him."

Turning around fully, I cupped his bearded cheeks in my hands. "Not for that, Hawkley. Never for that."

He closed his eyes, his lips flattening.

Stroking over his face, I sought to soothe him. "Hunter could be a bit of a hothead. Impulsive. Spontaneous. It was part of his charm. So damned determined, he never could take no for an answer."

I shook him lightly to get his attention. "Remember the snow globe costume?" I laughed. "That was his brainchild. No matter what we said, he would not be put off."

The remembrance of that debacle brought a small smile to his face.

"That determination was part of the reason for his success. He was complicated. Endearing. Charismatic. And chaotic. Lived his life unapologetically. And Hawk, he stopped listening to you around the age of zero."

His smile disappeared but his stormy eyes continued to search mine before shutting me out once again. The tension eased from his face, not in the way I would have wished, but in resignation.

When he opened his eyes, the veil had returned. "He was my brother."

"Okay, Hawk." I ran my fingers through his hair, tugging lightly on his curls, lightly scratching his scalp.

His eyes closed in pleasure, but when he opened them, he could not hide his anxiety. "Noelle," he began, "I want to keep quiet about us."

My hand froze in his hair, and I stared at him, my mind split. Two reasons. One, there was an 'us'. Two, he wanted to hide it.

He jiggled me in his arms. "Say something."

"There's an us?" I tentatively offered.

His face softened as he cradled me against him. "There's an us," he stated firmly.

He didn't sound particularly happy about it. Was it just my insecurity talking? I gently prodded, "You don't sound too happy about it?"

Holding me close, he pressed his cheek to the top of my head. "There's such a thing as being too happy, Noelle. Please. Can we just play it close to the vest for now?"

I nodded slowly against his chest, all kinds of disquiet buzzing in mine. *Too happy?* Then I gave myself a mental shake. Look where you are! You've just woken in *his* arms after spending the night in *his* bed after he buried *his* cock inside you after *holding you while you cried* after daring you to *kiss him.*

Wrapping my arms around his shoulders, I nestled closer, "Yes. We can do that for now."

He rewarded me with a tight squeeze, then slapped me on the ass. The sudden movement startled Bruce who leapt up, dug his tiny claws into the pillow, and sailed over Hawk like a flying squirrel.

"Ahh," he screamed as he tumbled off the bed onto his knees. He looked at me, eyes wide, face disgruntled. "Fuck, he's weird!"

Unable to stifle my grin, I stretched, arching my back and drawing his attention to my chest. "Well, that proves it. Two mornings in a row? You *are* afraid of my pussy."

Growling, he came at me, but I rolled out the other side. Wild laughter ensued as he chased me into the shower and dispelled any notion I had about his 'pussy phobia'.

Early that afternoon, I sprawled on my chosen chair. A plaid, fleece blanket covered my legs, but not my feet. Those hung over the arm, the fire Hawk built keeping them toasty warm. Bruce lay along the back of the chair, his tail twitching whenever something at the window caught his attention. I stared unseeing at the pages of my book, my mind churning with all I did not know.

"What do you do?"

He looked up from his book, bemused by my sudden question. "For work?"

I shrugged. "Yeah. After going to school for a decade, I figure you must have a big, cushy job somewhere," I teased.

He wagged his eyebrows. "I do have a big, cushy job right here at home."

"You work from home?" This surprised me. A strong leader and a naturally charismatic guy, I always pictured him surrounded by an energetic team.

"I do. I did the corporate thing for a while, but my heart wasn't in it. I opened my own consulting company where I overhaul antiquated networking systems for large companies like hotel chains, then offer training and support. And I do have a team, but they're online, and their primary job is customer support."

"Wow," I stared at him. "I had no idea. Your mom just said you work in customer service for the hotel industry."

He laughed. "I don't doubt that's what she said. I've explained what I do a million times and she boils it down to exactly that every time." His face split wide in a grin. "She's not wrong."

I cocked my head to the side. "Your system is installed at the Resort?" Sage Ridge Resort, Hawk's family's business, sprawled at the foot of Sage Ridge, the mountain for which it and the town were named. Being the first in town to establish a resort, they were able to avail themselves of the town name.

Nodding, he confirmed, "I perfected my system at Sage Ridge. And I have an office there, kick in whenever and wherever I'm needed."

"You still a good pool boy?" I teased.

He raised one haughty eyebrow. "I'll have you know I'm the best pool boy. I can still take out the trash like a champ and all the rest of the busboys only wish they had my talents."

Grinning, I responded, "I can't even count the hours I spent working at your parent's place. Every summer. Weekends. Special events. We all did."

So many memories, things I'd forgotten, others I'd purposefully pushed out of my mind. I realized my lips were curved in a happy smile. It had been a long time since thoughts of home had made me happy. Thinking about my childhood. Somehow, the triple tragedy of losing Hawk, then Hunter, then my sweet mother, overshadowed everything good that came before. Being there now, with Hawk, the clouds were parting.

"Do you remember the creek? How full it got in the spring?" He got a smug look on his handsome face.

I studied him, something niggling at the back of my brain, and I gasped, "My boobs!"

He laughed then grimaced, "I could have done without seeing Harley skinny-dipping, but it was well worth it to get a look at you, Noelle. Put that in my spank bank and kept it there for years." He smirked. "It's still there."

"Well, good!" I exclaimed, gratified. I cupped my breasts and ran my thumbs over my nipples.

His gaze sharpened on my hands, so I did it again just to see the heat flare in his eyes. "I have fabulous breasts. They deserve to be in everybody's spank bank," I teased.

His eyes came back to my face. Dark. Possessive. "Not everyone's, Noelle. Just mine."

I shrugged nonchalantly, my heart skipping in anticipation. "Oh, well, you waited so long to claim me, a girl can't just let all this goodness go to waste."

Tossing his book down, he swung his legs to the floor and barreled toward me.

At his sudden movement, Bruce flew off the back of my chair, sailed over my shoulder, and skidded across the floor as his nails failed to find purchase on the shiny hardwood.

I flailed, laughing, as I attempted to disentangle myself from the blanket so I could run. This worked to his advantage as he scooped me up and tossed me over his shoulder.

Laughing, I spanked his butt that flexed so enticingly in front of my face as he stalked toward his bedroom. "My pussy can't take any more today! She's developing a phobia... of hawks!"

His hand came down hard on my ass and ended with a squeeze. "That's good," he grunted. "Time to put that smart mouth to work."

Chapter 11 – Direct Hit

Lying warm and sated in Hawk's bed as he puttered around in the bathroom getting ready for the day, I sought out my cell phone to check the state of the roads.

Seven missed calls. All from my dad.

I pressed call.

"You doing okay, Christmas?" His voice sounded gruff, probably half worried, half just not wanting to know.

"Hey, Dad. I'm good. Sorry I missed your calls."

"Obviously not sitting around by your phone," he teased, then his voice turned serious. "Roads are clear."

"Yeah?"

"I'm thinking that's no longer good news. No one knows you're here. Yet. But I'm thinking finding you holed up with Hawkley may not be the best way for everyone to find out."

The splinter of disquiet I'd managed to ignore up until then began to throb. "He wants to keep things quiet."

"What?" My dad's voice, low and threatening, relayed his message loud and clear.

"I don't know, Dad. He carries a lot of guilt for some reason." I heard the shower turn off. "Can we talk about this when I get home?"

"That we can do. I'm going to head downtown and hit Beach Buns for fresh bread and chili. Give me a heads up when you're on your way."

"Yay," I cheered quietly, smiling wide as Hawk ducked out of the bathroom. Beach Buns was all about the bread, but when the cold rolled in, they rolled out their huge crock pot and put on the chili. "I'm looking forward to seeing you. Love you, Dad."

"Love you too. Love you like Christmas."

I ended the call and met Hawk's wary eyes.

"You spoke to your dad?"

"Yup."

"He knows you're here?"

"Yup," I popped the P.

He pressed his lips together in dismay. "The roads are open, but I'd hoped to steal another day, or two, before anyone knew you were here." He ran his fingers through his hair. "I guess that's not going to happen."

"It could," I offered quietly.

His gaze swung back to mine, the uncertainty in his eyes blasting a cavernous hole through the yearning in my heart, leaving me hollow and cold.

"Noelle..."

I held up a hand. "No. It's okay. You want to keep it quiet; we can keep it quiet."

With his hands on his hips, he stared at the floor and murmured, "Maybe we shouldn't do this, Noelle."

My lungs collapsed, stealing my breath, but my trained reactions came to my defense. "Lucky for you, it's not too late as no one knows. No one important, that is."

"Noelle..."

I raised my hand again, this time to stop him from speaking. "It's fine. I'm going to my dad's. Could you give me a boost?"

"Already done," he muttered.

My unprotected heart absorbed the hit and bled, but I smiled through the pain. "I'll be out of here in about twenty minutes." Without pausing or looking up, I swung my legs out of his bed and began to gather my things.

"You," he cleared his throat. "You want to stay for lunch?"

I stopped dead in my tracks and slowly spun to face him. And then I dropped the pretense and gave him the truth, "Even you cannot possibly be this obtuse."

Meeting my eyes, he winced, then scrubbed his hand over his face. "Noelle... I care so much-"

I care about you.

You're a wonderful woman.

I'm glad I met you.

You're going to make some man incredibly happy one day.

I'm sorry.

I met someone.

Fury, red hot and growing hotter by the second, combusted in a flash. "Don't! Don't fucking hand me the same GODDAMN tripe I've heard over and fucking over from every motherfucker I've ever shared my body with."

He flinched as my statement hit him squarely where it hurt.

"Yes, Hawkley, I have fucked other men. And guess what? Looks like I'll be doing it again in the not-so-distant future because you just proved you're not any different than the others." I swung my arm out to indicate all of him before placing my hand over my chest. "Despite everything, I still have hope I'll find someone to love me!" I laughed, my bitterness overflowing. "It's fragile," my voice cracked. "But it's there! And it's mine! And none of you have ever been able to take that from me!" I wiped the single defiant tear that dared to fall and continued. "And someday, someone will make all of this," I sneered, "worth it."

Turning on my heel, I moved to walk past him, the pile of my clothes in my arms.

He whispered my name as I passed but didn't try to stop me.

It wasn't until I had one foot out the door, Bruce in his carrier under my arm, that he got his shit together.

"No." A single word. A solitary syllable.

Without turning around, I clipped, "No what?"

"I don't want you to leave like this."

I cocked my head to the side, ready to unleash the sass, but suddenly tired. Tired of all of it. Of all of them.

Of myself.

"How would you like me to leave, Hawk?"

"Knowing I'm going to take a couple of days to get my head on straight. A couple of days to try to quiet the guilt. Knowing I'm going to text you. Every day. And we're going to make plans. And see one another. See if we have something that will last before we let everyone else in on it. On us." He took a breath. "I want you to leave knowing there's an us, that I'll text you later and call you in a few days."

My mind warred with my heart. My heart urged me to throw myself into his arms, press my mouth to his, and assure him we'd find our way. But my mind, well accustomed with how to play this game, knew the best offense was defense.

My back to him, I gave a short nod, and slammed out the door.

I drove around for an hour before I remembered what it did to my poor cat and headed home.

My dad took one look at my face and mutely opened his arms. "Do I need to kick his ass?"

I chuckled drily and nestled into my dad's strong arms. Why couldn't there be more men like him?

"I don't know what his problem is. He says he feels guilt. Apparently, Hunter wanted to marry me at the same time as Hawk started to notice me. He told me he's had feelings for me all this time but because of the guilt he never pursued me."

My dad hummed low in his throat. "I guess you showing up at his place forced the issue?"

"Something like that." I patted my dad on the back and slowly withdrew.

He looked at me thoughtfully, a frown on his face. "I can't say I'm overly surprised."

I looked at him in dismay as he ushered me over to the couch before he continued. "When we lost Hunter, we lost Hawkley as well."

My eyebrows rose before furrowing. "What do you mean?"

"You don't know because you left shortly after Hunter died, but Hawkley was never the same. He stopped smiling. Married that horrible woman who sucked the rest of the happiness out of him, though he didn't seem to care. I'd go so far as to say he barely noticed her."

He cocked his head exactly the way I did. "Later he built that house in the middle of the woods and quit his corporate job. Other than events at Sage Ridge, I barely see him at all. Lou says he rarely goes out as far as she knows. Doesn't date. At least no one he's ever introduced to her and Dan."

I sat silently, taking it all in, squireling the information away.

Finally, grimacing, he continued, "As much as it pains me to say it, if you want him, you'll have to be patient. Something inside him broke the day he lost his brother, and no one knows why or how or what to do to fix it." He met my eyes. "And trust me when I tell you, it's been a frequent topic of conversation over the years."

He was in pain.

I wouldn't add to it.

After carrying Bruce upstairs to hide under my bed, I pulled out my phone, and sent a text.

Just letting you know I'm home. Talk to you soon.

Thirty seconds later, three dots began to blink.

How is Bruce settling in?

Relief rolled over me in waves as I sat on the bed and scooted back until my back hit the headboard. Then I lay there on the same frilly teenage girl bed I first dreamed about him, a small smile tugging at my lips, and texted with my first love.

Chapter 12 – Temporarily

Stretching awake, I giggled, *giggled*, wondering what seventeen-year-old me would think if she knew she'd be here in this exact same spot, two decades later, still mooning after the same guy.

Thinking about it in those terms...

I quickly swung my legs out of bed before my musings destroyed my good mood. I couldn't sit around all day thinking about the two hours I spent texting Hawk. Although I totally could, catching up with Harley sounded better.

Body memories assailed me as I walked through the wide, welcoming lobby of The Sage Ridge Resort. Most of them were good, many so damn bittersweet they nearly caused me to stumble.

Memories from before my mom lost her battle. My sweet sixteen. My high school graduation. Weekends away with Harley and Lou to escape the boys. Although, those three usually managed to weasel in on our time at some point. Those weekends were mission impossible for them and they rose to the occasion.

It was here I had my first summer job, and Hawkley was my supervisor. All the girls tittered and laughed every time he walked by. At the time, I didn't understand the fury those giggles elicited in my gut. By the time he married Diane, which probably took place here as well, I understood all too well.

We gathered here after Hunter's funeral.

After my mom's funeral.

I winced at the thought we'd gather here for the next one as well.

A couple passed me, arms wrapped tight around one another, grinning into each other's faces.

"It's enough to make you want to hurl, right?"

I'd recognize that disdain for romance anywhere. I twirled around with a laugh to embrace my best friend before holding her hands out to get a good look at her.

"You look incredible!"

Harley twisted to the side, kicked out a hip, and patted her ass. "You mean this old thing?"

Narrow shoulders, small breasts, and trim waist atop round hips, thick thighs, and an ass that would not quit. With her dark hair liberally streaked with indigo, she looked like a rebellious pinup girl.

"Look at that bubble butt! You look hot, Harley! You need a motorcycle and some leathers to go with that ass!"

"I beg your pardon," Lou mock scolded as she came up behind me. "She doesn't need any further encouragement. She's crazy enough as she is."

"She's perfect!" I protested.

With a wink, Lou turned her warmth to her daughter, "That she is. As are you." Then holding my hand in both of hers, she assessed me in the way that mothers do. "What's the matter, lamb?"

Tears sprang to my eyes. Friggity-frack, I was turning into a leaky faucet. "I think it was just time to come home, Lou."

"Long past time, lamb. Long past." She gave me a squeeze. Her mouth in my ear, she sighed, "I'm glad you're here, my lamb. You look beautiful as always. Now let's see if we can't get you smiling."

Lou looked at her wristwatch. "I'm sorry, ladies, but I've gotta get to Novel-Tea. I'm late for Spill the Tea."

"What's Spill the Tea?" I asked.

Harley groaned, "You don't want to know."

Lou laughed and threw an arm around my waist. "I suppose you're old enough to know."

"I wish I wasn't," Harley grumbled.

Lou rolled her eyes, a sassy smile curving her lips. "Me and a whole slew of ladies young and old have a book club we call Spill the Tea."

I looked between her and Harley. "What's wrong with that?"

Harley, her voice dry, commanded, "Tell her what you read, mother."

Lou's eyebrows wagged and her smile widened. "Romance." She looked around surreptitiously before adding in a delighted whisper, "Sometimes erotica."

Harley groaned and covered her ears.

A burst of happiness erupted from my mouth. "I love that! Is it open to everyone? Can I come?"

Lou's eyes danced. "Absolutely! Michelle runs the group. Do you remember Michelle? I think she was a couple of years behind you in school." Lou wagged her eyebrows as she backed away. "She married a firefighter. I bet there's plenty of heat when she gets home on book club nights! I'll get her to forward you the details." With a final wave, she scooted away.

Harley took her place at my side. "Is she asking Michelle to forward the details of her sex life or the details of the book club?" Harley raised her eyebrows with a smirk. "This group might be racier than I thought."

I pressed my lips together.

Finally, she sighed. "Go ahead. Let it out."

"I cannot believe it! I cannot wait to join this group! Are you sure you don't want to come too?"

Harley's horrified face answered well before her uttered, 'fuck, no'.

I held up my hands in surrender with a laugh. "I won't ask again."

"See that you don't. We do not ever talk about book club."

I turned the imaginary key to my lips.

Looking up at me suspiciously, she huffed out a laugh. "Fuck, you're tall."

I wrapped my arm around her shoulders and pulled her close. "My shrimpy."

She slung an arm around my waist. "However, if Michelle dishes on her sex life, I want to know. Have you seen that man's muscles? Sigh. I bet she gets manhandled plenty."

I barked out a laugh. "You looking to get manhandled, shrimpy?"

"There could be worse things," she muttered then beamed at me. "I can't even tell you how happy I am that you're home. Are you staying? Looking for a job?"

I held up a hand and laughed, "Hold your horses, lady. I'm jobless at the moment, but I haven't decided if I'm staying or moving on. It depends where the jobs are."

And where things landed with Hawkley.

"The jobs are here," Harley enthused. "I'll gladly hand over event planning. That includes weddings where you have to deal with sickeningly sweet couples like the one that just walked out." She shuddered, "I almost prefer the bridezillas."

"You do not," I challenged.

"You're right. I don't. Can't stand those bitches."

Laughter bubbled up in my chest. "How on earth did you get assigned to weddings?"

Sliding me a narrow-eyed look, she explained, "Don't laugh or I really will make you do it. Our event planner left early due to pregnancy complications." She shrugged. "It just happened, and I haven't filled the position yet. You want it, it's yours."

"I've never done event planning, Harley."

She waved away my concerns. "You've been doing catering for ten years. Food is the most important part.

There are binders of info for the rest. How do you think I'm managing?"

Harley, despite her creativity with her appearance, excelled in numbers, logic, and community outreach. Like everyone else, she kicked in where needed. But I'd never describe her as particularly romantic.

"Um... not very well?"

She smirked. "It's all I can do not to gag. I'm not kidding."

"So, Paul still hasn't popped the question?" I inquired gently.

Her false cheer dropped as she looked to the floor before answering. "No. And he's beginning to talk about marriage being antiquated and unnecessary. And," her pretty mouth twisted, "much to my dismay, I find I'm an antiquated type of girl." She shrugged. "He's on his way out. I'm just not sure if he's going to end it or I am."

"He's an idiot." Paul pursued her relentlessly for over a year, and they'd been together for almost five. Harley had been ready for some time to take the next step. Paul kept her on the hook, waiting for the right time. "Do you still love him?"

"That's the thing," she smirked at herself. "Seeing all these couples, how wrapped up they are with each other, I'm beginning to wonder if I ever did."

I looked down. I'd always wondered the same but felt bad about it.

"What?" She demanded.

I wrinkled my nose then admitted, "I often wondered the same thing."

Her mouth dropped open. "Why didn't you say anything?"

I cocked my head to the side, "Didn't I?"

Harley's dark eyes went hazy. "Fuck. You did." She slapped a palm over her forehead and grumbled. "No one's ever accused me of being too bright."

"Aw, that's not it. Sometimes we just don't get that we're worth more than we're getting."

"Is that what happened with Hunka-Munka?"

"Barrett? No. I'm pretty sure he met someone else who flipped his switch. He didn't come right out and say it, but he gave me that impression. I was upset, but I didn't love him. I wish I did. Things might have been different. He's a good man. He treated me exactly the way a woman should be treated." I shrugged. "I guess he just wasn't meant for me. I miss him. A lot more than I thought I would. But I was never heartbroken. Not like I should have been if he was the one."

"Have you ever been in love?"

I looked away, unsure how to navigate this. I didn't want to lie to my best friend but telling her I'd been in love with her brother since I was eighteen might make things awkward. Especially if he moved on and I decided to stay.

Things were bad enough.

"You still have a thing for my brother?" she asked gently.

Startled, I swung round to meet her knowing eyes. I opened my mouth. Once. Twice. Nothing came out.

"So, it's like that." She nodded, eyes to the floor as she processed knowledge she thought she had but needed to have confirmed. Her eyes, when they came back to mine, overflowed with sadness. "Sorry for you, honey. Sorrier for him."

I took a deep breath. Should I tell her?

Before I could make up my mind, she changed the subject.

"So, Barrett. He was easy on the eyes, but inquiring minds want to know," she nudged me with her elbow, grinning. "He's kinky, isn't he? The quiet ones always are. Now that he's out of the picture and there's no chance of me running into him, you can tell me!"

I barked out a laugh but turned the imaginary key to my lips.

She flipped back dramatically on her chair. "I can't even get the good stuff vicariously."

I laughed and shook my head. "You really need to break up with Paul."

That night, I lay in my childhood bed after texting back and forth with Hawk for hours. We talked about everything, no subject out of bounds, except for Hunter. Not once did he bring him up. The few times I brought up memories that involved him, he steered the conversation elsewhere.

Unease cast a ripple over the surface of my happiness.

Pushing the worry aside, I turned my mind to the job offer Harley took great pains to assure me was legit.

If Hawkley committed, I would not hesitate. But knowing how much it hurt the first time he showed up with my replacement, I didn't want to be there to see another.

My thoughts shifted to dinner with my dad. My mom's empty chair. Bruce winding around his ankles as we ate and how I pretended not to notice the bits of fish that made their way under the table. His acknowledgment that my brother Max worked far too much and only managed to see him once or twice a month. His obvious happiness that I finally came 'home'.

Maybe I'd take the job.

Temporarily.

Chapter 13 - Once

"You don't seem that happy to be with me," I probed.

He looked at me briefly before returning his attention to the road. I could almost hear his thoughts working behind his eyes.

His deep voice in my ear when he called that morning sent chills down my spine while my shaking legs dropped me onto a kitchen chair. Bruce wound around my ankles where I sat frozen with nerves. Wondering if he might call it all off before we had a chance to begin.

At his dinner invitation, my free hand shot to the sky, and I kicked my legs up in celebration.

And knocked Bruce clear across the kitchen floor.

I spent most of the afternoon on my stomach offering him treats. Which he refused in favor of licking his nonexistent balls and staring at me belligerently from his one good eye.

When I left for Hawk's place, he still wouldn't talk to me.

I parked my car around the side of his house and walked up the path. Could he see me through the window?

Just as I reached the front door, he swung it open revealing a haircut and freshly trimmed beard, polo shirt and jeans, his shirt open at the collar. Somehow, he looked even fiercer than he had with the wild beard.

I blurted, "You're beautiful."

That brought a smile to his face. Something that seemed to be in short supply. He reached out for my hand and tugged me inside with a chuckle. "Isn't that my line?"

We were only inside for a few minutes, but by the time we got to his car, his good humor had disappeared.

So far, I'd gotten a different Hawkley every day. Today was no different. My initial excitement that morphed into heady anticipation as the afternoon wore on, now sat like a soggy lump of unease in my stomach.

"I actually am happy," he offered me a small smile, "extremely happy to be with you." Reaching across the seat, he picked my hand up off my lap and pressed my knuckles against his lips. Holding it there, his chest rose and fell with his deep breath. He gently squeezed and returned my hand to my thigh, covering it with his warm palm. "I feel guilty. I feel like I shouldn't get to have you."

Aw, it wasn't me then. My stomach lightened. I turned my hand to intertwine our fingers. "Because of Hunter."

"Mostly," he flicked his indicator, taking us onto the highway. Once he merged into traffic, he continued, "Max is going to kick my ass."

I laughed at the thought. My big brother going all, well, big brother.

His teeth flashed white in his beard, but he doubled down. "You think I'm kidding but I'm not. He will not like this. At all."

"Whyever not?" I asked, exasperated.

He shrugged. "It's the way with men. The idea of any man screwing your sister is distasteful." He shuddered. "But for it to be your bro? Someone you're close to? It's a betrayal."

"That's crazy!"

His eyebrows rose in challenge. "Is it? How about if Harley hooked up with Max?"

Jealousy unfurled in my gut. "Oh my gosh, I think I'd be jealous! I'd lose my confidante, wouldn't feel like I could let loose with her anymore."

"There you go," he laughed, his deep chuckle eliminating the last of my unease. "For guys it's a little more elemental."

"Don't you think it's different though? Hooking up as opposed to..." I trailed off suddenly aware of how much more certain I was of him than he was of me.

"As opposed to what?"

"As opposed to what we're doing?" I ventured softly.

He smiled sadly, "And what are we doing, Noelle? I'm not even prepared to take you out in town for fear someone sees us and reports back."

"What's the worst that could happen?"

My words wiped all expression off his face. He answered dully, "You'd be surprised."

Stroking his thumb across the pulse at my wrist, he turned the conversation, telling me stories about guests at the resort, catastrophes in the kitchen, romance drama between the staff, and some of the crazy events his mom pulled off over the years.

The highway rolled along beneath us, and it wasn't until I saw the sign that I realized where he was taking me. I twisted in my seat and grabbed his shoulder. "Are we going to Mistlevale?"

"Happy?" He looked over at my face and what he saw made him grin.

The happy bubbles inside me threatened to explode. "So happy! I haven't been here in years! Remember Harley and I used to beg you and Max to take us?"

"I do," he chuckled. "We should have taken you more often."

Mistlevale used to be a quaint, historic town with an equally historic name. Many years ago, as industry fled and the population dipped, the town got together and revamped itself into a tourist stop. Renovations began downtown at the city square first, and rippled outwards until it boasted one square mile of North Pole perfection.

Famous for its storefront windows that changed with the seasons, people flocked to its streets to take in the elaborate displays. But if you didn't go inside, you truly missed out. The toy store, made up to look like Santa's workshop, held mostly handmade and eco-friendly toys. At the back and behind glass lay an elaborate replica of the village itself with the addition of a fanciful train.

Likewise, the bakery, the deli, the craft store, the bookstore, and the restaurants all offered visual delights beyond their expected offerings. But the piece de resistance was the Christmas store. Set up like a winter wonderland, beautifully dressed Christmas trees displayed the ornaments for sale and created a path, the end of which led to every Christmas culinary delight you wish for and complimentary candy canes.

There were three fabulous restaurants in town. One, cafeteria style, served the multitudes with eateries serving food from all over the world.

The second, a diner, offered homestyle cooking from breakfast clear through to dinner. It was a warm hug on a cold day. That first sip of hot chocolate after shoveling the snow. Leftover turkey sandwiches at Grandma's the day after Christmas. Comfort food at its very best.

Ayana's offered something different. Candlelight and kisses. Soft lighting and sensual touches. A glass of wine in front of the fireplace. A bearskin rug after the kids went down for the night.

I'd been there many times with my family. Mom and Dad brought Max and me there for our 18th birthdays, high school and college graduations, Mom and Dad's 50th birthdays, any occasion worth marking, you could not go wrong at Ayana's.

I'd never, not ever, been on a date.

Over the years, I lost count of the number of proposals we witnessed. Max always sneered at the public nature of it, declaring it a spectacle.

I disagreed.

Like a sponge, I soaked up the emotions. Hope. Disbelief. Excitement. Beginnings. Awe. Love.

I dreamed of being asked, of saying yes.

The elaborate script on the sign for Ayana's beckoned me, but only when I was nearly under it, my mittened hand tucked into the crook of Hawkley's arm, did I realize we were going in.

My hand flexed involuntarily. My eyes stung.

In every fantasy, he'd been the one on bended knee.

Immediately, Hawk covered my hand with his. Tipping his chin down to look at me, he searched my eyes. "What's the matter? Do you not like this place? I made reservations but I can cancel them."

I gave myself a shake. "No, no. I love this place." I touched my free hand to my chest. "I'm just touched you went through so much trouble."

His eyebrows rose in surprise, then he dipped his face closer to mine. "Noelle, you're worth any and every amount of trouble."

Unable to speak, I stared back at him mutely, my lips pressed tight.

His mouth tipped up in amusement, but it did not dispel the sadness in his eyes. Before I could question it, he straightened, and with a gentle hand to my back, led me inside.

Crushed velvet, sparkling crystal, soft lighting, the kind of music you wanted to make love to. Rounded tables, curvy chairs, a sensual snow globe.

Conversation flowed easily between us through a truly delicious dinner as we reminisced about the past and filled in the missing decade between us.

"Was there ever anyone serious?" he fiddled with his napkin, systematically tearing it into confetti.

Why did this question make me wary? "There was potential a couple of times, but that potential was never realized before one of us broke it off."

"The fact that you're not married with kids is shocking to me. You were always so excited to watch the weddings at Sage Ridge."

"I still get excited when I see a wedding. I love weddings." I looked out the window. "They're beginnings and endings."

"What do you mean?"

I cocked my head to the side. "Well, romance novels often end with a wedding. It's the end of the journey."

"What's the destination?" he teased.

"Happily ever after," I blushed, my lips curving into a slightly embarrassed smile.

The frown I'd become accustomed to marred his forehead. "If anyone should have that, it's you."

I dropped my gaze to the table. "I'd have liked to have been married and had a couple of kids by now." *With you.* "It's what I want most," I admitted. "I can't seem to get past the initial couple of phases of a relationship before I call it off. I got closer with the last guy I think." I trailed off at the flash in his eyes.

"What happened?"

How much to tell? "We simply weren't in love in the end."

"Have you ever been in love?" he asked.

Chapter 14 — Eyes on Me

For a long time, I remained silent. Should I tell him? I'd decided not to hold back the next time I found a good man. Not only was Hawkley a good man, but he was also *the* man. If I couldn't go all in for him, could I go all in for anyone?

Was it too soon? I'd known him all my life, but this part was new. Sort of. I didn't want to lie, but it was too soon for the truth. At least, too soon for all of it.

"Once."

He looked at me for a long time while I fidgeted on the edge of my seat.

Wrapping my hair around my fingers, I opened my mouth to ask him the same question, then decided I didn't want to know. Looking into his beautiful, sad eyes, I decided I really didn't want to know.

He stood and held out his hand. "Should we go?"

I slipped my hand into his and he helped me to my feet, help I didn't need but would not deny seeing as it involved his hand wrapped around mine. He led me, his strong fingers gentle on the small of my back, to the coat check.

The attendant took our tickets, her appreciation of his dark, ruggedly handsome face obvious. *That's my mountain to climb, bitch. Back off.*

I smiled to myself. In my head I was truly a badass bitch. Not so much in real life.

"Ready?" His voice broke into my reverie as he held my coat open for me then smoothed it over my shoulders, his nose in my hair. Turning me around to face him, his stormy eyes held mine as he dragged the backs of his fingers down the lapels, fastening the buttons as he went.

My chest filled with air as the back of his knuckles brushed over my breasts.

I heard a soft gasp and looked up to find the attendant, her hand to her chest, lips parted, eyes on his hands.

Her eyes flitted up to mine and she smiled wide, and wagged her eyebrows in the universal message for, 'you go, girl'!

I decided I could be friends with her. I smiled at her, then Hawk's fingers brushed over my lower belly and my attention swung back to him. Impossibly, in every spot his hands brushed past, my skin burned and hungered for more. I blew out the breath I'd been holding.

"Good Lord," the attendant breathed. Fanning herself as she walked away, she called, "Have a good night!"

Hawk offered her a perfunctory nod and led me, half-dazed, out of the restaurant.

He touched me so innocently, but with such focused intensity, she could feel it from three feet away. Awareness snapped between us. A magnet pulling me into his orbit, my entire being attuned to him.

My first date at Ayana's surpassed my wildest teenage imaginings. Far from being a teenager anymore, the imaginings I indulged on the quiet ride home would have sent teenage me under her bed.

He kept a hand on me the whole way home. When he merged onto the highway and needed two hands, he pulled my hand over to his thigh. He laced our fingers together. Cupped his palm over my leg.

Used to being alone, the quiet didn't bother me. It wasn't until Hawk spoke that I realized he might have misinterpreted my silence.

At the stop sign leading onto Sage Ridge's main road, he tugged my hand to pull my attention away from our linked fingers. "Are you okay, Noelle?"

I squeezed his hand and turned my smile on him. "Never better," I replied, the huskiness of my voice revealing the train of my thought and darkening his eyes.

"Come home with me," he demanded, his eyes slightly wild. "Will you do that? Will you come home with me?"

"Of course," I smiled.

He rubbed a rough hand over his face and didn't smile back. "I don't know if I can give you what you deserve. If I were a better man..." he petered off.

The flash of headlights illuminated the back window. Hawk looked at the rearview mirror then back to the road as he rolled through the intersection.

I sat with my hands folded in my lap, my fingers twirling around each other.

He gripped the wheel with both of his.

"But I'm not a better man, Noelle. You need to know that. If you come home with me, you need to know that."

Are you going to go all in or not? "Take me home with you, Hawk." I paused then reminded him of my truth. "There's nowhere else I'd rather be."

Foregoing the offered drink, I took his hand and led him to his bedroom.

He smiled at me, amused, muttering, "I'm not really a man who takes a woman's lead."

I cocked my head to the side and teased, "Even if it's me?"

"I could perhaps make an exception for you," he acquiesced, gently pulling me flush to his chest and wrapping my arm around his back.

My other hand rested over his beating heart. I splayed my fingers wide and pressed, reveling in the proof of *feeling* beneath my palm.

Tunneling both of his hands through the hair at my temples, he took his time gathering my hair into his fist and held me immobile as his lips brushed softly over mine. "Will you follow my lead?"

"Yes," I answered immediately.

His eyes flashed with heat even as his lips tightened with irritation.

I whispered, "Don't punish me because you weren't there, and I won't punish you for marrying a woman who wasn't me."

Taking a deep breath, he pressed his forehead to mine. "I'll try not to, Noelle." With his fist wrapped around my hair, he pulled my head back just enough to arch my body further into his and captured my gaze. "Take everything off, Noelle. Sit on the edge of the bed. Eyes on me."

He dropped my hair and moved back a step.

I bent my head to release the buttons on my blouse.

Suddenly, he was back, his finger firmly pressing my chin upward. "Noelle, eyes on me."

My mouth went dry. This was a different level of intimacy. Intense connection. I tried to swallow. Tried to speak. Settled on nodding instead.

I followed his path around the room while I removed my clothes, hanging my blouse on the end of his bed, shimmying my round hips out of my jeans. Stepping out of them.

He placed candles at intervals, lighting them as he went. "These are new," he told me calmly. "I don't normally keep a stock of candles. I bought them today in hopes you'd be here with me." He lit a candle and trailed his eyes up my body. "I want to be able to see you."

My imperfect body was mine to offer. I'd long since gotten over my insecurities. Holding his eyes, I reached around and unclipped my bra. It, too, fell to the floor.

"Beautiful," he praised as he set out another candle, lit it, and moved onto the next.

Hooking my thumbs around the edge of my panties, I pushed them down my thighs, walked to his bed, and sat on the edge.

Tossing the lighter onto his dresser, he wasted no time crossing to me, his movement causing the candlelight to flicker wildly. "Lean back on your hands," he ordered. "Drop your head back. Relax."

I heard the soft flicks of the buttons on his shirt, the near silent brush of it falling down his arms, the ends of it barely trailing over my quaking knees. The stiff button of his jeans, the rasp of his zipper.

The desperate desire to see.

A deeper need to please.

His finger drew a line beginning at my bottom lip, curving over my chin, trailing down my throat, dipping between my breasts, sliding over my soft tummy to rest on my tightly closed thighs.

He tapped my flank. "Open."

I parted my thighs. Stuttered out a breath.

Dropping to his knees, he grasped my ankles and placed my feet on his shoulders. His voice soft, he licked the inside of my ankle. "Watch, Noelle."

Drunk with desire, righting my head took effort. Seeing my body spread open for him sent a shudder through my frame. And when he dropped his mouth to my core, my body bowed, seeking more.

"When you need to, you can lie back but don't move your feet from my shoulders."

My eyes greedily drank in the sight of his dark head between my thighs, that perfect mouth latched onto my clit, his tongue by turns lashing and soothing.

All the more intense for his lack of attention anywhere else.

Concentrating on keeping my feet in place, I dug my fingers into the blankets, striving to watch for as long as I could stand it.

Hard, soft, fast, slow, deep, light, frantic for more.

My hips began to move of their own volition. I fell back, hands over my head, grasping the blankets, bracing as his wide shoulders pressed my calves back onto my thighs, shifting me across the bed as he went at me.

Sensitized from his lips, his tongue, his beard, his fucking teeth, I teetered between wanting more and needing to escape. The first flutter hit, and my body seized.

He pressed the flat of his tongue hard against my clit then swept it inside me before returning to my clit and spinning me out of control.

My body flew apart. I bowed up, grasped the back of his dark head and mashed my pussy into his face as I came, a guttural, inhuman moan escaping my throat.

I released him, but he didn't stop.

His mouth chased me across the bed, his hands wrapped around my hips, as I scrambled for reprieve.

"Enough!" I cried. "Enough!"

Throwing my legs around his hips, his mouth glistening, he reared up over me. "I say when it's enough, Noelle."

Lining up, he sank deep.

I cried out at the invasion, and he ground his hips in further, eliciting a gasp. Withdrawing to the tip, he swiveled his hips, massaging the ring of swollen flesh at my opening, then plunged back in, again and again, until my body welcomed him.

Hands open on the bed above my head, back arched, thighs spreading wide around his hips, I gave myself over to him.

Nothing sweeter.

His hand to the back of my knee, he pushed himself up and ground his pelvis against my tender flesh.

Nothing better than having him inside me.

My walls fluttered around him, waves of pleasure tugging me under.

I'd take what he gave me.

Dropping to his elbow, he took my mouth, my taste on his lips. Bracing his knees wide, he pounded into me, seeking his own release.

Whatever he gave me.

Yanking my head back, he latched his mouth onto my collarbone, drove inside me, and released his seed, my name a prayer on his lips as he gentled his hold on me.

For as long as he was willing to give it.

I held his head in my hands and pressed my cheek against his temple.

And if he fled, I'd have this to remember.

Chapter 15 - Home

My dad drummed his fingers on the kitchen table, eyes aimed toward the window. His voice gruff, he tried again to say what he'd been trying to say for the past five minutes.

"Noelle. In no way am I trying to tell you what to do. I just want..."

Finally, I took pity on him. "Dad, I'm not going to take offense. Just tell me what's on your mind. Is it about me being at Hawk's last night?"

Grimacing, he answered, "Yes and no. I don't care about you being with him. I think," he blew out a breath, "I think he's going to break your heart."

"Why?" I whispered.

A wariness shadowed his eyes as they met mine. "He's not sure," he reached for my hand. "And you are. And I don't want to lose you for another ten years if he hurts you again."

"What do you mean again?" I asked more sharply than I intended.

Lacing his fingers together on the table, he again looked out the window. "I know something happened between the two of you. Before Hunter passed. Before Hawk brought that woman home." He faced me. "I don't know what happened, but I don't want history to repeat itself."

I opened my mouth, but he raised a hand to ask for another minute. I noted that I inherited that mannerism from my dad as well.

"At the same time, I love him like he's mine. He's been hurting so long, and I know you'd be the best thing to ever happen to him. I'm not so sure he'll be good for you."

"So, what do I do?" I shook my head, at a loss.

"Honey," he sighed. "I wish I knew. But whatever happens, I'm here for you. And as much as I wish things were easy for you, sometimes you need to fight for the good stuff."

"Did you have to fight for Mom?"

"Not in the early years, but we had our tough times. As good as things look from the outside, we're all a little broken, and sometimes those jagged edges cut deep."

My dad's softly spoken words stayed with me as I hurried across the parking lot and through the lobby of Sage Ridge. Still unsure about the wisdom of what I was about to do, I continued on.

Inside, I bypassed the front desk and knocked briskly on Harley's office door.

"It's open," she called.

As soon as I stuck my head in, she brightened. "Noelle! Come in! What are you doing here?"

"Looking for a job, boss lady," I half-joked.

Harley's eyes narrowed then went wide. "You're serious." Her smile split wide open as she screeched, "You're serious!"

I held my palms up but she barreled around her desk to grasp my hands. "I'm so happy! You'll fall in love with Sage Ridge again and you'll stay forever and I'll never *in my life* have to plan another wedding!"

I threw my head back and laughed. It was difficult, if not impossible to be around Harley for any amount of time and not laugh. "Truly, Harley, I need you to be serious for a few minutes."

"Right, right," she chanted as she paced away from me then darted behind her desk. Sitting poker straight, she laced her fingers together on her desk and grinned at me. "You were saying?"

"I'd like to take the job on a temporary basis. Until I decide if I'm staying or going. I have no objection to you continuing your search for a replacement and I'll step aside if you find someone."

"Nope," Harley sliced a hand through the air. "With Christmas coming, it's almost impossible to hire anyone. The soonest I'd be able to start a search would be January. And by then you will have decided to stay, so, no need." She smiled cheekily, beaming with excitement.

"I have another concern, one I'm not sure if I should talk to you or your mom. Who oversees long-term bookings?"

"Mom," she answered decisively. "I'll page her. While we wait for her, I'll go over your responsibilities with you."

While there were lots of bookings, planning didn't pick up until late January. From then it was full speed ahead until October. At which point corporate events took center stage.

Those I could handle in my sleep.

Harley showed me to my new office and explained the ancient binder system they still used.

The software would take a bit longer to work out, but it wasn't anything I hadn't done before. Before the end of the day, Lou came by and made it official.

"I wanted to ask you about renting one of the suites or cottages for the next few months."

"Sure, lamb. Lots are available right now. Take your pick."

"Lou, I have a cat..."

"Oh. Well," she paused. "You'll have to take one of the cottages, then." She drummed her fingers on the desk. "Do you want furnished or unfurnished?"

"Furnished, but I'll take unfurnished if you prefer."

"No, no. Take 3D. It's close to the parking lot and it's got a great view. And it's furnished."

"That's excellent! How much is it and how do you bill? Weekly? Bi-weekly? Monthly?"

"I'll talk to Dan and let you know, lamb."

"Let her know what?" Dan's booming voice filled my tiny office.

Tall and barrel-chested, friendly and charismatic, Hunter would have grown to be just like him.

It pierced me.

"Dan!"

He opened his arms. "How's my girl?"

"Better now," I beamed.

"Yeah?" He drew back to look at me, his eyes kind. "How's that?"

"Well, I've got a job and a place of my own for the next little while until I plan my next steps. I'm home and can catch up with everybody." *And I'm sleeping with your son.* "What more could I want?"

I could think of one thing.

But I hadn't heard from him since I left that morning, and I didn't want to push too hard.

"You want me to round up Hawk and Max and get your stuff moved in?"

The idea of seeing Hawk in front of Dan. And Lou. And Harley. And, oh, Lord, Max, made me feel faint.

His eyes sharpened on my face. "You okay there, honey?"

"I'm good, Dan. I don't honestly have much. Most of it is still in my car. And with the place fully stocked, anything I don't need will be staying in the boxes."

"I'll help her," Harley slung her arm over my shoulders. Or tried to.

I rounded her shoulders with my arm and hers dropped to a much more comfortable height at my waist. "Should we get a bottle of wine?" I asked.

She grinned up at me. "Most definitely!"

My dad insisted on helping and, of course, Lou and Dan showed up as well. It took less than thirty minutes to get everything into the cottage and hang my clothes in the closet.

After they left, I folded the fleece Sage Ridge blanket off the bed and replaced it with my own comforter. I positioned my jewelry box that housed the few pieces of jewelry I loved, as well as the ribbon I arguably loved more, on the dresser. A few framed photos on either side completed my unpacking and personalized the place as much as ever.

Other than Bruce.

Harley threw herself back on the bed and star-fished. "I think your cat is kind of weird," Harley commented.

"So I've been told," I smiled, thinking of Hawk's skittishness around my mini cyclops.

"Who else says he's weird?"

"Hmm? What?" I shrugged. Heat crawled up my chest. "A few people." I flopped down beside her on my back. "I don't think he's weird."

"He's a bit skittish," she countered.

"Most cats are."

She rolled onto her side to face me, and I followed suit. "I don't think we've ever had cats. Either of our families."

"No," I confirmed. "We've always been dog people. It's taken time to learn to speak cat. I'm still not good at it."

Her eyes twinkled. "That's probably why he's weird. You've made him socially awkward."

I laughed. "I don't doubt it. You want to come to the store with me to buy him a birdhouse?"

Harley's brow furrowed. "You want to buy your cat a birdhouse?"

"Not to live in, Harley," I explained exasperatedly. "To hang outside the window. So, he can watch the birds."

"You mean a bird feeder? You really can't speak cat. Or bird, apparently."

"Shut up," I grumped before grabbing her hand and pulling her off the bed.

In the end, I bought a bird feeder, bird seed, a kitty window seat, a climbing gym, and a hand-felted mushroom house that cost more than my monthly car payment.

I'd never felt more at home.

Chapter 16 - Taquitos

Panting, I grabbed my cell and accepted the call. "Hey!"

"Why are you out of breath?" Max barked. He took his role as big brother seriously.

Juggling my keys, I opened my door and tossed them on the counter. "I'm good," I teased. "How are you?"

I grabbed a glass from the cabinet and filled it with water from the tap before guzzling it down. I'd forgotten just how good Sage Ridge water tasted. As if I dipped my face into the spring at the foot of Hailey's Falls.

"Noelle," he growled.

"Really? That's so interesting!" No matter how old I got, that bratty little sister vibe kicked in whenever Max showed up in all his big brother glory.

"Right," he clipped. "I'm coming over."

"What? No!" I laughed. "I'm stinky and sweaty. Hello? Max?" I shook my head as I realized he hung up on me.

One of the best things about living on the resort was the easy access to hiking trails and the gym facilities on site. I'd partaken of both that morning, and I needed a shower. Badly.

I affixed a sticky note to the door informing Max I was in the shower and sprinted through my routine. Throwing my wet hair back into a soft ponytail, I came out just in time to witness the frown that stole across his face as he tore my note off the door.

His dark brows snapped down as he knocked louder. As incensed as he was by my note, he did not notice me slinking over to the door where I stood grinning at him from the other side of the glass.

When he raised his fist to knock again, I knocked back.

He jumped, his hand going to his chest, much like mine did when surprised. I swung open the door. "Did I scare you, old man?" I teased. "Want me to get you an aspirin to chew?"

I was tall but Max was capital T tall. In one step he was behind me, my head tucked under his arm, his knuckles rubbing my scalp. "You're a troublemaker," he groused.

"Is this news?" I wheezed through my laughter as I struggled to free my head. "Are you losing your memory as well? How's your hearing?"

"You don't put a note on your door advertising that you're naked and alone and vulnerable in the shower, squirt."

"It didn't say I was alone," I huffed at his waist.

"I'm going to stuff your nose in my pit," he threatened.

"Ew," I smacked him. "Grow up!"

"Me?" He released my head and cupped my face in his hands as he took his first good look at me. "You started it."

"I started it? Really?" I asked softly as I studied him right back. "Want to call Dad and tell on me?"

Pulling me in for a hug, he grumbled, "What good would it do? He always took your side."

I snorted out an unladylike laugh as his arms tightened around me.

"It's good to see you."

I wrapped my arms over his heavy coat, lay my head on his big chest, and sighed. "It's good to be seen."

After a moment, he broke the silence. "You going to make me a snack?"

Thankfully, some things never changed. "I can do that." Turning to go into the kitchen while he ditched his coat, I rhymed off the tastier contents of my fridge.

We debated the merits of each as he pulled up a stool to the breakfast bar and finally settled on taquitos.

I puttered around the kitchen, choosing glasses, getting drinks, taking down plates, and pondered the wisdom of opening some of my boxes. Using my own things.

Not that my things were anything to write home about. I mentally shrugged. I could buy new things. Things that made me happy when I looked at them. What would I buy?

I pictured warmly familiar patterns and glassware. Things that were packed in other boxes, boxes Dad packed up after Mom passed. The things she insisted be set aside for me.

After all this time, I wanted them.

"Noelle?"

My head snapped up. "What? Sorry! Got lost in my thoughts."

"What were you thinking about?"

"Mom's dishes," I admitted.

"You finally going to take them?" he challenged.

"Thinking about it. Why does it bother you so much?" I'd never understood the way he reacted when I moved, and he never explained.

"Because when you left, you left everything except your car, your clothes, and a few pictures. You brought nothing of home. Nothing of Mom. Nothing of Dad. Or me. I honestly thought you were leaving us behind. I worried we wouldn't even hear from you; you were such a mess."

His words sent me back to that dark time when the growing pile of losses whittled away at my ability to cope.

It appeared he wasn't the only one who had never explained. "I think," I began carefully, "the pain of losing Mom, seeing Dad fall apart," I swallowed hard as the memories kicked off hard and rose to the surface, "seeing you the way you were, it just hurt too much. I couldn't tolerate it."

That and the risk of running into Hawk with Diane every time they came into town. I wondered when he built his house. Was it possible she was old news by then?

"You stayed away for almost ten years. You rarely came home. Was there any other reason? Anything I should know about?"

"What?" I exclaimed, my heart skittering. "What do you mean?"

"Did someone hurt you?" He chewed on the inside of his bottom lip. "Did a man touch you? Hurt you?"

"What? No! My God, Max! I'm so sorry you thought that!"

He waved a hand. "It was just one of many theories."

"Well, now you know. No longer any reason to theorize," I chirped.

His eyes narrowed in concentration.

Pretending I didn't notice, I grabbed the oven mitts and pulled the gooey chicken and cheese goodness from the oven and dished it up.

Sitting on a stool beside my big brother, I reveled in the easy relationship we shared. Max chatted about his work (busy), his dating life (nonexistent), and his (unrequited) travel dreams.

Relaxing back on the barstool next to him, I was unprepared for his sharp turn in subject.

"What happened with the veterinarian? You seemed to like him."

Surprisingly, tears sprang to my eyes. I had not once cried over Barrett other than that one tear. A disbelieving bark of laughter escaped my lips. "I don't know why I'm emotional. I didn't even cry when he first broke up with me, never mind now!"

Unfazed, Max continued, "Did you love him?"

I thought about Barrett, remembered his rare smiles, his tender attention. "You know, I think I could have, maybe I did, but I never let myself go. Not really."

"Disconnected," he hummed.

I held my hand up. "Oh, no! No psychoanalyzing me."

His face split into a boyish grin. How much younger he looked when he smiled! That singular dimple, the one that creased his cheek when he smiled as well as when he nervously chewed his lip.

Mom could never resist that dimple.

"I wouldn't dare!" He held up one finger. "Can I ask you one question?"

I groaned and lay my forehead down on my crossed arms on the counter. "Go ahead!"

"Have you felt more connected since you came home?"

I stilled. Taking in his question, thinking about how much more alive I felt. The sense of home. The memories that permeated the very air of this town. Harley starfishing on my bed. Dan's big laugh. Lou's tight hug. Dad's gentle wisdom. Max's worry hidden beneath his big brother antics.

Hawk.

Finally, I nodded my bowed head. "Yes."

"That's good, Noelle," he murmured. "That's really good."

"I think so," I agreed softly.

"Have you seen everybody?" he asked gently.

"Mostly." I kept my answer vague.

"Have you been out to the cemetery?" he pushed.

"She's not there, Max," I retorted. "Neither is he."

He leaned against the backrest and tipped his beer into his mouth with a sigh. "Don't I know it."

Chapter 17 – Time

"Gross!" I complained, peeling my leggings off my sweaty legs. "I'm disgusting."

Thursday after work, I drove directly to Hawk's place where he immediately tumbled me into bed. By Sunday morning, not having stepped one foot out of the house, and despite the beauty we created between the sheets, we both needed to escape the confines of his walls.

Rising early, we bundled up, filled our thermos at Tim Horton's, and headed for the trail at Wildflower Bluff. We'd been gifted with a thaw but knew the reprieve would be short-lived. The snow would return with a vengeance, and then the trail would close for the winter. But for today, the sunshine cleared our way.

Always a good hike, when we reached the lookout, a large, flat area that overlooked Silver Lake, we rewarded ourselves with a rest and drank our coffees.

I examined the bench he chose. "Is this the bench we carved our names in?"

The first time the five of us hiked up here without an adult, we left our mark. Nobody got in trouble that time.

Carving your name into the benches at the top of the trail was a time-honored tradition.

"Yup." He sipped his coffee.

"You didn't even look!" I cried.

Rounding my shoulders with his arm, he cuddled me into his side. "I come up here all the time and I always sit on this bench." He jerked his chin to the side. "It's back there."

I ran round to the back of the bench and traced the letters, worn and faded by time.

Like my ribbon.

Like me.

"Up here, the world is quiet," I mused, walking back around. "A person can hear themselves think." I snuggled back in under his arm.

"When was the last time you hiked this trail?" he asked.

"Ten years ago?" I said it like a question, but I knew. A few days before I left, Harley and I climbed it and polished off a bottle of wine at the top. Probably not our best decision, but it was a difficult time for both of us.

"I love being up here," he confessed. "It's peaceful. I don't think about anything when I'm here. At all. I just take it in."

"Hunter hated it," I laughed, tears stinging my eyes. Looking around, I noticed the detritus of waste left behind. "I hate when people leave their garbage up here."

Hawk stood abruptly. "Let's pick it up and head back."

Surprised by the sudden change but distracted by the issue of the garbage, I let it go. I'd accepted his changeable moods as his new normal. We'd all changed.

The past couple of weeks with him surpassed my sweetest dreams. Every available moment we found, we spent together. We'd regained the easy camaraderie of our youth but added the excitement of new love.

Well, old love for me, but new for him.

Hopefully.

By the time we made it back home, the sun was high, and the temperature had risen by several degrees.

And we were drenched in sweat.

"You look like you peed yourself," he laughed.

"So! Look at you, Mr. Wet T-shirt contest!"

"All I want to do is lie down on that bed," he looked with longing at the sheets we rumpled so sweetly the night before.

"Shower," I advised. "Shower first."

He agreed, walking his naked butt ahead of me into the bathroom, smiling cheekily over his shoulder. "No funny business," he asserted. "I can barely stand."

I snorted. "No funny business. Are you telling me if I dropped to my knees you'd say 'no, thanks'?"

"Don't!" he stopped in the doorway, his voice warm with humor. "I do not want to get a hard on right now."

I moved in close, twisted sideways, and brushed my naked breasts against his ribs as I passed. "Oops," I quietly taunted.

I didn't even see his hand, but I felt it half a second after it cracked my ass. My mouth fell open. "Hawk!" I sputtered. "You can't just *spank* someone!"

"I just did," he answered smugly.

My eyes dropped to look at his hand but got caught on his erection. I smiled triumphantly. "Ha! My work here is done," I sauntered over to the shower and bent over, taunting him, to turn on the water.

Hawk remained in the doorway with his hands braced on the frame, the muscles in his arms and chest on glorious display, looking down at his dick. "Sorry, buddy. If she takes us there, I don't think I'll be able to stand. You're going to have to wait."

A fit of giggles bubbled up in my chest, but I repressed them as I made a show of bending over to talk to my vagina. "It's okay, sister. We've got excellent toys at home. We don't need him and his little buddy."

"Little?" he exclaimed, stalking toward me. "Who are you calling little?" Pulling me against his chest, he grinned down into my face and reached past me to test the water. "I should take you outside and throw you in the snow, but this will have to do."

With that, he lifted me off my feet and stepped into the shower where the full force of the freezing water hit me.

"Ah, Hawk, you asshole!" I screamed, smacking his back.

He spun me away from the spray, laughing and gasping as it hit him instead while he hurried to adjust the temperature.

"That was mean!" I frowned, my arms wrapped around my shivering frame.

He grinned at me. "But funny."

"Yes," I admitted begrudgingly. "It was funny." I smiled at a memory. "Remember when we all went up to the cottage at Moose Lake and Hunter poured freezing water over the edge of the shower curtain on your dad? Startled him so badly your dad pulled the whole curtain down."

"And stood there naked and gaping while the five of us stared back?" Hawk laughed. "Come here," he held out his hand. "It's hot now."

I grinned. "Harley and I ran out of there so fast. I couldn't look your dad in the face for years."

Holding my hand, he tugged me under the water, dropping a gentle kiss onto my shoulder.

"The man is hung," he teased. "It's where I get it from."

"Oh my gosh, stop talking!"

We made short work of our shower as he held true to his word that nothing but nothing would happen.

He got out first and passed me a bath sheet which made him a truly hot commodity in my book. Getting out of the shower in the cold ranked in the top five things I hated most about winter. It may even have been number one followed by slush, power outages, icy roads, and scraping my car off in the morning.

The volume of his complaints showed me he was not a fan either. Wrapped in his enormous bath sheets, we jumped into his bed and pulled the heavy blankets up over our shoulders.

At that moment, the exertion from our early morning hike caught up with me. My limbs heavy, I groaned, "I can't move."

"Moving is overrated," he huffed. "I thought I was fit, but after this morning I'm not so sure."

Turning on my side, I folded my arm under my head and studied his profile.

Strong nose, firm lips, crazy beard that did crazier things to my breasts and thighs. He smiled up at the ceiling, the fine lines at the corners of his eyes crinkling in a way that called to my heart and my lips.

"You're staring at me again," he chuckled, turning on his side to mirror me.

"You're beautiful," I said.

He snorted. "Women are beautiful, Noelle." He ran a gentle finger from my temple to my chin. "You're beautiful." His eyes warmed on my face. "I'm a stud," he teased.

"You are a stud," I confirmed, hearing the smile in my voice.

Since we'd started, a warm sense of belonging became my daily companion.

My eyes ran around his face, delighting in him, in being so close to him. I held up my hand and, his eyes soft, he pressed his palm to mine.

Watching his reaction, I confessed, "I don't want us to be a secret anymore."

His face fell. When he went to pull his hand away, I quickly laced my fingers through his. "Don't. Don't pull away unless you're doing it for real."

"I'm not," he firmly denied. "Noelle, there are things... if we tell them...I..." He closed his eyes and tucked his chin to his chest. "When they find out, we're going to fall apart."

I gently squeezed his fingers. "How can you say that?"

He shook off my hand and gathered me in his arms instead.

"Hawk? How can you say that?" I worked to get my hands between us, to put some space between us so I could see his face.

"Shh, baby, please." His fingers knotted into my hair, his face bowed into my neck, he rolled me under him.

His solid weight should have been a comfort, but the thud of his heart and the trembling of his large frame alarmed me. "What's wrong?"

I ran my hands up and down his strong back, pressing him closer, knowing I'd never become accustomed to the wonder of him in my arms.

Scared out of my mind that I wouldn't have the opportunity.

"Hawk," I whispered.

"Please," he pleaded, low. "Please give me more time." His fingers bit into the soft flesh of my hip. "I'll figure it out." His knee pushed my thighs apart, nesting his groin in the cradle of my pelvis. "Wrap your legs around me."

And like that, he clung to me.

Eyes wide, my brain scrambled to discern a possible cause for his angst. This couldn't still be about Hunter, could it?

"Hawk, is this still about Hunter?" I asked softly.

He wrapped his arms around me tightly, forcing a grunt from my mouth, but he didn't let go. "There are things I need to tell you...tell everyone...but I'm not ready." His chest expanded with a deep breath, nearly crushing mine. "Everything will fall apart, Noelle. And I can't let that happen. Not yet." Pushing up to his elbow, his mouth gently covered mine.

A tentative exploration. Whisper soft. A tentative request.

I opened to him, and he groaned. Deepening the kiss, he rolled his hips, the evidence of his desire awakening mine.

"I need to have you," he murmured against my lips between kisses. "Can I have you?"

The vulnerable note of uncertainty in his voice corralled my spinning thoughts to laser focus on him. "Yes, Hawk. You can always have me."

His mouth fused to mine, no longer tentative, no longer begging, he demanded my response. The hair on his chest rasping against my breasts, his tongue whorling around mine, licking inside my mouth, drawing me into his. Slipping his hand under my butt, he tipped my pelvis, and dipped inside, back and forth, inch by inch, until fully seated.

"Noelle, Noelle," he chanted, driving inside me, his eyes screwed shut. "You were always meant to be mine. Always." His beard chafed the tender skin of my throat as his lips endeavored to kiss every available inch of skin within reach. "And I was always meant to be yours."

Such sweet words spilling from his lips should have sent my soul soaring. I struggled to grasp the truth behind the words, hidden as it was behind the wary ache in my heart.

I ran my hands up and down his back, feeling his muscles undulate as he moved over me, his breath quickening against my face as he buried himself so deep inside me his ghosts would never find him.

His words, not those of a man in love, but a desperate plea, a painful yearning, a grieving for something not yet lost.

What would it take to hold this man? What could I give that I hadn't? Was I still holding back?

Rearing up over me, his hand cupped the back of my head. "Stay with me, baby," he murmured against my lips. "Want you to come with me."

His stormy eyes held mine, their glossy sheen not lost on me.

I nodded and gave him my mouth.

Tilted my hips, taking him deeper.

My head fell back as he ground against my clit.

"That's it, baby," he praised. "That's it."

The slight buzz that accompanied the complete giving over of myself kicked in, and my body melted against him.

"There you go, beautiful girl. My beautiful girl." His lips danced over my eyelids, the crests of my cheekbones.

I could feel it coming, the wave building, the pressure mounting.

Prickly heat tingled, my flesh engorged further, gripping him tightly, demanding fulfillment.

A ripple of pleasure.

The most exquisite of warnings.

A violent shudder as waves of euphoria engulfed me and obliterated every thought in my head.

Floating in him, in us, the faintest awareness of reality, the world reduced to his hands, his body, his breath, his release deep inside me as he spilled what was only ever meant to be mine.

Chapter 18 – Cloud Nine

He rolled to his back, taking me with him. I lost him from inside me but gained a comfortable resting place for my head on his firm chest, his strong, steady heartbeat beneath my ear, one of his hands in my hair, the other cupping my hip.

Wrapped up in him.

The past few weeks together passed in a happy blur. Seeing as how he was never far from my thoughts, I spent my days in much the same state.

Even Harley, not known for her powers of observation, noticed.

Several times.

"What is going on with you?" she laughed. "You walk around like you're on cloud nine!"

"I'm happy," I shrugged. "It's good to be home."

She walked around me playfully, pretending to inspect me, her eyes narrowed to slits. "You're not walking bow-legged but I'm pretty sure there's a man," she declared. "Only a really good dick can bring about a change like the one I've seen in you." With her pretty lips pursed together, she braced her hands on her hips. "Come clean, Noelle."

Oh, how I wanted to! Especially in that moment, the light of happiness in her eyes, happiness for me. We shared everything. We always had. It might be a little weird for her that the 'good dick' she referenced belonged to her brother, but we could get past that. I teetered with indecision but thankfully held true to my promise to Hawk.

"Harley, if I meet someone new, you'll be the first to know." Not technically a lie, it was definitely within the spirit of a lie. With great effort I stilled the twirling of my fingers and returned her gaze.

She looked uncertain for a moment, her eyes questioning. "Okay," she decided. "I believe you."

I maintained my innocent expression, but inside, I positively rotted with guilt. You don't grow up that close to someone, closer than a sister, and lie to them about one of the most important things to ever happen to you in your life.

Even if it involved her brother.

Especially when it involved her brother.

It got worse when she showed up at my place unannounced when Hawk was there. It may have seemed like a foolish risk to have him there, but he parked on the other side of the resort, and people were used to seeing his truck parked outside at all hours.

It was not unlike him to arrive in his truck and take a different vehicle home. Many times he took a snowmobile home through one of the trails that wound around the lake.

He'd taken me out several times when I stayed with him at his place. Bundled up tightly against the cold, the sound of the motor echoing through the night until we reached our destination. Cutting the engine, we sheltered in a copse of trees he knew well, and stood in our own snow globe, nothing between us and the light of heaven but time.

"I feel closer to him here," he murmured.

It was the first time he'd ever brought up his brother. "I can see why. He loved it out here," I smiled.

"He loved a lot of things," he agreed without looking at me.

I snorted. Time to bring a few things into the light.

Hawk looked at me in surprise.

"Hawk, he loved women. Plural. Many women. We were friends, remember. He shared about his conquests with me. He often asked me about guys I dated and never showed an ounce of jealousy. If he wanted me for himself, he would have said."

A pained look crossed his face.

I latched onto his arm and gave him a little shake. "He never said. Not once. Not a single sign that he felt anything other than sisterly affection. If anything," I mused, "he probably had an idea that it would be great to settle down and take over the resort." I laughed. "He probably decided I'd make a great partner. I don't believe he harbored some great, unrequited love for me. Not one bit."

"Would you have gone out with him?"

"No."

"How can you be sure?"

Should I tell him? Would he freak out if I used the L-word?

"Because I wanted you," I compromised and gave him half of the truth. "I told you even then. Hunter was not on my romantic radar. Even if you didn't exist, the way he went through women? I wouldn't have taken him seriously enough to find out if there could have been anything between us." I sighed, more than ready to put the Hunter issue behind us and move forward. "It would never have happened. Never."

He took in my words, his eyes begging for absolution. For a sin that didn't exist.

"What do I need to give you? What do I need to say so you can free yourself from this?"

His arm shot out and he yanked me into his chest, his other hand cupping the back of my head. "Noelle... so sweet. I knew you would be, but even with what I thought I knew," he swallowed hard, "if I'd known the truth of you, I never would have been able to stay away."

Wrapping my arms around his back, I held him as tightly as I could through the layers of coats and sweaters. I uttered more truth into his chest. Voiceless truth.

I love you. I pressed my nose into his coat, his scent, my lips moving soundlessly.

I love you. The strength of his chest under my cheek.

I have always loved you. I breathed him in, my hands fisted in his coat, aching to say it aloud.

Aching to tell the world. Yearning for him even as I held him in my arms. Held him in my heart. Because I didn't have all of him.

And I worried he wasn't holding quite so tightly onto me.

This, the only shadow over the past few weeks, his continued insistence on secrecy.

He squeezed my hip, bringing me back into the present. "Are you okay?"

"I'm scared."

He jerked at my admission and pulled back to stare down into my face. "Scared? Why?"

"In every relationship I've ever had, I've always held part of myself back. With you, you're so interwoven into my life and heart and mind, I couldn't even if I tried."

"And that scares you," he stated, his arms circling around my back.

I tipped my chin back to see his face. "You could break my heart."

His stormy eyes looked into mine. He opened his mouth to speak, but nothing came out. Then, retreating behind his closed lids, he gathered me into his arms and pressed kisses to the side of my face.

I arched against him, aching for words that didn't come.

It wasn't until the next morning that he offered me something to hold onto.

Setting my coffee down on the table, he swung into the chair next to mine, folded his arms on the table, and stared at me.

"What?" I laughed. "Do I have toothpaste on my face?"

He didn't smile back. "You're perfect, Noelle. Utterly perfect." His eyes raced over my face.

Too serious. He was much too serious. "What? What is it?" I whispered, my heart in my throat.

"Give me until the Christmas party to come to terms with everything. Then we'll sit down and talk. And we'll tell everyone we're together."

I shot up straight in my chair. "Yeah?"

His mouth tilted into a sweet smile, though his eyes remained sad. "Yeah."

I slid over onto his lap and looped my arms around his neck. "I'm going to make you so happy, Hawkley," I promised. "I'm going to chase away the sadness in your eyes. I'm going to beat it back. You're going to see."

"You do make me happy, baby. Happier than I deserve to be. Happier than I ever imagined a person could be."

I hugged him tight, happiness lending strength to my arms. "Eek!"

Chuckling, he wrapped me up and rocked me back and forth.

"I'm going to keep making you happy, Hawk. That's a promise."

A promise that would prove difficult to keep.

Chapter 19 - Limits

"Daire's coming to the party?"

At home, curled up in my mother's favorite chair, I waited for my dad. Every year, the first week of December, Sage Ridge hosted a staff Christmas party. I had missed every single one for the past ten years, but nothing would keep me away from this one. Hawk gave tonight as the deadline, and he'd given me no reason to doubt him.

We weren't going together, but I pictured us walking out together by the end of the night. Our families surprised but happy.

Fantasies of weddings and babies danced through my dreams, asleep and awake. It didn't help that my job revolved around planning those blessed nuptials for other couples. Now, every idea or wish list item expressed by a bride or groom went through my mental Hawk-Noelle wedding checklist. I wondered how involved he'd want to be. Probably not very, I smiled.

"He is," Max grinned. "Do you still have a crush on him? He's pretty interested in seeing you again."

Lost in thoughts of Hawk, it took me a moment to remember my question. Surprised that he'd want to fix me up with a friend, I raised an imperious eyebrow. "And you're okay with that?"

His mouth twisted. "Not if I think about it too long, but he's a good guy. Why wouldn't I want you to have a good guy?"

That boded well, I thought happily.

Max laughed, "So you are excited to see him again!"

"No, no, I just think it's funny. Harley had a massive crush on him, not me. Why is he coming anyway? Have you guys kept in touch all these years?"

"Yes, and we also run into each other occasionally through loose work circles. He's considering a job offer here in town."

"Is he a shrink, too?" I teased.

"No, actually, he's a kindergarten teacher."

My mouth dropped open. "You're kidding!"

His brow furrowed. "What's wrong with that?"

"Wrong?" I laughed and patted his chest. "Absolutely nothing is wrong with that. You poor man, you just don't understand women."

"Well," he growled, "explain it then!"

"A man who looks like that, tall, lean, wide shoulders, that rockstar hair, those eyes, in a profession where he's caring for small children? I bet all the single moms are all over him."

"So, it's an ovary thing," he groused.

"It's an ovary thing," I agreed.

"And ovaries don't get excited about psychologists I'm guessing?"

I gave him a mock sympathy face. "They shrivel up into little raisins and spitball messages to the vagina warning of a drought."

"I'm going to warm up the car," he grumbled. "You laugh but it's a problem. The next woman I meet who has potential, I'm not telling her what I do."

"That's unethical," I called after him.

"Only if she's a patient!" he yelled back.

Pulling out my cell phone, I quickly texted Harley to give her the news. Hoping she'd finally broken up with Paul.

No such luck. Paul was the first person I saw when I walked in with Dad and Max. Coming out of the bathroom, he was still tucking in his shirt. I shuddered. I had no idea what Harley saw in him.

Him wanting her, I could understand. Based on the way he treated her and the asinine things he said, he had no comprehension of his good fortune.

"Don't shake hands," I murmured to Max.

He grimaced as Paul strode forward with his hand extended. "Max, how are you?"

Telling Paul that Max was a psychologist and could not help but analyze everyone he met was a stroke of genius on my part. It ensured an Oscar-worthy performance every time they crossed paths.

"I wish I had popcorn," I murmured.

Max slanted me a dirty look while Paul grabbed his hand and pumped it aggressively, adding a slap to his back to round out the 'good ole boy, I'm an Alpha, you're an Alpha, wouldn't you like to be an Alpha, too' routine.

I hummed the old Dr. Pepper tune under my breath, knowing Max would understand.

"Hello, Paul," I said as I moved away. "Point me in Harley's direction?"

"You can't miss her," he joked. "She looks like a cherry."

He elbowed Max. "You know, round and juicy? She's wearing a red dress that's probably a size or two too small but with an ass like that? I'm not complaining!"

"You do realize Harley is like a sister to me, right Paul?"

He laughed heartily, "She's not like a sister to me, man."

Max's smile did not reach his eyes.

I thought to warn Paul to brace for his imminent evisceration, but he deserved whatever Max dealt out. The man had his limits.

I slipped away just as Paul realized his error.

Searching for both Harley and Hawk, I spied Daire instead. He'd just walked through the doors and was immediately flanked on either side by the high school senior girls we hired to help with the event.

I laughed out loud.

He must have heard me because his chin lifted, and he found me. When he smiled, I remembered it wasn't just Harley who had a crush.

"Daire! Lovely to see you," I gushed, rescuing him from his teenage admirers. "You didn't bring your husband with you this evening?"

His eyes glinted with amusement. "Now, Noelle, you know I'm not married anymore," he teased.

The girls looked back and forth between us in an attempt to discern the truth.

Looping my arm through his elbow, I thanked the girls and led him away.

Dipping his head toward me, he smiled, "Thanks for the rescue. I can't imagine a fairer damsel for the job."

"Flattery will get you everywhere," I assured him.

"You owe me now," he said warmly, patting my hand at his elbow.

I raised my eyebrows in surprise. "You mean you owe me."

"No," he shook his head with a smirk. "If those girls talk the way I think they will, you just killed my love life."

I laughed and slapped a hand over my mouth. "My gosh, you're right!" I pretended to study him. "I think you'll be okay. Anyways, Sage Ridge's ovaries could use a break."

"Sage Ridge's what?" he leaned down, his eyes alight.

"You're a kindergarten teacher. The way you look? Ovaries. Exploding everywhere." I demonstrated with my hands. "If this rumor circulates, just think of all the single moms who won't be bringing you casseroles."

"You've rescued me twice," he determined.

I nodded firmly. "I have." I scanned the area for Hawk and Harley. "Do you remember Harley?"

"Harley?" he pondered. "She the little bitty thing you used to hang out with?"

"Yes!"

"Is she still tiny?"

I smirked. "Only in the right places."

He chuckled. "Noelle, how I missed your humor. Tell me you're not married," he demanded. "Or engaged. Or otherwise tied up."

"I am indeed tied up," I quipped.

I couldn't deny his attention was a welcome balm. Except for the fact it drew my attention to my growing insecurity about Hawkley keeping us a secret.

"You have any inclination to disentangle yourself?"

Grinning up at him, I chirped, "Not a one!"

"And who is the lucky bastard?" He looked around. "Is he here?"

"Um," I stalled for time. "I'm not sure..."

Thankfully, Harley grabbed my hand and spun me around. Looking over my shoulder, she stared up at Daire, her pretty mouth hanging open. "Is this the guy?" she stage-whispered. Badly.

"No," I hushed her, then turned to Daire. "Daire, you remember Harley? Harley, Daire is Max's friend from college. He stayed with us a million years ago when we were young and fresh."

"You both look plenty fresh," Daire replied. His mouth twitched as he surreptitiously took Harley in.

I could not tell what he thought of her, but when Paul stomped up, teasing Harley about her dress, there was no mistaking his irritation.

Now that fine man would be worthy of Harley, at least on the outside. I'd have to get to know him again to see if the inside lived up to the promise of his looks.

I smoothed my emerald green dress over my hips. With tight sleeves and a plunging neckline, the silky wraparound flowed over my hips, and flared gently to my knees. With my silver stilettos and my mother's pear-shaped diamond pendant that I wore only on the most special of occasions, I was ready for Hawk's and my debut.

It wasn't until we sat down to dinner that Hawk arrived. Apologizing for being late, he assured everyone that he had no intentions of holding dinner up any further. Greeting people as he made his way down the table, I sat on the edge of my seat waiting for him to get to me.

Seeing Daire, he stopped and held out a hand. "Great to see you again, Daire. Max tells me you might move up here?"

I smiled widely, bouncing in my seat a little as I waited for him to turn to me.

"Yes, I'm seriously thinking about it," Daire answered. "Hoping to settle down." Glancing at me, he added, "Hoping Noelle might be interested in weighing in."

Startled, I looked up at Daire for a moment before swinging back to Hawk to check his reaction.

Other than a brief tightening of his mouth, he didn't react at all.

I smiled up at him happily. "Hawk, you look wonderful," I purred.

A coldly polite smile on his face, Hawk finally looked at me. Rather, he looked through me. "You look lovely, Noelle. It's nice to see you again."

My face froze around a smile I hoped looked at least somewhat natural. The acrid taste of shame filled my mouth. My breath came quicker as my heart worked to keep up with the surge of adrenalin.

Too caught up in the storm of my emotions, I did not see him walk away.

Daire's voice broke into my thoughts. "Whoa, he's pretty cool to you. You guys aren't close anymore?" Daire studied me quietly.

Only a few short hours ago, we were as close as two people could get. "Oh, you know how these things are…" I trailed off.

I did not in fact know how these things were.

The evening progressed, dinner ended, and people began circulating. Hawk diligently avoided my gaze, and I slipped further and further into confusion.

Daire could not have done worse than having me as a table companion. It must have been a novel experience for him. I didn't imagine he suffered much rejection.

Had I so gravely misjudged the situation?

Did I want a future with him so badly I'd made more out of us than what we were?

Was Hunter really the problem? Or was there something else going on?

The longer he ignored me, the greater my resolve grew. Max had his limits, and as I was discovering, so did I.

Chapter 20 - Set Up

Daire leaned closer, his ice blue eyes intent on my face. "Is he your entanglement?"

"Who?" I asked, my eyes wide.

His eyes crinkled at the corners. "You're a terrible liar."

I pressed my lips together and attempted to pull up my most imperious look, saw the challenge alight in his eyes, and gave up the ghost. "Yes. But he wants to keep us under wraps."

At that, Daire's face turned serious. "I don't think I have to tell you this but I'm going to. If I had your hand in mine, your eyes following me around, fuck, if I had you in my life, in my bed, I would not be keeping it a secret." His eyes searched mine, knowing he was voicing the very thing I desired. Shaking his head, he took my hand in his. "You deserve better."

My first inclination was to defend Hawk, but I would not be that woman. "I know," I whispered.

He gave me a gentle squeeze. "I like you, Noelle. If it comes to it, look me up. I won't say no."

Before I could answer, he pushed back from the table and excused himself. I watched him walk over to Max and pull up an empty chair.

Stricken by that shameful exposure, I looked down at my lap, my fingers twirling the ends of my hair. Needing reassurance, I looked to Hawk only to find his sharp, stormy eyes already trained on my face, the light snuffed out.

A minute later he rose from the table and headed for the lobby.

My need for reassurance ratcheted up and I followed him out. When I didn't find him in the lobby, I went through the employees only door to the long hall that housed the offices. I found him in his office at the end of the hall.

He sat facing his desk, his back to the door, long legs stretched out in front of him.

I knocked on the door to alert him of my presence and walked in. "Hawk? What are you doing, honey?"

Frowning, he gripped the arms of the chair and slanted his eyes toward me. "What did Daire say to you?"

"Daire?" I asked, stalling for time.

"Yes, Noelle," he turned his head to meet my eyes. "Daire."

"He asked if we were together," I began as I edged my way closer.

Immediately, his brows drew together and he barked, "What did you tell him?"

Shocked by his reaction, I drew back. "I said yes. I tried to lie but I'm not a good liar."

He rubbed a harsh hand over his face and growled.

My patience fled, my shame flared, and I rose to my own defense. Hands on hips, I narrowed my eyes. "You know, I could give myself to you. All of me. Anything you want, anything you need, I'll give you. But I can't tear myself down for you."

His eyes snapped with ice as his entire body attuned to me. "What the hell does that mean?"

"I mean," I began, my voice rising with my temper. "I'm not going to be anyone's dirty secret."

His mouth fell open in shock, then he scoffed, "You're not a dirty secret!"

"But I am a secret," I pushed, leaning toward him.

"No," he pushed back, sitting forward, "we're a secret. But maybe we shouldn't be anything. Maybe you should be with Daire. He's interested in you."

"Don't get off topic. Daire is not and never has been a part of this." I took a breath to calm myself. My voice, when I continued, reverberated with the pain of every loss, every rejection. "I don't want to be a secret. I feel cheap. And I have never felt cheap in any of my relationships. Disposable in the end, but never cheap."

Standing, he reached out a hand for me to come to him. "I've never treated you anything less than precious to me," he stated firmly. "You are precious to me."

I crossed my arms over my chest and hugged myself. "Keeping us a secret is treating me less than precious," I argued. "I'm lying to everyone I love. Everyone we love! It's not right and I can't do it anymore. We need to come clean."

"What the hell is going on?"

A startled scream flew from my mouth, and I skittered backward at the sudden intrusion of Max's booming voice.

His sharp gaze darted back and forth between us. Whatever he saw in Hawk's face wrenched a growl from his chest and he barreled forward, his fist twisted in the front of Hawk's shirt as he continued forward and slammed him against the wall.

"Max! No!" I cried, running forward and hanging onto his arm.

"Cheap?" he whispered menacingly, his nose almost brushing Hawk's. "Did she say 'cheap'?"

I gasped, lacerated by the word I, myself, had provided.

Hawk stared back at Max, his eyes lifeless.

The sight turned the blood in my veins to ice.

I shouldn't have pushed.

I should have treasured what we had, what we were building.

I should have given him more time.

With both hands wrapped around Max's bicep, I felt the vibrations of the adrenalin strumming through him. I yanked on his arm and cajoled, "Max, you have to stop!"

His eyes spared me half a glance and his whole body tensed as he leaned further into Hawk's space. Shaking him roughly, he sneered, "You sack of shit, you're not worth the effort."

Hawk looked sick, his face pained, the first sign of life since Max came in the room and it wasn't a good one.

I kept waiting for him to defend himself, defend us, but he said not one thing.

Releasing his shirt and slamming him once more into the wall, Max then turned to me. He opened his mouth to speak then snapped it shut, his lips turning white with the effort to suppress words I surely did not want to hear.

My breath stuttered out of me as he stalked away. I dropped my chin to my chest and panted out a shocked breath. The relief was short-lived.

"How long?"

I spun to find Harley looking at me, hurt and anger shining in her eyes.

"How long?" she demanded, her voice shaking.

"Six weeks," I whispered.

Her mouth fell open. "Six weeks? Six *weeks*?" She stared at me, her eyes wide. "You've lied to me for six weeks, Noelle?" Her gaze dropped to the floor for a pregnant moment before she looked back up. "So many times, so many opportunities and you never once said."

I moved to go to her, but she stayed me with her hand.

"No. Not right now, Noelle."

She looked at her brother, leaning against the wall, his head down before looking back at me. "I told you he was fragile," she hissed.

"Harley," I pleaded.

"I can't right now," she snapped, her heels clicking across the floor as she left me alone with Hawkley.

Spinning on my heel, I went to Hawk. I needed to pick up the pieces, and quickly, before I lost it all.

"Did you do it on purpose?" he asked dully.

Disbelief rendered me dizzy as the hits kept coming. "What?" I whispered, hoping against hope he'd take it back.

"Did you set me up?" He bit off each word. "Did you want Max and Harley to come back here?"

"No!" I protested. "I don't know how you could even think that!"

Pushing away from the wall, his fractured heart visible behind his eyes, he stared down at me, "I told you what would happen. You couldn't leave well enough alone." Hands hanging at his sides, he dropped his chin to his chest.

I raised my hand to cover his heart.

He stepped back, heaved in a deep breath, his eyes darting around the room as if looking for an escape.

"Hawk," I whispered. "What is going on?" Surely people knowing about us did not warrant this much drama.

Barely sparing me a glance, he uttered three words. "We are done."

My mouth fell open. *What?* "No, Hawk, no," I countered softly. I launched myself at him, my hands going to his chest. "It'll be okay, Hawk. They just need time to adjust."

"No, Noelle," he wrapped his hands around my wrists. For a long moment he paused, pressing my hands tighter to his chest, his eyes closing before gently pulling them away. He released me and stepped back.

Oh, God. This was it.

Have you given it all? Have you held anything back?

"Hawkley," I looked up into his face. "It'll be okay. I love-"

Stepping back, his neck corded, his vein pulsing, the fury he'd held in check now palpable, he roared, "It will never be okay! We. Are. Done."

I reeled back, my hand over my breaking heart. Disbelief rendering me speechless.

Spinning on his heel, he picked up his chair and flung it against the wall where it smashed on impact.

"No," I mewled, as he fell apart. I backed up, my hands over my mouth, stunned by the force of his rage. This mood I'd never encountered. How did we get to this crazy place where I didn't even know him?

Picking up a leg, he smashed it against the wall again and again until only splinters remained. His chest heaving, he stood with his hands braced against the wall.

I took a single, tentative, step forward. "Hawk?"

Roaring, he drew back his fist, slammed it into the wall, and walked out, sparing me not a glance. Drops of blood spilled from his split knuckles, marking a trail to the devastation he left in his wake.

"Oh, God," I whispered. Half in disbelief, half in supplication.

Staggering back into a chair, I leaned forward and hugged my knees. His face. His furious face. Those lifeless eyes.

We are done.

No. No way.

My head shot up. Was he going to drive? I didn't have time to break down, I needed to stop him.

By the time I made it to the front door, he was gone. Through the window, I watched as his car sped past.

A knock on the door.

It's your son.

There was an accident.

Hunter is gone.

'Drive carefully, darling,' my heart cried, my hand splayed on the glass until his taillights winked out of sight.

I stood facing the window, staring into the past, threading an imaginary ribbon through my fingers as I prayed that history would not repeat itself.

A new set of footsteps sounded behind me. I turned to face the next onslaught only to see my dad, wary eyes alert, heading straight for me.

Two steps away, he held out his hand.

I grasped it like a lifeline, and he pulled me into his side. Still taller than me, but shorter than he used to be, that change, a blistering reminder of another loss yet to come.

I gulped.

Felt myself being ushered forward.

A door closed.

Lou's office. Warm with wood, lit with stained glass. Covered in family photos.

He turned me into his chest, his tight hug holding me together.

I curled into him.

My body stiffened.

Oh, no no no no no.

Keep it together.

My brain replayed the events of the last few minutes, the last few hours, the last few weeks, and further back to the day at the pool before returning to Hawk's furious face.

"We are done."

The air thinned. I gasped for breath.

"You're okay, Noelle," my dad murmured, rubbing my back.

"Oh, God..." I looked around for an anchor, something to hold my attention, but the world swam in front of me.

"Breathe, honey," he urged.

A gentle hand stroked my hair, Lou's voice sounding behind me. "Let it out, darling girl."

It? I shook my head. Twisted my hands in my dad's sweater. I was no longer sure where I ended, and 'it' began.

I swallowed my sobs, but they shot right back up, breaking from my lips in strangled cries, seizing hold of my lungs in their quest to escape.

If I let it out, I'd never be the same. That tight control kept me from the abyss. If I let go, my grief would consume me.

Lou's gentle hands cupped my shoulders, ran down my arms, and unfurled my fists before taking me from my father.

I caught sight of his beloved face ravaged by a renewal of his own grief as Dan's arms came around him.

Lou turned me into her motherly arms and nestled me against her softness. Reminding me of what I had.

What I lost.

My neck arched back, fighting for room to rein it in, swallow it down, push it away, but it had grown to be bigger than I was and would not be contained.

The sounds that escaped my body frightened me, but Lou held firm. "It's a long, long time coming, darling. Let it out."

My heart in my hands.

Don't go there.

A knock at the door.

It's your son.

A telephone call.

Mom is sick.

We need to talk.

I've met someone.

Hawk.

We are done.

Three little words.

A handful of syllables.

A lifetime of afters.

"Hawk," I cried, my voice rasping. A decade of grief saturated that single syllable, then wrenched it from the very heart of me, and split me wide open.

My body bowed forward, caving in, my walls in flames. I clung to Lou, her softness, her familiar smell, her arms an oasis in the desert, as the loop played on. As my heart bled, my soul keened, and my walls fell into a smoldering pile of ash at my feet.

I began to shake.

And Lou held firm, her voice in my ear.

Incapable of discerning any meaning from her words, the sound of her voice alone threw a line to rescue me from my isolation, to pull me from my self-imposed pit.

The reality of all I'd lost waited at the top as I pushed my way out. Like a baby coming into the air, the first breath burned. I squeezed my eyes shut at the shock and clung to Lou. To what I still had.

For as long as I had her.

I swallowed.

Convulsed.

The first tear fell.

I allowed that.

Then the second, and a third I did not permit.

"I love you, Lou," I blubbered.

Dan coughed behind me and cleared his throat.

"Aw, my lamb," she stroked my hair and held me tighter, her voice strained. "I love you, too."

I pulled back so I could see her face. I had to tell her. I had to tell somebody. I had no idea if my celestial emails were working, and I needed someone to know.

I grasped her arms. "I miss my mom," I whispered.

A garbled sound came from my dad. I ignored it, focused desperately on Lou's eyes. I needed another lifeline and I hoped somehow she held that one as well.

"I miss her, too, lamb."

I nodded in acceptance and took a deep breath. Tried to release her, but my hands would not obey the message from my brain.

I nodded again, clinging desperately.

"What else, lamb?" she prodded.

My eyes flew back to hers. "Hunter," I blurted, and grew alarmed as tears sprang to her eyes. "I'm sorry!"

"No," she shook me lightly. "Never apologize for bringing up his name. That's how we keep him alive." Her eyes searched mine. "What else?"

This was harder. Fresher. Soul-deep.

I swallowed convulsively. Tried to keep it in, but this pain, too, demanded to be shared.

"Hawk." His name came out with a deep, guttural sob.

"I know, lamb." Lou's eyes held compassion. Acceptance. Love.

"Oh, no," I moaned. My chest constricted as I struggled to hold in the worst of it. I wrapped my arms around my head to hide my face, give myself space to pull myself together, but there was no holding back the deluge.

The sharp edge of his rejection.

The anguish of seeing him with his arms around her.

The loss of my mother.

Leaving my family.

The lonely silence of my self-imposed isolation.

And losing him again after learning just how beautiful it was to hold him.

My heartache, so deeply buried, erupted with a wail.

I tried to step back, to turn away, to hide, but Lou held firm.

"I've loved him for so long," I blubbered, batting away my tears. "I told him, but he didn't want me," I confessed, my words garbled and broken. "And then Hunter died, and it hurt, and everyone fell apart."

"Yes, lamb. I hear you, sweetheart," she murmured at intervals, as she took it all from me.

"I couldn't see him with her," I gulped, my stomach working to physically expel the wretched images of him and Diane burned into my brain.

I gagged, choking on the mucous in my throat.

I pressed the back of my wrist to my mouth.

My tears fell faster.

My voice rose.

"Then my mom got sick and... and... she left us. I wanted to stay home. I wanted to, but I couldn't stay. And I'm so sorry, Dad," I spluttered to Lou, unable to face my father. "I'm so sorry!" I cried. "I'll make it up to you. I'll make it up to everyone."

"Nothing to make up for, lamb," she assured me, drawing my face into her neck.

The dam broke. With my fingers drilling bruises into her shoulders, I hid inside her strength and let the tears fall. Tears that drained and cleansed, leaving me both hollow and lighter.

I breathed in her familiar perfume, let it fill my senses, calm me, taking the place of the rancid sorrow I'd held inside for so long.

Behind me, my father bowed his gray head over mine and put his arms around Lou and me.

And Dan.

With his bearlike chest and his massive reach, he wrapped his arms around all of us.

Heavy with fatigue, I sagged between them.

Only then did they take me home.

Chapter 21 – Love Him

Back at home in my childhood bedroom, I woke slowly to the sound of a soft knock at my door. My heart leapt in my chest.

Hawk.

Sitting up quickly, I called out, "Come in!"

Dad opened the door and winced at the look on my face. "I'm sorry, honey." A cup of coffee in his hand, he crossed to my bed and sat on the side.

"How many times have you sat in this exact spot?" I asked, my voice gritty from the night before. "I bet you didn't think you'd still be doing this at thirty-five years old, did you?"

He shook his head sadly. "I'll do it when you're eighty-five."

Tears sprung to my eyes, and I impatiently wiped them away. "Friggity-frack! I've barely cried in ten years and now I can't seem to stop."

Setting my coffee on the nightstand, a small, sad smile on his face, he said, "Lou's right. It's been a long time coming."

"Dad," I whispered, thinking of the drama that unfolded the night before. "What have I done?"

"Nothing," he shook his head firmly. "Our family has been broken for a long time. First, we lost Hunter, then Hawk disappeared inside his head. Not that long afterwards Mom got sick and we lost her, too. Then you stopped coming home, Max does nothing but work, and Harley's temper goes off at the slightest provocation."

"And what about you, Lou, and Dan?"

"You can't weather those kinds of losses and not change. But where you kids withdrew into yourselves, we turned to each other." He looked at me thoughtfully. "Do you know I moved in with Lou and Dan for six months after mom passed? I couldn't stay here without her."

"I'm so sorry, Dad," I murmured, stricken. "I should have been here. I should have been home."

"No, Noelle. What I needed, I got from Dan and Lou. But I don't think you got what you needed to heal."

Ignoring his last statement, I asked, "Do you want to sell this place? Start over?"

This time when he smiled, humor glinted in his eyes. "You couldn't get me out of here with a crowbar." He looked around my room. "Every crack and crevice carries a memory. Most of them, good. All of them, precious. My happiness, the proof of a love well lived, permeates these walls and lives with me still." He cocked his head as he looked at me. "It's that connection to Mom, to Max, to you, that keeps me going."

Connection.

The very thing I'd run from ten years ago. Shutting down to block out the pain.

"Connection," I repeated.

"It's everywhere. You just need to let it in when it finds you." He looked at the floor for a moment, absentmindedly tapping his fingers on his knee. "You're like me, you know. You and Max both."

"What do you mean?"

"Mom," he smiled, "Mom loved with abandon. She chased me relentlessly. Courageously," he corrected. "I was scared of what she made me feel. It got worse after we had you and Max. I remember asking her about it once. How she could love so freely without worrying about losing one of us."

Yes.

God, I wish she was here.

"What did she say?" I asked, my attention rapt.

He smiled wistfully. "She was surprised. Said the fact that she could lose one of us at any time was the precise reason she loved us the way she did." His eyes, softened by time and memories, looked far away. "I intend to leave every piece of my heart here on earth. Not taking any of it with me. Going to spend it all. Spend it all on you..." When he came back to the present, his eyes glittered with unspent tears.

My father and I had never talked about feelings before. That was my mother's forte. I'd never once asked him how he felt about Mom's passing. And he'd never asked me. I ventured one more question. One that terrified me. "You still miss her the same way, Dad?" I whispered.

"No, darlin'. I miss her more."

I miss her more.

Some losses produce an ache that never fades.

The cost of the connection we crave.

His words stayed with me, replacing the awful loop from the past twelve hours. They stayed with me while I showered and dressed and ate breakfast.

They stayed with me when I drove through the gates of the Sage Ridge Resort later that afternoon and parked outside my temporary home.

Hunter was everywhere here.

So was my mom.

We all were.

They stayed with me when I slipped the key in my lock and scooped up a belligerent Bruce who was so happy to see me, he couldn't put forth the effort to play hard to get.

They stayed with me the next day when I hit the bluffs again. The trail to the top had closed, but the path down to the beach welcomed me. I could almost hear us laughing, the sound echoing back through time with the churning of the waves.

And they stayed with me all through that long night when I heard not one word from Hawk.

They were with me still when I walked into work Monday morning and knocked briskly on Harley's office door.

Betraying her mood, Harley barked, "Who is it?"

I froze, wondering how to answer. It's your bestie? Not your favorite person at the moment? The woman who shagged your brother and would happily do so again?

I heard a feminine growl come from the other side of the door. I raised my eyebrows and grinned to myself. Time to take the bull by the horns.

Opening the door, I sang, "Good morning, bestie."

Harley's brows lowered, and she raised a hand. "I am not in the mood for this right now."

"I get it," I replied. I stepped inside and registered the exact moment her nose caught a whiff of the deep-fried bear claw covered in cinnamon and cream cheese. Setting it on her desk with her regular coffee order, I pulled up a chair. "If I go, I'll take the bear claw with me."

It was not a huge gamble. Harley rarely ate breakfast, often suffered from low blood sugar from forgetting to eat, got migraines due to her caffeine addiction, and harbored a major sweet tooth.

"You can stay for as long as it takes me to eat it," she grudgingly allowed.

"Can I speak?"

Looking at me sidelong, she grumbled, "Let me at least enjoy the first bite before you start."

When we were kids, there were only two offices set up for use along this back hallway. The rest of the rooms, Harley's present office included, sat empty.

When she was on bite number three, I pounced. "This was our room."

With her index finger full of cream cheese and halfway up to her mouth, she paused. "What?"

I circled my finger in the air to encompass the room. "This was our room. The year your mom started working here full time, she and your dad gave us this room. We had a dollhouse over there," I pointed to her bookshelf, "and I believe...I can't believe we did this, but I believe 'the portal to hell' is behind your fish tank."

She smirked. "It's still there. I wouldn't let them fill it in when they renovated the offices. Hawk's office is on the other side. We had a tiny door installed."

I smiled at her. "I can't believe we didn't get in trouble for that."

"Some of us did," she laughed. "Hawkley took the fall for all of us even though it was Max and Hunter's idea."

"And we were fully invested," I murmured.

Harley carefully contemplated the surface of her desk. "He always felt so responsible for all of us." She looked up at me, a challenge in her eyes. "He took Hunter's death the hardest. I lost both my brothers that day."

"I know it's not the same, but I lost them, too."

Her frustration boiling over, she demanded, "Why would you get involved with him, Noelle? You had to know screwing around with him would not end well."

I looked her in the eye, making sure she heard each word. "I'm in love with him. I've been in love with him for over a decade. He's the reason I left, the reason I haven't been able to make it with anyone else." I shrugged. "I'm not screwing around."

Harley's eyes widened at my bald revelation. "A decade?" she whispered.

"More," I whispered back.

She leaned over her desk, still whispering, and suddenly we were back to us. "Why didn't you ever tell him?"

"I did. Right before Hunter's accident." A tear slipped down my cheek. They were so commonplace at this point, I barely noticed. "He told me he wasn't interested."

"Bastard," she scowled, then grinned at me.

I grinned back, then got serious. "I'm sorry I lied to you, but I had to respect his feelings. It was a lose-lose situation for me. I've loved him for so long, if he was finally going to give us a shot, I had to take it."

"Of course," she murmured. "I'm sorry, Noelle."

"Love you, Harley. Never would have lied to you if I could have done this any other way."

Coming around the desk, she perched on my lap, her short, little legs swinging, and threw her arms around my neck. With her forehead pressed to mine, she promised, "I'm here, okay?"

I nodded, swallowing around the lump in my throat, one more kind word away from bawling. Again.

A brisk knock on Harley's door sounded half a second before the door swung open. "Hey, Harley. I got here as soon as I - for fuck's sake, do I even want to know?" Max complained.

Harley winked at me. "It's purely platonic, Max."

166

He huffed out an irritated breath. "Good. I've got nothing against lesbians. Or throuples. But how the hell would this work? A total mind-fuck."

"We're not a throuple. Ew, Max. That's my brother." Harley shifted off my lap and pushed him into a chair. "Want some of my bear claw?"

"Ah, that's how you got in," he mused, throwing me a bemused look before sarcastically adding, "Nice to see she was your first stop."

I gave him my best cat's smile. "She wasn't."

That got his attention. "What do you mean?"

At the look on my face, he sat back and groaned. "What did you do?"

"I might have ordered you some reading material to help you get used to the idea of me boning your best friend."

"Fuck," he stood, hands on his hips as he glared at me. "Do you have to put it like that?" His eyes darted around the room. "You did something to my office?"

"Yup," I gloated. "And you're forgiven."

He pointed at his own chest, his face a mask of surprise. "I'm forgiven?"

"Yes," I replied evenly. "But if you ever put your hands on Hawkley because of me again, you and I are going to have trouble. I've loved that man my entire adult life. I don't know if he loves me, yet, but he wants me. For some reason only known to him and God, he doesn't feel like he should have me."

Max seemed to deflate at my confession. "But you want him."

"I do. Always have." *All in.* "Always will."

"Well, fuck me," Max breathed. He contemplated me for a moment, then that damned dimple flashed. "What can I do?"

I leaned forward, eager to begin my campaign. "Love him."

Chapter 22 - My Sweet Girl

I'd grown used to my office. I added a few throw pillows I found in town and bought myself a mug just for work. I'd even hung a framed painting I found in my childhood bedroom that I fell in love with a million years ago.

I sat staring at that painting while I contemplated my situation. Stage one of my campaign to win Hawk consisted in showing him that our family would accept our relationship.

For her part, in true Harley fashion, she planned to unleash her Mama bear on her brother, berating him for keeping me a secret, and in that way, showing her support. Harley rarely exposed her tender underbelly. A tiny bulldozer, she showed her love and support the only way she could. Which made it all the more incomprehensible that she put up with Paul.

Max promised to go see Hawk just as soon as he cleared out the shipment of romance novels featuring heroines falling in love with their best friend's brother or their brother's best friend. Knowing Max would be at the receiving end of endless amounts of ribbing from the women who worked with him amused me to no end.

Other than that, I had little to smile about.

I weaved my ribbon through my fingers. Since the Christmas party, it lived in my pocket or my purse. A comfort and a reminder. Though I wasn't so sure anymore what it was supposed to remind me of.

With stage one underway, I turned my thoughts to my next step. I knew part of the key lay in reducing his guilt around Hunter. Another lay in simply loving and appreciating him until he could see his worthiness. Though, as Max pointed out, not knowing 'his reasons for believing himself undeserving of happiness presented a considerable obstacle'.

Those were his exact words. Harley nearly pissed herself laughing at Max's psycho-speech.

One of Max's best qualities was his ability to laugh at himself. As usual, by the time he left Harley, his dimple appeared to be permanently drilled into his cheek.

A soft knock at my door drew my attention.

"Hi, Lou," I called softly, my heart filling with all the goodness that was having her in my life. "Come on in."

She shook her head. "Come on, honey. I'm taking you out for lunch."

I shot up. "Is everything okay?"

"Nothing new has happened but I think it's time to go over some of the old. And I'm feeling a deep need to check in with you and I'd like to do that over a leisurely lunch so I have time to do that."

"I'll grab my purse," I replied, crossing to grab my coat and scarf on my way. "Where are we going?"

"The closest thing to home we can get without going home," Lou answered.

Sitting in the passenger seat of Lou's ancient SUV assailed me with more memories. She refused to get rid of it. Even went so far as to have the entire engine replaced much to Dan's agonized amusement.

How many times had the five of us piled in here to get dropped off and picked up at school? The movies? The mall on the outskirts of town? Most everywhere else in town, we could walk. But those three places, on the outskirts of town, required a drive.

Or snowmobiles.

We'd only done that once when we were teens. The hell we caught for that stunt didn't bear thinking about. Even all these years later, I shuddered at the memory.

"Are you cold?" Lou reached to turn up the heat.

"No," I huffed out a laugh. "I was thinking about the time we took the snowmobiles to go to the movies."

Lou flicked the indicator to take the turn and laughed. "Child, that was one of the few times I'd ever seen your mama truly angry." She shook her head. "Dan, too. He always took your antics with a shrug, but when Hawkley and Hunter came in holding Harley between them with her sprained ankle? He had to leave the house."

Lou slid into an available spot at the curb and led me inside Susie Q's. Of course. Perhaps it was not the best place to have a private conversation, but it was, like she said, home.

Susie, herself, greeted us at the door. "Well, I'll be a monkey's uncle!" she exclaimed with her hands on her hips. "Look what the cat dragged in! Come here, girl. Give your Aunt Susie a hug."

Before I could properly respond, Susie jostled me into a bone-crushing hug. "Good to have you back home!" She pinched my ribs. "Let's get some meat on those bones!"

"Oof," my breath escaped in a puff of hair that morphed into a delighted laugh. "Susie! I've missed you," I confessed honestly.

She patted my cheek gently and beamed up at me. "Me too, doll. Me too."

Reaching a hand back for Lou's, Susie led us to a corner table. Giving Lou a quick kiss on her cheek, she promised to call her to catch up before leaving us.

"She's still a hurricane," I noted with a smile.

"Hope she never changes," Lou agreed.

When we ordered dessert, Susie's treat, Lou got around to the reason she wanted to go out for lunch.

"I think by now you've figured out that Hunter's death changed Hawkley," she frowned. "It was a dark time for all of us and I fear, in my grief, I neglected to mother my other two children. I don't think either of them have properly grieved, if there is such a thing as properly grieving.

"Dan, Harley and I talk about Hunter all the time, but Hawkley never mentions him. It's like he's dead to him in every way. As if he never existed. And I know that's not true. I see the pain in his eyes whenever Hunter is mentioned, but he never speaks of him.

"I don't think the very mention of his name should still cause him this much grief," she finished.

Despite her words, Lou's eyes clearly professed her continual suffering.

"I think everybody grieves in their own way, Lou. And you're a wonderful mother."

She lay her hand over mine. "Thank you, lamb." She looked away for a moment before turning back to me. "I try. Everybody grieves differently, this is true, but the signs of healing look pretty much the same. And I see none of those in Hawkley."

"Do you know we celebrate his birthday every year? We don't put a number on the cake, though Harley insists we have a cake." She smiled. "That girl has a terrible sweet tooth."

"She does," I laughed in agreement.

Her face softened with good memories. "We do it to remember. We eat too much, talk about old times, family vacations, the trouble you all got into. The Portal to Hell that we all knew was Hunter's brainchild for which Hawkley took the fall." Her smile faded. "Hawkley never comes," she whispered. "Not once in ten years. It's like he's taking the fall for this as well."

"He feels guilty," I blurted.

Her gaze sharpened on my face, "Why?"

My mouth snapped shut, unsure what to say.

She waved me away. "He's obviously spoken to you about it and that's," she took a deep breath, "that's a really good sign. I don't want you to betray his confidence," she paused. "I'm going to speak to you as a mother. His mother."

I scrunched my brows, unsure where she was going.

Looking at me intently, she squeezed my hand. "Don't give up on him. I haven't seen this much life in him since we lost Hunter."

"You've seen a change?" I asked, eager for any encouragement.

"Yes. A big change." Her lips trembled and her voice shook. "I want my son back and if you're the change that's come over him, I want more of it."

"I want that, too," I agreed softly.

She didn't look any happier at my admission as our server placed my cheesecake and her apple crumble on the table in front of us.

"I have more to say, lamb," she murmured.

Then she stopped talking. My stomach clenched with what might be coming. I cleared my throat. "But it's okay with you if we're together?"

"Oh, yes," her smile, quick and radiant, reassured me. "Never doubt that. Your mother and I used to dream about it." She laughed. "We also dreamed about Max and Harley. Can you imagine those two together?"

I snorted. "No. They'd kill each other. Actually..." I laughed.

Lou finished, "She'd kill him."

"Exactly!"

"Eat your dessert. I want to tell you about me and your mother."

Stories I'd heard before, as well as a few new ones, she shared them all. Long after I finished my dessert and Lou paid the bill, she spoke of her friendship with my mother.

"I miss her," I smiled, nodding madly and blinking back my tears.

"Oh, lamb, I know. You haven't healed either." She pressed her lips together. "I hope you and Hawk can heal together. I hope that with every fiber of my being. But. Because I love you dearly and your mother will always, always, be my best friend, I'm going to speak for her."

A chill raced over me leaving goosebumps in its wake. As if I might actually hear my mother's voice after all these years.

"Don't settle for less than you deserve. And you, my sweet girl," tears sprang to both of our eyes at her use of my mother's endearment for me, "You deserve the world."

Chapter 23 - Gamble

Slumped behind my desk, I closed my eyes, grateful I had no appointments and no event set up to oversee. Nine days had passed since Hawk walked out on me after the Christmas party, and I'd been riding an emotional rollercoaster ever since.

After the initial shock, I'd focused on my campaign to, well, heal him. I truly believed a visit from Harley and Max would have been enough. Stage two could not begin until he contacted me.

Except he still hadn't contacted me.

Six weeks of living in each other's pockets, followed by nine days of radio silence.

My resolve to wait on him was fading. And the hope I held onto so tightly began to ooze through my fingers. I refused to think about it. Every time the thought popped up, I banished it to the far recesses of my mind.

Not having much to do at work made the minutes pass like hours. I paced the confines of my small office until I swear I wore a groove in the floorboards.

I crossed to the filing cabinet where the 'ancient texts' as Harley and I had dubbed them were housed. Binders and binders of notes, pictures, and resources from every event at Sage Ridge over the past ten years.

Over the past ten years.

The part of my brain invested in self-preservation urged me to move on. The rest of it, slave as it was to my rabid curiosity, would not let it go.

Dragging my finger along the spines, I continued my internal argument until I found the year I wanted.

My hands shook as I spread it open on my desk and began to leaf through the pages until I found what I was looking for.

Hawkley Bennett and Diane Mason.

My lip curled up in distaste.

Close it. Nothing good can come from this.

With one eye closed and the other squinting, I turned the pages of their file to ensure there were no pictures of the bride and groom tucked in with the samples and the notes and the illustrated design for the venue set-up.

No part of my brain wanted to see that.

With that settled, I leaned over my desk and took in every word. Every mention of the bride elicited a snarl. She was demanding and complained about the fabric of the napkins, the dishes, the cutlery, the size of the head table, and the platform for the band. They had a band? I didn't even think Hawk danced.

I sat back in my seat and slammed the binder shut. I did not want to see the notes on how it all eventually went down.

Did they have a first dance? Of course, they did. Even their song choice was noted. Did he pick it? Did she? Was it their song?

It was a stupid song, anyway.

Stupid, stupid, stupid. I hit my forehead with the heel of my hand. I knew nothing good would come from looking in that file.

I stared out my office window. The edge of Sage Ridge, its silvery pines, just visible. I focused on that point until it blurred while my mind dragged me into the past.

"Hawk?" To my eternal embarrassment, my voice cracked. "Can I talk to you?"

He smiled easily, wiping his hands off on the towel he carried in his back pocket when he was on pool duty. "Sure. What do you need?"

I pointed to the deck chairs. The pool area was deserted. It always was at this time of night. "Can we sit?"

His face creased with concern. "Are you okay?"

"What? Yes!" I rushed to reassure him. "It's just... important. And it can't wait any longer."

He waved me to go ahead of him. I sat back in a lounge chair and put my feet up. I needed all the physical support I could get. But in that position, I was practically lying down.

Feeling incredibly vulnerable, I shifted my legs, one on either side of the chair and sat forward. No. That wouldn't do at all. Like an invitation. Which was great if he took me up on it, but maybe not the best if the conversation went south and he didn't want to.

Go south, that is.

Ha.

I swung my right leg over to join my left which put my back to him. Also, less than ideal.

His deep chuckle sounded behind me. "Noelle, what the hell are you doing?"

My chair jerked as he flopped onto the bottom and yanked my legs up, draping them over one of his.

"Oh," I gasped. It had been a long time since I'd touched him. Every point of contact between us tingled with awareness.

His hand, still wrapped around my ankle, seemed to flex and release as he stared down at it. Transfixed.

Hope swelled in my chest as the moment dragged on.

"Hawk," I whispered. "Do you think…"

His head whipped up to face me, his expression intense, almost angry. "Don't."

"Don't what?" My voice trembled.

"Don't go there. It's not in the cards for us."

I'd come that far, I didn't want to leave without being sure to shoot my shot. "But I think…"

Standing, he gently placed my legs on the lounge chair. With both hands wrapped around my ankles, he gave me a gentle squeeze. "I'm sorry, Noelle," he muttered. Then without looking at me, he walked away.

A lump the size of a golf ball lodged in my throat as I sat and stared at the stillness of the water.

I could feel it even now. At twenty-four, I was no teenage girl in the throes of her first crush, I'd loved him silently for years at that point. His outright rejection was not a case of simple humiliation.

It crushed me.

Then Hunter passed.

Hawk brought Diane home.

My mom got sick.

The walls of the town closed in and, as soon as I could, I left.

After that I visited, taking care to avoid Hawk and Diane, but I couldn't move home.

For nearly a decade I flitted from town to town and man to man. Never giving either more than my bare minimum.

Except for Barrett. And in the end, I screwed that up as well by holding too much of myself back. Unwilling to lose anything else.

April's words came back to me. *'I hate to see you alone. You're far too beautiful, inside and out.'*

Maybe I was simply destined to be alone. Twirling the ends of my hair around my finger, I contemplated the possibility. It wasn't what I wanted. Growing up with the examples set forth by my parents and Hawk's, I knew love could be beautiful.

And I wanted it. I'd always wanted it, but those losses so close together sent my poor heart into hiding. Now I was ready to give all of me, and Hawk didn't want anything to do with me.

Don't go there.

I'm sorry, Noelle.

We. Are. Done.

Standing, I snatched my coat, hat, and scarf off the hook. It was far too cold for a walk, but I needed to escape. I opened my Pokemon Go app to clock my steps and hatch my eggs.

Staring down at the small screen, I opened my office door and crashed into a wall. A wall that smelled like sin. A wall that exclaimed, 'Oof'.

"Mothertrucker!" I exclaimed, bouncing off. I looked up. "Daire? What are you doing back here?"

"Lou said I could come back and knock on your door." His eyes shifted down to my phone and a sexy grin stole over his face. "Are you playing Pokemon Go?"

I looked down at my phone, my tiny virtual pet ready to rumble. "Uh, yeah?"

"Fuck me," he laughed. "You're adorable. Where are you going all bundled up? It's freezing outside."

His unexpected presence, his words, that cologne, his sexy smile, and worst of all, getting caught with my Pokemon out, befuddled my mind.

"Uh, I just needed to get out for a bit…" I trailed off.

"Come on," he invited, throwing his arm around me for a second and giving me a brief squeeze. "I'll take you out for a coffee."

"Um," I tried to think.

He stopped and faced me. "You wanted to get out, right?"

"Well, yes," I nodded.

"Right," he adjusted my scarf around my neck. "Let's go. Your timing is perfect."

Before my brain could catch up, I found myself sitting across from him at The Beanery sipping hot chocolate and chatting away as the afternoon sun sunk low in the sky. I began to laugh.

He raised his eyebrows, his mouth tilting up. "What?"

"You're very smooth," I accused.

He grinned unrepentantly.

I laughed but the awkwardness of the situation could not be ignored. "I'm, uh, at least I think I'm *involved*-"

"Noelle," he began. "I'm sorry to cut you off. I don't want you to be uncomfortable. I know things are complicated at the moment. I just wanted you to know, if they become less complicated, I intend to be here. In this spot. Across the table from you. As well as in other places. In close proximity to you."

My mouth fell open and I sat staring at him, my mind a tangled mess. Questions I'd asked and answered a hundred times over the years came surging back to the forefront of my mind.

Could he be the one?

What if things with Hawk never worked out? Did I want to be alone?

What seemed like a simple but grand plan, love him, proved to be anything but in its execution.

And across from me sat a man I'd crushed on as a teenager. A man who looked like a rock star but taught kindergarten. A man who was tender and nurturing, and unless my radar was off, that nurturing would take good care of me under many different and exciting circumstances. He expressed his interest and intentions clearly. No games. Here was a man I could easily fall for.

If I didn't already love Hawk.

I looked into my nearly empty mug. The man across the table stood for the past ten years. Running from the hard stuff. Safeguarding my heart. Afraid to go all in with what I truly wanted.

But, oh the sweetness of being pursued.

Feeling wanted.

An intoxicating aphrodisiac.

One I would have to resist if I wanted any chance at all with Hawkley.

I raised my chin and met his eyes.

His beautiful lips pressed together momentarily, then he stood and rounded the back of my chair, pulling it out like the gentleman he'd always been. "I'll drive you home now," he murmured.

Touching his forefinger to my chin, he pushed it upward.

Panic flashed at the thought he might kiss me.

He shook his head ever so slightly. "I'm not going to kiss you. Not now. But I want you to remember what I said." He applied slightly more pressure, and I wondered just how deep the gentleman act went. "Will you do that?"

"Yes." The temptation to fall into him and let him sweep all the rejection away, even if it offered only a moment's reprieve, rode me hard.

Hawkley's furious face the last time I saw him.

The hurt in his eyes.

I stepped back.

"Thank you for the hot chocolate."

"My pleasure," he replied easily, his intensity dissipated. "My heart is still intact and we're still friends."

I laughed. "Well, that's good. I could use more friends."

"Be sure to count me in that number," he smiled.

We didn't speak on the way home. Would it be awkward saying goodbye? Thankfully, Max and Harley were waiting at my door with pizza.

Max's eyes darted between Daire and me, filled with questions I had no intention of answering.

He held his fist out to Daire. "Was just about to message you to meet us here. Just wanted to make sure Noelle was cool with us landing on her." Turning to me, he continued, "You okay to have dinner with us?"

Daire's eyes flicked to mine. In light of what he'd just revealed it was perhaps not the best move but there was no way to say no without awakening suspicion.

By the slight twist of his lips and the glint of humor in his eyes, Daire knew my predicament and had no intention of helping me out by distancing himself.

"It smells good," I replied. Seeing a hint of anxiety in Max's eyes, I assured him, "I'm glad you're here."

He relaxed until we got inside.

"Be careful of the cat, Daire," Max warned. "It's a bit... off."

I laughed. "He's not 'off'. He's perfect."

Bruce sauntered past all of us and went straight to Daire, winding around his legs and head-butting his knees.

Daire leaned down and scooped him up, causing all of us to stiffen, awaiting Bruce's mighty reprimands.

"Don't worry," Daire informed us, "I speak cat."

Bruce purred in his arms, his tail swishing under Daire's arm.

"See?" he looked at me smugly at which point Bruce sunk his tiny teeth in the pad of Daire's thumb.

"Fuck!" he exclaimed, quickly releasing Bruce.

"I thought you knew how to speak cat?" I teased.

"I do!" he assured me. "He just asked me to put him down."

For the first time in a week, I laughed. And I continued to laugh as he and Max entertained Harley and me with stories from their college years.

Hours later, with Bruce wrapped around my head in my bed, I wondered if I was the world's biggest fool to pass up a good guy like Daire in favor of taking a gamble on Hawkley.

Chapter 24 - Better

By Wednesday, day eleven, I couldn't bear the endless, empty workday ahead, and I needed a reprieve from the pitying looks that landed on me at regular intervals. If we'd been a secret before, we were definitely not anymore.

"Bruce? I think it's long past time to introduce you to your namesake."

Holding up a DVD, because for some movies you had to go old school, I continued, "This is Bruce Willis. This is a man. The man. Triple threat. Fierce, funny, and fuckable."

By the end of the movie, I'd gone through almost an entire box of tissues. "I know, Bruce. I'm not fierce. Not at all. Not even a little bit."

The detritus of my binge lay scattered over the surface of the coffee table. Where I fully intended on leaving it. My heart was a crime scene, and here lay the evidence. Seeing the mess was bizarrely satisfying. I decided not to examine it too closely. Introspection was Max's deal, not mine.

I had just tossed another used tissue onto the growing pile when the doorbell rang.

Sitting forward on the couch with my elbows on my knees, I sighed deeply. Maybe if I ignored them, they'd go away.

The doorbell rang again.

Through the peephole I watched the delivery man retreat down my path. Swinging the door open, I called out a thank you and looked down to find a box wrapped in a swath of paper and plastic. Peeking inside, a tiny indoor garden awaited me.

"Oh!" I could handle sympathy if it came like this. Bringing it inside, I peeled off the paper.

A bowl, shallow and wide, housed tiny flowers interspersed among a variety of succulents. Tiny ceramic gnomes and forest creatures frolicked between them.

My fingers trembled, knowing who sent it but fearing the letdown if I was wrong, as I opened the card.

A simple 'H' scrawled across the card revealed little of his intent in sending me this gift, but I understood the reference.

My mother's collection of garden gnomes delighted me as a child, embarrassed me as a teen, and destroyed me as an adult when she left them to me.

Noelle,

There is magic in the world. I know this to be true based on the wonder of all that is you. Open your heart and you'll find it.

I love you always.

Mama.

It was Hawkley who found me taking a hammer to her gnomes.

It was Hawkley who wrestled the tool from my hands, and Hawkley who rescued the remaining statues from my grief-stricken tirade.

I showed him the note and watched as tears came to his eyes.

He swallowed hard and nodded before handing the note back. "She's right you know," his voice cracked. "If anyone deserves magic, it's you."

Kind words.

They'd always been my undoing.

From him, they were kryptonite.

My anger melted away and I crumpled. His arms caught me as he followed me down to the hard ground and rocked me as I silently grieved, sucking in great gulps of air in my effort not to cry.

I often wondered what happened to the survivors, but I never asked. If my dad got rid of them, if they lay in a landfill somewhere, I didn't want to know. My mother's final gift to me and I destroyed it. So long as I didn't ask, I could picture them tucked away in a shed or a closet somewhere. Not at my dad's place. I'd searched every nook and cranny. But somewhere.

Inside, I cleared the coffee table and set the fairy garden at the center.

"Don't touch it, Mr. Willis," I whispered. "This is important to Mama."

Suddenly fatigued beyond measure, not understanding the intent behind Hawk's gift, and more than a little angry at its ambiguity, I went to bed and slept through to the next morning.

Resolved to stick to my routine, I marched into work on Thursday determined to continue familiarizing myself with the different aspects of my job. Enmeshed in pricing, supply lists, and vendors, lunch rolled around without me noticing until Eva from reception knocked on my door with a brown paper bag in her hands.

The smells emanating from the bag made my mouth water.

"Somebody likes you, that's for sure," she quipped as she left it on my desk and sailed back out.

My stomach growled. The last bite of food I'd sent down the chute was during yesterday's afternoon binge fest.

No card. No paper. Nothing.

But inside, a takeaway container from Ayana's with the same meal I'd eaten when he took me weeks ago.

This message was slightly easier to interpret but I couldn't be sure unless he spelled it out for me. And I was not ready to ask him. In case his answer killed my hope.

Friday, much to my dismay, passed without incident. With a heavy heart, I opened my door at the end of the day, tossed my purse and coat on the chair, and flopped onto the couch.

Bruce leaped up, walked up my body to stand on my chest, stared down into my face and loudly demanded his dinner.

"You want to eat? Of course, you do," I murmured. "Let's go get you some food. In the tiny kitchen, I opened a can while he urged me to go faster. "You hungry, Mr. Willis?" I crooned.

Feeling his head butt me on my thigh, I hurried to get the food into his bowl, knowing what followed the -

"Ouch! Bruce!" I rubbed my ass where he nipped me and quickly put the bowl down on the floor. "Don't bite Mommy's bum!" I grumbled. "I think you're the one who doesn't speak cat! You're a monster!"

Pacing around my tiny living room, I pondered the wisdom in texting Hawk. Was it my move? Was there such a thing as moves at our age?

I didn't want to push him too fast.

I didn't want to know yet if this was his way of saying goodbye.

The doorbell rang and I whipped around to face it. Moving slowly, instinctively knowing he was on the other side, I opened it without shifting the privacy blinds.

"Hi," I croaked, my heart in my throat.

He stood on my front step, looking much the same as he did when he woke me in my car. Faded jeans, beanie pulled over his curls, lumber jacket buttoned to the chin, a heavy frown pinned firmly in place.

"I tried to stay away but I visited you every night," he gruffly confessed.

My mouth fell open. Stepping back, I opened the door wider to invite him in.

"Saw Daire come out of your place on Thursday. Stayed away Friday and Saturday. Didn't want to see him come out again. Wanted to give you a chance to move on."

"Nothing happened," I whispered, wondering why we were standing in the doorway, desperately wanting him to come in.

"You should have the opportunity to move on. I should just let you have that option." He frowned down at me, his eyes as sad and stormy as I'd ever seen them. "I can't give you that option."

"Do you want to come in?" I finally breathed.

Instead of answering, he looked over his shoulder at his truck. "I parked right in front, and I'd like to keep doing that for as long as you'll let me."

I backed up, a tremulous smile on my lips, tears balanced on the tightrope of my eyelids.

Pushing me gently backward, his hand splayed over my stomach, he explained further, "Where everyone can see and know we're together. I want to take you out in town, hold your hand, kiss you whenever I want."

I nodded vigorously but no words came out.

"Do you want that, Noelle? With me? Because baby," he cupped my face in his big hands and continued on in a whisper, "I'm a mess and I don't see that changing anytime soon. Are you sure you want to put up with the up and down that being with me is going to entail?"

"Yes," I croaked. "I'm sure. Always been sure. Always will be sure."

His eyes searched mine as he whispered, "You deserve better."

Smoothing my hands from his abdomen to his chest, I grasped the front of his shirt. "Then give me better."

Chapter 25 - Consequences

Walking down Main Street Saturday morning with my cold hand tucked into the crook of his elbow felt all kinds of right.

On my birthday no less, possibly the best one I'd ever had. I woke that morning with Hawk in my bed and a shiny silver bangle clasped around my wrist.

With less than a week until Christmas, visitors had descended on our tiny village in full force. Sage Ridge, known for its seasonal festivals and celebrations, was no slouch at Christmas either. All four corners of the town square offered sweets for the tummy and treats for the eyes. Our giant Christmas tree reigned over all from the center of the square.

Plenty of locals bustled about as well. I lost count of how many people did a double take when they saw us together. Hawk made no mention of it, but I wondered if the attention bothered him.

When your family went through a tragedy, you became somewhat of an unwilling spectacle. Your presence, a thrilling reminder of the fickle nature of fate. Their sorrow for you, outweighed only by their gratitude that it bypassed their household. The pitying looks. The ducking away when they didn't know what to say.

But this type of attention didn't bother me at all. It would be terrible if he walked away from me again. I gave my head a little shake. No good came from thinking like that.

Hawk flexed his arm around my hand to get my attention.

I turned and looked into his eyes. Eyes that had seen me in every mood and had reflected every mood back to me at some point or another. Eyes I could read as easily as my own. Eyes that hid something, that something being *the thing* that stood between us and the future I envisaged for us.

His brow furrowed. "Are you okay?"

"Yes," I assured him, the warmth of his concern crowding out my worry. "I'm more than okay." I tightened my grip on his elbow. "I'm happy."

His lips curved in a sexy grin. "Good," he muttered. "You deserve to be happy."

"Yeah?" I teased.

"Definitely. And I'm going to see that you're ecstatically happy when I get you home."

I wrapped my other arm around his and pressed my breasts against his arm. "Might take a while."

His lips quirked. "I'm up for the challenge." Turning his body into mine, he backed me out of the pedestrian traffic until my back hit the wall. Looking down at me, he raised one thick eyebrow toward the handful of purchases he carried. "How much longer are we going to be shopping?"

I'd bought for Max, my dad, and Bruce. I may have gone a little bit overboard on my cat if Hawk's rolled eyes were anything to go by. I knew what I wanted for Lou and Dan; I just hadn't found the right one yet. But Harley was my wild card. I'd know the perfect gift when I saw it. Hawk's gift, the only one I bought early, was already safely ensconced at his parents' place.

I tilted my head. Sweetly saccharine, I patted his cheek softly and teased. "You have to be patient, sweetie." Fascinated, I watched his eyes darken.

"You're a brat," he asserted, his jaw clenching.

I raised my brows in surprise. Did he mean in bed? Was I? I thought about Barrett, if we'd had this dynamic.

A second later Hawk's hand wrapped around my jaw. "I don't like to think about you with anyone else. Don't think about him. Not when I'm standing here in front of you."

I began to tease him but the intensity in his gaze stopped me. "I don't think I'm a brat," I whispered. "I think I'm testing your parameters."

His eyes softened as his long fingers stroked my throat. "You want me to test yours? Is that what this is about?"

My eyelids fluttered shut. Did I want to be tested? I swallowed just as his thumb grazed over my Adam's apple.

"Mouth dry, baby? Want me to put something in it?"

My lips parted as my eyes snapped back open, darting from side to side before returning to his. "Yes?"

His thumb stroked the line of my jaw. "You feeling a little unhinged? Want me to take the reins?"

"Yes." Of that, I was sure.

He hummed, satisfied with my answer. "For every ten minutes you make me wait, you'll earn yourself a consequence."

Being friends since childhood had given me a false sense of familiarity. I suddenly suspected I'd barely scratched the surface of his sensuality. I wondered what kind of consequences he had in mind.

I protested weakly, "But I still have so much to get..."

He dipped his knees and caught my eyes. "I'm counting on it."

An hour later, I panted on my hands and knees, my arms stretched over my head. "Hawk...please..."

By my count, I'd earned three consequences. I considered the fact I finished my shopping within thirty minutes a minor miracle, but the uncertainty of what was coming turned out to be fierce motivation.

I barely spoke to him as I rushed from store to store, catching his eye now and then, my heart skipping a beat at the heated amusement in his. By the time we reached his house, my nerves were stretched taut like the strings of a violin.

He ushered me up his front path, unlocked the door, and set my bags to the side.

With my back to him, I placed my purse and gloves on the chest behind the door and reached for the top button of my coat.

As soon as the front door closed, his mood changed. Awareness crackled between us.

I stuttered, "Do I, uh, need a safe word?"

He snorted. "Stop, no, or wait will work just fine."

His hands came to my shoulders, and he turned me gently to face him. Cupping my face between his large palms, he brushed his mouth across my lips. "Everything will be for your eventual pleasure."

I swallowed. "Eventual?"

His lips tipped up on one side. "It wouldn't be a consequence if it was easy. Take off your coat and hang it on the hook."

I turned toward the hook.

"Face me, Noelle. I always want your attention on me unless I tell you otherwise."

I could bare my body with ease, but giving him access to my face, especially when he could read my every expression, boasted of a deeper intimacy. A greater exposure.

With shaking fingers, I released the buttons and let my coat fall down my arms to my hands. Quickly glancing to the side, I hung up my coat and turned back to face him.

Tossing his coat to the side, he undid the buttons at the cuffs of his shirt and rolled them up his forearms. "Shirt and bra, please."

I pointed at the floor at my feet. "Here?"

He smiled. "Right there is perfect."

I glanced at the front door to my right. There was no glass, but it wasn't locked either. I pointed toward the door. "The door is right there…" My voice petered off.

"Thank you, Noelle. I know where my door is. Shirt and bra, please."

My brows lowered at his words.

"Tick tock, baby." He crossed his arms over his wide chest and rested back on his heels.

The muscles in his forearms flexed across his chest. What the heck, I mentally shrugged. I wanted to play his game; I knew I did. What I didn't want was to earn any further consequences until I understood how he played.

I made quick work of the buttons on my blouse and flicked the front clasp of my bra open. Pressing my arms back, I allowed both to fall to the floor behind me, my chin raised proudly as I met his eyes the way he demanded.

He dropped his arms to his sides and stepped toward me, halving the space between us. "Everything else off."

My eyes skittered to the door before returning to his face.

He watched me patiently. What was the worst that could happen? We'd be embarrassed? Caught bare-assed? I huffed out a tiny laugh to myself.

His eyes crinkled with amusement as if he knew my thoughts. Maybe he did.

Holding his gaze, I hooked my thumbs into my jeans, grabbing my panties on the way, and slid them both over the top of my hips.

His eyes skated the length of my body. On his way back up, at my pelvis, his lips parted with a tiny huff of breath.

Gratified to see the power shift to me, I wiggled my hips and slid my pants over my bum and down my thighs to the floor, watching as desire flushed his cheeks. My socks followed and I stood before him, fighting my smile.

One step and his mouth brushed across my forehead. He tilted his chin down, a silent demand for my eyes, which I gave him. Bending his neck, he brushed his mouth across my cheekbone and traced the shell of my ear with the tip of his tongue until his teeth rasped my earlobe.

"Good girl."

And that quickly, the power shifted back.

Knees weak, my eyes drifted shut. I reached for him, laying my hand over his chest to steady myself.

"Eyes, Noelle," he breathed. "You don't want to miss this."

I forced my eyes open and watched as he dropped to his knees before me.

His chest inflated as he breathed me in. Running one hand down the length of my leg, he stopped at my ankle and tapped it firmly before wrapping his fingers around it.

I shifted my weight to my other leg and allowed him to pull my leg up and over his shoulder. From there, I expected the teasing to be merciless.

It wasn't.

Parting me with his thumbs, he dove in.

The back of my head and both of my palms hit the wall while the leg over his shoulder slammed down against his back, holding him to me.

"Sorry!" I gasped.

"Don't be," he muttered. With both hands scooping behind me to cup my cheeks, he pulled me closer.

My passion rose quickly, and I panicked at the thought he might pull away. I tightened my leg around his back.

He chuckled against me then dug his fingers into my soft flesh, wrapped his lips around my swollen bud, and suckled me gently into his mouth.

The first wave hit, and my hand found the top of his head. Curling my fingers into his hair I held him in place until it became too much.

Whimpering, I drew back, pushing gently on top of his head.

Leaping to his feet, he gently covered my mouth with his then scooped me up and carried me to his bed.

I looped my arms around his neck. I'd gotten off easy. My lips curved softly upward, deeply satisfied.

Half an hour and three orgasms later, I begged for release. On my knees, my wrists lashed together and secured to the headboard, I pressed my forehead into the mattress. Hawkley's hard thighs pressed along the back of mine as he slowly pumped in and out. "Hawk ...please..."

"Give me one more, Noelle. One more and I'll call it a night," he urged. "Come on, sweetheart. You came on my face. You came on my fingers. You came on your own fingers for me." His hands ran soothingly up and down my spine. "I know you're tired, but I want to feel you come on my cock."

His dirty words strummed my clit as surely as his hands and his tongue.

A deep moan built in my womb and traveled upward.

"Yes, sweetheart." He spat on his fingers and reached around to rub a tight circle around my clit. My body bucked beneath him.

"That's it, baby." Circle. "Let go." Circle. He swelled inside me. "Give it to me, Noelle," he demanded. "I want it."

The tension built, my body fighting the almost intolerable pleasure until the tension suddenly dissipated, and my ribs hit the mattress. Back arching deeply, hips tilting up in offering, I accepted the fire as it lazily rolled through me.

"Good girl," he grunted, dragging his hands up to my hips to hold me in place, his movements becoming purposeful in seeking his own release. "One orgasm is a gift. Four orgasms are a consequence."

The last word escaped on a gasp as he emptied inside me, making my thighs slick with our combined release.

Rolling me to my side, he pulled the end of the scarf to free my wrists and brushed my hair back from my face.

I licked my dry lips. "So," I croaked, "the consequence to shopping too long is fucking me to death?"

Laughing, he pulled me into his arms. "It's not a bad way to go," he teased.

Chapter 26 - Sanctimonious

Max's house did not look like the quintessential bachelor's pad. Classy and comfortable. A warm hug but a slap upside the head if you tried to put your feet up on the coffee table.

Even his Christmas decorations consisted of only the most tasteful of greenery with a touch of tulle.

From the moment you stepped through the door, the whole house welcomed you. No unnecessary clutter. Soft, muted walls, vibrant rugs and throw pillows.

Max inherited all the interior decorating genes leaving exactly none for me. The one time I bought a throw pillow, it turned out to be a dog bed.

Unsurprisingly considering our afternoon activities, we were the last ones to arrive. Harley and Daire sat on either end of one of the couches while Max sat across from them, his expression carefully blank.

I laughed at the sight. "You look like you're in couples' counseling and things aren't going well," I joked.

Harley narrowed her eyes at Daire who cocked his head and smiled politely back at her. "Well, this half of the couple has had enough for now."

Daire briefly dipped his chin. "For now," he agreed, which only seemed to rile Harley further.

Standing up, she flounced from the room.

Hawk's jaw tightened. He glared at Daire. "What's going on?"

Max stood and intercepted his death glare. "We were talking about Paul. Harley brought up the subject. Daire gave his opinion. Which I share," he added. "Harley didn't take it too well."

"What did he say?" I breathed.

Daire leaned back against the couch as Max moved out of the way. "I said she needed to find someone who appreciated her instead of hanging onto a loser who didn't know his ass from his elbow."

Hawkley grinned. "I imagine she didn't take that too well."

Daire ran his hand over the top of his head and huffed out a laugh. "She told me where I could shove my elbow. Which is not anatomically possible, by the way."

I laughed and disengaged myself from under Hawkley's possessive arm. "I'm going to go check on her."

I found her in Max's bedroom, curled up on his bed.

"Hello, shrimp," I called softly.

"Argh," she grunted. "Why can I not keep my mouth shut with anyone other than Paul?"

I lay down facing her. "I don't know. Why can't you open your mouth with Paul?"

She sighed. Uncharacteristically, a tear slipped past her defenses. "Because I've become accustomed to gritting my teeth. If I ever let loose on that man, he might never recover."

"Why are you with him?" I ventured softly.

Harley's eyes flashed.

I held up my hands in a surrender pose. "I'm asking, not judging. Why are you with him? Give me the good."

"He's not a terrible person. He can be sweet occasionally..." she began. Her brows lowering, she pinned me with her gaze. "The truth is, he's an ass! But he's the best I've been able to do, and I don't want to be alone."

"Does he ever make you happy?"

"Sometimes," she grumbled. "Occasionally. Once in a while." She sighed, then twisted her mouth into a smirk. "Not anymore."

"Have you tried to talk to him?"

"Yes." She rolled onto her back, Harley-speak for 'I'm going to tell you, but I can't look at you while I do it'.

"I told him how it makes me feel when he makes comments about my looks. About my body."

I could feel my temper rising. "What did he say?"

She threw her arm over her eyes. "He told me I needed to lose weight. For my health," she spat.

I rolled to my back, Noelle-speak for 'I'm going to speak my mind and I don't want you to hit me so I'm exposing my tender underbelly'.

"He's an ass. You should dump him. Might I even say, he's a loser who doesn't know his ass from his elbow and you should find someone who appreciates you."

Harley snorted. Then huffed. Then began to laugh. "I overreacted a bit in there."

"Hmm."

"I told Daire to stick his nosy elbow up his sanctimonious ass."

I snorted. He hadn't told us that part. "Sanctimonious?"

Harley turned to face me, her eyes dancing. "It was an honest compliment. Have you seen that man's ass? It is morally superior to any other I've seen."

I nodded enthusiastically while at the same time turning an invisible key at my lips.

"Is my brother jealous?" she whispered.

"Insanely so," I whispered back.

Her eyes widened. "I could have so much fun with this."

"Please don't!"

Harley opened her mouth to tease me, but I cut her off. "If you do, I'll tell you all the ways he punishes me."

"Ew!" She covered her ears. "No. No! Okay, you win!"

I nodded sagely.

Her smile slowly faded and the sadness she fought to conceal broke through. "I have to break up with Paul." She closed her eyes. "I just don't know if there's anyone better for me out there. I want kids. I want a dog. I want a man who loves me."

"I know." I reached for her hand. "It's not him. The longer you stay with him, the longer you'll have to wait to get all those things you want."

"You're right." She rolled onto her back.

"Are you ready to go back out there?"

"You go first. I'll be there in a minute. Have to prepare to apologize," she snarled.

I hugged her and heaved myself from the bed. In stocking feet, I slipped down the hall back to the living room. Just as I was about to enter the room, I heard my name.

"You have a thing for Noelle."

"I do."

"Are you going to be a problem for her?"

"No. I have no intention of causing trouble for you. For either of you," Daire stressed. "I'm not in love with her. I can walk away. But she's a great girl." There was a long pause. I imagined them lining up, readying to fight. I was just about to walk in when Daire continued. "If you choose to walk away from her again, I won't be so generous."

"Those who eavesdrop seldom hear anything good."

Max's voice behind me made me jump.

"You nearly made me scream," I hissed.

"It's not like I was trying to sneak up on you!"

"Where were you?"

"In the bathroom."

"What were you doing in there?"

"Really, Noelle? You want the details?"

I scowled.

He laughed and pulled me along the hall and back into the living room.

Hawkley and Daire seemed to have negotiated a truce because the rest of the evening went smoothly.

Especially after Harley returned from her self-imposed time out.

The conversation stuttered a bit when she entered the room before picking back up. Then, as it happens with these things, it came to a roaring halt.

"Oh, for fuck's sake," she exclaimed. "He's an ass. A giant ass. And there is nothing remotely sanctimonious about it."

All three men stared at her expectantly.

She threw up her hands. "And I'm going to break up with him."

A chorus of three replied, "When?"

She huffed out an unconvincing laugh. "Before Christmas."

Chapter 27 - Love

Christmas Eve morning dawned bright, the light bouncing off freshly fallen snow. Bruce curled up on my chest, his tiny paws making bread on my breasts.

"You like those, buddy?" I scratched his raggedy ears. "Yeah. You're not the only one. No scratching, ok?"

Turning his head, he nuzzled into my hand. I gave him what he wanted knowing his tolerance for my attention was often fleeting.

"Where's Hawkley, Bruce? Is he having coffee?"

Standing up, Bruce arched his back, turned around to present his butt to me, an action I'd been assured was a gift, and settled back down for a butt scratch.

My attention drifted to the sliver of light peeking through the crack in the curtains.

Hawk hadn't been himself since the evening at Max's place. Like, somehow, he'd been muted, becoming a shallow reflection of himself.

In my mind, I called it the darkness. It kept him up late every night, tossing and turning when he finally succumbed to sleep. One night he woke me up, grunting and crying out in his sleep.

He didn't seem to remember it the next morning.

Then last night, surprisingly, he went to bed much earlier than usual.

Hours later, when I carefully slipped into bed beside him, he woke up immediately and reached for me.

"Hey," I whispered. "Sorry to wake you."

"Noelle," he whispered, rolling me under him, nudging my thighs with his knee. "Let me in, baby."

I parted my thighs around his lean hips.

He found my entrance and slowly worked his way inside, his eyelids fluttering shut. Holding himself up on his elbows, he pressed his forehead to mine, whispering my name like a prayer.

This Hawkley, I hadn't met yet. The urge to soothe, to comfort, rode me hard. I stroked the length of his back. Pressed my body to his. Tipped my chin up to dust his scruffy jaw with kisses until my body accepted him.

With his hands on either side of my head, he rolled his hips, nudging the secret spaces deep inside me.

My eyelids fluttered shut.

"So sweet." he pressed closer and swiveled his hips, delivering delicious friction to my sensitive flesh. His sweet lips worshiped my closed eyelids with gentle kisses.

His body quaked. He needed me.

I spread my thighs wide, drawing my knees up to hug his ribs, my feet curved around on his back, my hands flexing over the muscles in his strong shoulders.

Whispered words of adoration fell from his lips as he sought to bury himself deeper, and he rubbed his scruffy cheek against mine.

"Too good for me," he murmured against my mouth, "but I'm keeping you anyway."

"Hawk?"

Covering my mouth with his, gently licking inside, his tongue begged entrance I would never deny as he kept up his maddeningly slow pace.

"Shh," he soothed, his thumbs rubbing circles over my temples before gently closing my eyes. "Don't speak. Just feel me the way I want to feel you. To remember. To hold this memory instead of-"

My mind raced. Instead of what?

"Stay with me, sweetheart," he urged, covering my mouth again and again, licking, nipping, tasting, teasing.

Joining.

How long I'd dreamed of this.

How much sweeter and deeper and sadder and more intense than I imagined. Beautiful. Exquisite. So thankful I didn't know. How would I have survived if I'd known what I'd lost?

He was my missing piece.

My missing peace.

The one my soul called for, the one my heart ached to hold, to heal.

To love.

His fingers tightened in my hair as he reared up over me, his own thighs spread wide as he strove to eliminate the space between us, demanding my response, groaning as I clenched around him, giving him what he wanted.

"Noelle... Noelle," he murmured against my mouth as I came down, one hand gliding down to capture my hip as he rocked harder, chasing his own release. "My good girl, my sweet girl, my girl, my girl, my girl-"

His back bowed and his forehead pressed to mine. Gentle puffs of air caressed my face as he panted out his release before wrapping his arms around me.

"My girl," he breathed into my neck.

Rolling to his back, he dragged me up his chest.

I tried to lift my head. To question. To reassure.

"Shh. Don't speak." His hands tight in my hair, he pressed my head to his heart and quickly fell back to sleep.

Not once opening his eyes.

I blinked away the beauty and confusion of the night before.

I shifted, preparing to gently transfer Bruce to the floor. Sensing my movement, he beat me to it, digging his pointy feet into my chest as he launched off my chest. I massaged my poor boobs as I walked out to my living room to look for Hawk.

A post-it on the door drew my attention.

OUT FOR A WALK. BE BACK IN A FEW HOURS. HAWK. XX

I turned the sticky square around and around. Who takes hours long walks in this temperature?

Just before lunch, I heard his key turn in the lock.

"Hawk? You okay?"

He darted a glance at my face and nodded slowly, his face ruddy from the cold. "I'm okay."

"You're not quite yourself," I ventured.

Hanging his coat on the hook, he turned and pulled me into his arms. "No."

Hearing his honest answer coupled with him nestling me into his arms soothed the worry that had grown over the course of the morning. "Want to talk about it?"

He sighed. "I don't know what to call it. It's not depression, exactly. More like dread. As if the knowledge that he's gone creeps up on me and the loss feels brand new again."

"That sounds awful. How often does it happen?"

"A few times a year." Turning his head to the side, he lay his cheek against the top of my head.

"The walking helps?"

"It does. It gives me time to push it back. Sometimes I just need a bit of time and space to push it back."

"What can I do for you?" Would he be like this tomorrow? Did he need counseling? Was this PTSD? Survivor's guilt? No, that didn't make sense.

His deep chuckle roused me from my thoughts. "Your brain is overheating. I'm okay now. I promise. What do you want to do today? We've got the whole day."

"Do you want to be bad?"

Squeezing me tighter, he swayed back and forth. "Weren't we bad enough last night? And the night before? You're going to wear me out," he teased lightly.

"Not that kind of bad, old man," I laughed. "Want to take a walk on the wild side?"

He leaned back to look at me, his eyes crinkling at the corners. "The wild side, hm?"

"Yeah." I smiled impishly. "We'll take the snowmobiles downtown to Mary Lou's and stock up on candies. All our old favorites. Then we'll ride down to Krippy's Chippy and pick up fish and chips to bring home. We can watch a movie, eat our num nums. And then, if you can stay awake, we can try to sneak onto Carousel Island!"

His eyebrows shot up. "Sneak onto Carousel Island? To ride the ponies? How are we going to do that?"

Disgruntled, I furrowed my brow. "I haven't figured that part out yet."

He hummed. "Lucky for you I still have the key."

My head flew back in shock. "What?"

His half smile failed to lift the sadness in his eyes. "Hunter left me his things. He still had the keys we made."

Tears came to my eyes, but he brushed them away as he agreed with my plan. "Let's go be bad."

The trip to town took longer than we expected. Which was only partially my fault. There were still too many stores I hadn't visited.

"I thought we were going to Mary Lou's for treats?"

"Hm," I paused to look in the window of the art co-op, waving to the owner who was knee deep in shards of glass. "I think Rachel's making Harley's lamp! She called this morning to say she'd drop it off on her way home tonight." I waved excitedly and Rachel laughed, pointing to her watch to indicate she still had time.

I stuck my head in the door. "We're just going to Mary Lou's and Krippy's, then we're heading home. What time do you think you'll be by?"

"Give me a couple of hours. I'll send Pete to drop it off. There are a few more things I have to get done..." She petered off, her attention drawn back to the exquisite piece of glass in her hands.

"It looks beautiful, Rachel," I squealed.

She looked up as if surprised I was still there. She waved me away, promising, "It will be."

I closed the door and met Hawkley's amused eyes. "What? If you didn't rush me through my shopping, I'd have had a chance to talk to everyone."

Brushing the backs of his fingers over my face, he smiled into my eyes. "You looking for more punishment?"

I threw my arms around his neck, the glint of my bangle between the cuff of my coat and my mitten a happy thrill. "No. I'm looking for candy. Let's go to Mary Lou's and see what Anita brought in for Christmas!"

Going to Mary Lou's was like drawing back Oz's curtain. All the wonders of the candy universe could be found in her shop.

She bustled back and forth, filling our little bags and recommending more. "You kids going home after this?"

"We're heading to Krippy's first to pick up dinner," Hawk said, pointedly looking at the time. "We've got to get there before it closes."

"Hang on." Anita grabbed her cell and held it up to her ear. "Kristen? I'm sending your order over with Hawkley and Noelle. Is Brittany still cooking? These guys want dinner."

She listened for a moment, then looked at Hawk expectantly. "What's your order?"

Leaning over to give her a quick kiss on the cheek, he answered, "Two number threes with extra coleslaw and a number four on the side."

Anita blushed to the roots of her bright red hair and put her mouth back to the phone. "You got that? Good. I'll send them over."

We almost didn't make it to the carousel. After stuffing ourselves with deep fried fish and chips, onion rings, extra coleslaw, and sending our blood sugar into orbit, we passed out on the couch.

Waking just as *Love Actually* came to an end, I tugged on Hawk's hand. "Hawkley! You want to go? We can make it there before midnight and be there as it turns to Christmas Day!"

Blinking sleepy eyes, his hair a mess, I began to reconsider. All of a sudden, climbing into bed and messing his hair up even more seemed a lot more appealing.

His deep chuckle did nothing to dampen my ideas and everything to dampen my knickers.

"Let's go, baby. Christmas only comes once a year. And this year it's special."

There are winter nights when the blanket of snow deadens all sound. When the wind sleeps. The trees stand still. And the twinkling of the stars alone betrays the movement of the universe. That night was one of those.

Once we cut the engines, only the crunch of our footsteps broke the silence until the gears of the carousel slowly came to life. Hawkley jumped on first then held his hand out for me.

Sitting on my chosen pony, Hawkley standing beside me with his arms loosely encircling my waist, I took a deep breath.

Let the memories in.

The silent echo of laughter.

Love was, most definitely, all around me.

Chapter 28 - Santa, baby.

Waking up Christmas morning with my butt pressed against Hawk's hip ranked in my top ten best feelings ever. I wiggled against him. My voice husky with sleep, I asked, "You awake?"

"Mm-hmm," he hummed.

I wiggled my butt again, more forcefully. "Come and cuddle me."

"Can't," he answered shortly.

"Why not?"

"Your cat is on my head. Don't make any sudden movements. I don't want him to scratch my eyes out when he tears across the bed."

"Are you scared?" I guffawed.

"Terrified," he replied.

I twisted around to face him. The soft white winter morning shone on his beautiful face and my cat was indeed wrapped around his head, his tail hooked under his chin.

The only thing Hawkley moved were his eyes.

I leaned up on my elbow. "You've got quite a predicament there," I noted.

Bruce opened his eye and winked at me.

Is it possible to wink with only one eye? Wouldn't every blink be a wink? No, there was a distinct attitude that went along with winking and Bruce had definitely just winked.

"I think Bruce likes you now," I smiled.

"The feeling is not mutual," he growled.

Bruce chose that moment to stretch and knead his paws into Hawk's hair.

With his eyes screwed shut, Hawk waited for the torture to stop. "Think you could lift him off of me?"

"But," I rolled onto my stomach and rested my chin on my palms. "You're bonding."

"I'll bond you in a minute," he threatened.

"Promise?"

"Noelle, I have a present for you but if you don't get your psychotic cat off my head, I won't give it to you until tomorrow."

I didn't think he'd had time to get me a present on top of the birthday present he'd already given me. I sat up abruptly and clapped my hands over my cheeks, squealing, "You got me a present?"

Bruce startled, leaping to his feet and flying out the door while Hawk screamed and rolled off the bed, hitting the floor with a heavy thud.

"Ow, fuck!"

I peered over the edge of the bed, working to keep my face straight. "You okay?" I cocked my head to the side. "I wonder if Max has any advice to help with your pussy phobia?"

Looking at me sideways, he reached up and pulled me down with him then straddled me while I laughed. Taking both of my wrists, he pushed my arms up over my head and gently encased both of them in one hand.

His body stretched out over me, I took in the entire length of his torso, from his magnificently sculpted chest to where his hips poised directly over my groin.

"Oh, I like this," I breathed.

His eyes turned to slits, with a light in them I didn't much like.

"Hawkley," I warned.

He trailed the fingers of his other hand down my arm to end with a circle in my armpit.

"No," I squirmed underneath him. "That's cruel and unusual punishment!"

The final syllable came out with a barking laugh, like a sea lion as he dug his fingers into my pit.

"No, Hawkley," I laughed. "I have to pee!"

"Looks like you've got quite a predicament there," he teased, his fingers skimming my waist and digging into my ribs before returning to my armpits.

"Please," I begged. "I can't take any more!"

"Hm," he skimmed his hand lightly up and down my arm.

I forced myself to relax. Tensing only made the tickling worse.

"You were talking about phobias?" he teased, grinning.

"No," I shook my head adamantly, trying and failing to buck him off. "I was talking about Christmas morning blow jobs and how we have to make our own Christmas traditions!"

Studying my face, he considered my words, then released me. "Go pee. Quickly. Then come right back. If you do a good job, I'll give you your present despite your bad behavior."

We were almost late.

But I got my present.

Every Christmas I could remember, we spent with Hawk's family, the tradition ending for me when Diane entered the picture. Even after their marriage ended, I could not bring myself to attend.

It had been ten years.

A wave of nostalgia hit me as soon as we walked in the door. The evergreen boughs on the fireplace mantle, the ceramic Christmas village nestled among the branches, Hunter's Christmas train, the one he lit on fire one year because he wanted smoke to come out of the chimney. The tree stood tall and proud in the same corner as always, and Lou's mother's nativity sat on the table in the hall.

Had I not walked in with my hand safely tucked into Hawk's, those memories might have sucked me under. As it was, I grieved the lost years, my eyes greedily soaking up every detail, and delighting in every hint of familiarity.

My dad helped us with our packages and our coats. "Merry Christmas, Christmas," he smiled, pulling me into a hug.

"Merry Christmas, Pops," I whispered.

So many lost years. My chest heaved with a suppressed sob, but I yanked my control back around me and pulled back to smile at my dad. "Merry Christmas, Pops," I told him again.

Unable to speak, Dad moved to Hawk and hugged him warmly. "Merry Christmas, son."

The endearment wasn't new, but with us being together, the meaning changed. What would it be like if we were married, and he actually was his son-in-law?

Married. Me in the white dress. Hawk dressed to the nines. Definitely not in gray like his first wedding. My stomach soured. I'd dreamed of marrying Hawk at Sage Ridge, but I didn't want anything from our wedding to remind him of his first.

Realizing how far my mind had wandered, and the fact that he hadn't even given me those three little words, I gave my head a shake and huffed out a laugh. We weren't even engaged, and I was planning the wedding.

I'd been planning that wedding for about fifteen years.

Lou and Dan bustled over as we made our way into the living room. "Well? Was Santa good to you?" she asked, nodding at Hawkley.

"Santa was very good to me," I purred, tilting my head to showcase the pear-shaped diamond earrings he bought to match my mother's necklace.

"Nice," she nodded her approval. "Was Santa good to you, Hawkley?"

He grinned. "She had to improvise a bit, but I have no complaints."

"Oh my gosh, Hawk," I cut in, my face flaming. "Your present is under this tree."

"Why is it under this tree?"

Why, indeed. Because less than a week ago I didn't think I'd be waking up with him on Christmas morning. Once he came back, I deemed his new body board too big to cart back and forth. And I wanted to ensure he got it in case he changed his mind about me. About us. I shrugged. "It's just the way it worked out."

Something in my face gave me away.

Leaning over, he kissed me lightly on the mouth. "Thank you in advance. From now on, feel free to keep my gift at home with you. Because that's where I'll be."

His words lit up my entire body. I beamed at him, surprised my eyes didn't light up like twin headlights.

Harley showed next, sans Paul, followed by Max shortly afterward. It wasn't until after dinner that Hawkley began to show signs of stress.

Tummies full of turkey, family story time arrived, and everyone had a story to tell. Every time Hunter's name came up, Hawk's body tensed as if bracing for a hit, afraid of what he might hear? Or feel?

"Are you okay?"

His stormy eyes met mine, and this time he waited a beat before shuttering his pain.

223

"We'll go soon, okay?"

He shook his head, murmuring, "I don't want to ruin your first Christmas back."

"The only thing that could ruin this most perfect day would be if you were unhappy. Let's go now while everything is still shiny and bright." I leaned in, my breasts brushing against his abdomen. "We'll celebrate more at home."

Smiling down at me, his eyes lit with interest. "Yeah?"

I nodded and twinkled up at him. "You need more exposure therapy for your phobia."

Pulling me close, he pressed his mouth against my ear, his voice low. "For that, you're sitting on my face."

"That's not exactly a deterrent," I answered breathily, the visual in my head parting my lips.

His sharp eyes missed nothing. "You're already there in your head." He pressed his lips to my forehead. "Time to say goodbye."

Chapter 29 - All of Me

In the days following Christmas, the darkness hounded him.

It didn't drag him under and send him into hibernation, but it accompanied him like an unwelcome guest, announcing its presence in every room. A detectable heaviness no amount of teasing or loving could lift.

And it was no wonder. Under the practiced smile that never reached his eyes, lay an ancient, open wound.

How could he blame himself?

He'd always taken responsibility for all of us, perhaps that was the problem?

He avoided talking about it. Instead, he took off on long walks, leaving for hours at a time, only marginally more settled when he returned.

Laying side-by-side in his bed after one of his marathon walks, I stroked his unruly hair back off his forehead.

Bruce curled up in the curve of Hawk's bent knees. They'd become friends of a sort. It could be the fact that Hawk outfitted his house for Bruce by adding a cat tree at each wall of windows, and two plush beds, one of which lay in the corner of our bedroom. I'd have been jealous of their blossoming bromance if I wasn't so proud of both of them.

"Have you ever spoken to anyone about this? Professionally?"

Keeping his eyes closed, he rested his hand on my thigh and released a deep sigh. "This happens every year when Mom throws the birthday dinner. She doesn't understand why I don't go."

"Why don't you go?" I asked softly. "I feel like we should."

"You can go if you want to, Noelle," he answered tiredly, "but I've been through this argument with my mom every year. Please don't make it something I have to go through with you as well."

"No," I replied at once.

"You can go."

"I'm going to stay with you."

"I usually like to do something he and I used to do on his birthday."

"Can I go with you guys this year?"

He opened his eyes and looked into mine. "You want to come with us?" he uttered softly.

"Only if I won't be in the way," I whispered back.

Closing his eyes to shutter the pain, he leaned his forehead against mine. "You could never be in the way. You are the way, the way I want to take forward. My past mistakes keep dragging me back."

"What mistakes?" I tried again, hoping against hope that this time he'd give me an answer.

For a long moment, he was quiet, then, finally, he shook his head and closed his eyes. "I just get down at this time of year. It starts at Christmas and lasts until his birthday." He paused. "It also happens around Hallowe'en and the anniversary of his death. I miss him. I think about how things might have been different." He opened his eyes and offered me a weakly sardonic half-smile. "You don't deserve this up and down bullshit."

"What could you have possibly done differently, Hawk? You weren't even in the car," I challenged him but stopped at the flash of agony in his eyes. "You feel responsible."

"I am responsible," he confessed.

When I opened my mouth to respond, he placed his index finger across my lips. "That's the most I've ever spoken about Hunter. I can't do any more today. Okay?"

Everything in me wanted to dig deep, drill down, and exhume the beast that did its best to devour him three times a year. Perhaps I had more in common with Max than I thought.

Instead of answering, I rolled on top of him and looped my arms around his neck. "You can be my bodyboard."

His arms encircled me, his hands cradling my ribs. "I love being your bodyboard. We going to go out on the lake in the summer?"

"Of course! We're going to do it all, baby."

Well into the second week of January, I watched him struggle. I ached to see his smiles all but disappear. His hands and mouth greedy and insatiable in the hours between dusk and dawn, I gave him the comfort his body craved. Still, his mood darkened by the day, a downward spiral until the day before Hunter's birthday when he couldn't get out of bed.

When I'd left Hawkley at my place that morning, he assured me he planned to get up and head back to his place to work. Worry niggled at my brain all morning. Finally, right before lunch, I texted him. When he didn't answer, I headed home to check on him.

I closed my eyes at my door, almost afraid to open it. He wouldn't do anything stupid. He wouldn't.

I walked in quietly, noting Bruce did not run out to greet me before punishing me for my absence. Moving quietly, I peeked into the bedroom where a giant, Hawk-shaped lump lay still beneath the covers. Bruce lay curled against his stomach.

I circled round the bed. Watched his eyes as he tracked my movements.

"Baby," I called softly, sliding onto the bed behind him, twisting to curve my body around his back and tucking my knees behind his. I looped my arm over his waist and stuck my hand up his shirt to lay over his wounded heart.

"I'll be okay, Noelle," he reassured me, his voice monotone. "This is the hardest day. I know they're going to be all together tomorrow, and, in a way, Hunter will be there, too, and I won't be."

"Did you change your mind? Do you want to go?" I pushed up on my elbow and lay my cheek against his arm.

"No. I can't. I... just can't ... because... "

I lifted my head to see him.

He stared into space, lost in time. Finally, he spoke, his voice low and controlled. "I lied to you."

About what? My heart stuttered in my chest. *Please, God. I closed my eyes. Don't let me be disposable to him.*

Pushing concern for myself aside, I concentrated on him. Rubbing soothing circles over his tender heart, I asked, "About what?"

Silence stretched between us to the point I thought he'd fallen asleep when he covered my hand with his. "Can we talk about this tomorrow? I'll tell you everything tomorrow. Today... tonight... could you just hold me?"

Tall and strong on the outside. So very capable. Successful. Controlled.

On the inside, much like the rest of us.

Ever so slightly broken.

"I can do that, baby." I kissed his naked shoulder and sat up on the edge of the bed, quickly stripping down to my panties before slipping back under the covers.

I tucked my nose into his curly hair. Splayed my hand protectively over his heart. Pressed a whisper of a kiss behind his ear.

"I've got you, Hawkley. Sleep."

His lack of sleep over the past few weeks caught up with him and he slept clear through until morning.

At six, I slipped from the bed, pulled my hair up into a ponytail, and headed for the kitchen to make coffee and start on breakfast. After skipping dinner the day before, we both needed to eat.

At nine, the shower started. I slipped his eggs and sausage into the pan, popped his bread into the toaster, and set the table. I put the food down just as he walked in.

To my surprise, he looked better. Almost like the fever had broken.

He crossed straight to me and looped his arms around my waist and touched his forehead to mine. "Thank you."

"Anytime," I replied lightly. Then promised, "Every time."

He closed his eyes tight, then nodded. Breathed deep. "Should we eat?"

Hawk pulled his chair closer to mine and sat down to eat, his hand on my thigh. His breakfast disappeared in record time. I'd been snacking all morning while I waited for him so mine did not go down quite as quickly.

He sat back in his chair, his hand over his belly. "Delicious, sweetheart. Thank you."

I assessed his face with a smile. "You're welcome."

"Are you coming with us today?"

I put my fork down and shoved my empty plate away. "If you want me?"

"I want you," he assured me, answering all my unasked questions. "I want you, Noelle. I..." He twisted round to face me, spinning me so that my knees lined up with his. Wrapping his hands around my thighs, he offered me a half smile. "It's probably not the time, but why waste any of it? I love you, Noelle. I've loved you for a long time. In fact, I can pinpoint right to the day, to the hour, I knew I loved you. That I would love you always."

My eyes skittered back and forth between his. "I should feel happy," I whispered, "but I feel scared. Is there a but?"

"No," he shook his head firmly, no hint of shutters over his eyes. "There is no but. I love you. I love you more than life. I suspect I will always love you." He paused. "Do you love me?"

Vulnerable. For me.

I leaned close to him, my hands cupping his neck. "I can't pinpoint the time I knew for sure. I think in some capacity, I've always loved you. I always will."

Standing, and pulling me up with him, he pulled me close and cupped the side of my face, his long fingers delving into my hair as he angled my head up. Looking at me intently, he smiled faintly. "You've made me un-fucking-believably happy. I want you to know that. I've never felt happiness like this in my life." His eyes turned slightly desperate. He shook me slightly. "I want more of it."

"You're going to have it, Hawkley. You're going to have all of me," I asserted.

"Noelle…" He tucked my hair behind my ear. "I need to be able to give you all of me."

231

Chapter 30 – Tonight

My heart dropped to the floor just as the floor dropped out of my world because I knew what was coming. "Hawk..." I breathed.

"Let's sit down." Taking my hand, he led me to the couch that was not mine, in the cabin I rented by the week.

"I'm ready to talk about Hunter. To tell you what happened. The part I lied about."

"I'm listening," I promised, working to still the panic in my chest. I spoke through wooden lips, my fingers as cold as they'd ever been, including the night I slept out the storm at the bottom of his driveway.

"I told you Hunter loved you first. That I was only beginning to develop romantic feelings for you. I told you about his one-year plan, how he intended to get the promotion and date and get other women out of his system before pursuing you."

"Yes." Everything in me wanted to cover my ears and run for the bluffs. Climb to the top. Lie down among the wildflowers that flooded them in the spring.

"As you know, he continued to date. A lot. I assumed he wasn't serious about you, and my feelings grew."

I nodded.

He took my cold fingers in between his warm palms and rubbed life into them.

I'd wanted this truth. I'd asked for it. Begged for it. Knew, instinctively, I needed to take it from him. I turned my hands over and clasped his. I spoke, my voice strong and steady, "Go on, sweetheart. I'm listening."

"I planned to talk to your dad. With our families being as close as they are, I didn't want him to think I wasn't serious."

I smiled. "That's sweet, baby. I like that. So different from the punishing Hawkley who doesn't let me shop," I teased, hoping to elicit a smile.

His beautiful lips tipped up, a spark of delight reaching his eyes. "I've no doubt you would have earned lots of punishments, my beautiful girl."

I smiled back.

His smile faded as he searched my eyes for permission to carry on. "I need to finish. I feel like if I don't tell you now, I'll never be able to tell anybody, and I don't think I can continue like this. The guilt, Noelle," his voice rasped as he twisted to sit back against the couch.

I threw my leg over his lap and straddled him, cupping his bearded cheeks in my palms. "Truth."

"Truth." He nodded. "Hunter came home. Told me he was ready to move on with you. He was so excited." He smiled. "You know how he was when he had a plan."

I laughed even as tears pooled in my eyes as I witnessed the avalanche of emotions crushing the man beneath me.

"He asked me to be his best man." He met my eyes. "I was heartbroken. Jealous. But he was my brother and he claimed you first. I told myself I'd get over you," he confessed.

He leaned his head on the back of the couch and swallowed hard. "A couple of days later, you tried to talk to me, and I turned you away." He looked away, gritting his teeth. "I went home and fucking cried."

I pressed my fingers into the hair at the nape of his neck, massaging the taut muscles. "No, Hawkley," I whispered, tears filling my eyes. So much time wasted. "Why didn't you tell him?"

His Adam's apple bobbed in his throat.

I pressed a kiss to his trembling mouth.

A flash of old anger tightened his jaw.

"Then he started dating that model who worked at Susie Q's. Do you remember?"

I sat up straighter. "Yes, I do, actually. I hated her. She couldn't keep her eyes off you."

"Well, she was more than happy to take a spin with Hunter. And did. After a week of watching him joke around with you and go home with her, I confronted him. He told me she'd be the last one. That you weren't in love with him yet, so it didn't matter. It wasn't like he was hurting you."

"He wasn't," I agreed quietly, still struggling to piece things together. Knowing I was missing some vital piece of information.

"I..." His face contorted and he looked down, breathing out heavily. When he raised his chin, he looked straight through me. "I told him I wanted you. Told him you wanted me, too." He swallowed, looked up at the ceiling. "Oh, fuck," he blinked back tears, his voice shaking. "Told him I was falling in love with you."

He sucked in a breath and exhaled a sob he quickly swallowed. His chest heaved.

Tears streamed unchecked down my face, collected in the divot of my collarbone, and emptied down between my breasts. I hung onto him tightly. Hugging him with my thighs, holding his beautiful face in my hands.

His voice strangled, a look of horror and disbelief flitting over his face, he continued brokenly, "He took my car. The one he found for me to rebuild. I went to my parents' place to wait for him. You and Harley were sitting on the front porch..."

"Oh, no," the final piece fell into place, and it was tragic. My body went limp, my hands dropped from his face. I stared at him, mouth open in shock.

"The officer came to the door..."

I sprang back to life and wrapped my arms around him. "Oh, God, Hawk... it's okay. I hear you, baby. I get it," I assured him.

His arms locked around me as he rocked us back and forth.

"So much crying. Mom's screams. Dad," his voice broke, "My dad... the noises he made... Harley's," he gulped, "...face."

I remembered.

I lived this nightmare with him.

Relived it almost every day.

"And you, baby?" I stroked his hair, kissed up and down the side of his face, pressed closer. "Where were you in all this?"

I knew exactly where he was. He stood at the outskirts. His hands in his pockets. Face blank, eyes bleak. I thought he was in shock. I guess he was, but I never guessed the extent of the reason why. I lost him that day, too. We all did.

His fingertips dug into my back. His body bowed tight as he pressed his face between my breasts, a guttural cry escaping. His tears joined mine in the valley of my breasts. A river of tears. "I lost...you that day." He dragged in a shuddering breath, rocked deeper, fingers bruising my ribs as he clung to me. "I lost ...him that day. I lost ...me that day. And they lost everything because of me."

I held on.

Shared his grief.

Held his guilt.

Assuaged his horror.

When his tears abated, I pushed up to my knees and wrapped myself around him. "I'm sorry, Hawkley. I'm sorry that happened to you." Leaning back, I held his face in my hands and stared into his glossy eyes and gave him back the truth. "Hunter would die a thousand deaths if he knew what this did to you. It was not your fault, baby. It was a fucking tragic accident. It was not your fault."

His body heaved. He bent his neck back to pull in a breath, his eyes wild, then fell apart in my arms, body shaking, hands gripping my shirt tight then smoothing it down over my back over and over.

"I miss him."

"Every day, I miss him."

"Our last words..."

I ran my hands over every part of him I could reach. "I know, baby. But know this. No two brothers loved each other the way you two did. He would have gotten over it. He would have been your best man. And he would have absolutely spit-fire roasted you for stealing me away from him when he gave his speech."

He rewarded me with a wet, garbled laugh. Slowly his body calmed, his hands at my back became more purposeful, his mouth hit my throat, a hiccup escaping as he gently bit down and kissed it better. "Noelle," he gritted out, his voice tight. "Need you."

"Yes, Hawk. Always yes."

Unsnapping his jeans, he shifted me to my back on the floor, ripped my panties down my legs, and covered me with his mouth. Frantically, he brought me to orgasm. Then, rearing up over me, he pushed his jeans over his ass. Body quaking, eyes wild, he lined up and drove inside me. His hand around the back of my neck, he yanked my face up to his and filled my mouth with my taste on his tongue, the salt of his tears on his lips, as he cried out his release inside me.

Lying on the floor in an exhausted heap, he looked at me, his eyes finally clear. He offered me a smile that faded all too quickly, "I need to go away for a while."

The blood drained from my face. A wave of nausea churned in my stomach. Gathering my heels beneath me, I made to skitter away from him.

He lurched forward and grabbed me, pulling me onto his lap where I curled into a protective ball. "No, baby. Not like that. I'll be back. I just need to say goodbye to him. And I need to tell my family what I told you. And I need to do it in my own way." He ran his hand down my side and pressed his mouth to the top of my head. "I'll be back. I love you. I'll be back."

"When are you leaving?"

He paused.

"Now."

Chapter 31 - Infinite

One week ago, I would not have guessed I'd be standing outside my door in the cold.

Alone.

I tucked my ribbon into my jeans pocket, studiously ignoring the shrinking size of the waistband. Still in shock that Hawkley left so abruptly after pouring his heart out.

Was he scared like me? Would he cut and run? Avoid the risk? Evade the pain?

He's coming back.

Is he? What if one of his revelations tells him I'm not for him?

Perhaps he's been hanging onto me because he's been living in the past all these years?

The thoughts were crowding in, and I needed to clear them. Wrapping my scarf tighter around my face, I opened my Pokemon app to track my steps and took off for Carousel Island. What was supposed to be a day spent celebrating Hunter with Hawk turned into a day without either of them.

I couldn't shake the suspicion I would somehow be disposable at the end of it all.

How much could 'I love you' mean if the outcome was the same?

The old habit of pulling up and heading out tempted me. It didn't make sense. What would I gain by leaving?

I trudged along, the icy, snow-laden trail enforcing my slow pace. The trail joined the boardwalk around Silver Lake, then circled the bluffs, and continued along the edge of Crystal Beach to the footbridge. The roar of the wind blocked everything out, and I could hear myself think.

It was simple, really. The payoff was an escape from the blistering uncertainty of not knowing when the rug would be pulled out from under me.

Of the four romantic relationships I'd had since I left home, Barrett came the closest to breaking down my resistance. For all his fierce looks, he was a gentle giant and he'd treated me with care. Showed me what I deserved from a man.

Healed what the others broke.

And yet, it didn't come close to the tenderness with which Hawk handled me.

When he was there.

Was that what we were to be? A cycle of having him for a time only to lose him again?

I reached the footbridge and crossed over. The park was lonely. Anyone with a functioning brain cell was cuddled up on their couch with a blanket on a day like this. The temperature had risen to above freezing overnight, but it brought a dampness that penetrated every layer meant to keep me warm.

Circling the carousel, I found the pony I rode when Hawk and I snuck in with Hunter's keys. Instead of swinging my leg over, I went in search of a different pony. It took me fifteen minutes to find it. Bending low, I peered at the inside of the back leg. Reaching out, I traced the letters we carved into it a million years ago.

I huffed out a laugh. We were kind of bad, but we never meant anybody any harm.

"Hunter, I miss you," I whispered. Wrapping my hand around the leg, I leaned my forehead against the pony's frozen side and cried for the boy I loved. The friend I lost. The brilliant man and all the light that his death extinguished.

"You're always here, though." I stroked the pony's side.

What would Old Man Gillie think if he saw our little act of vandalism? He'd always been kind to us and had an especially soft spot for Hunter.

Lou brought Hunter to ride the carousel every day when he was small. If she didn't, he screamed the house down.

I smiled. Passionately persistent from birth.

More memories surfaced. Hunter racing up the hill to the carousel, his hand raised in a high five. "Hey, old buddy!"

Old Man Gillie laughing in response as he slapped his hand. "How ya doin' little buddy?" Even when Hunter towered over him by several inches, the script never altered.

I patted the pony's chest and came in contact with a metal plate. Going down to my knees, I crawled around to look.

For Hunter. Ride on, little buddy.

I covered my mouth with my hand and sobbed.

He knew. All this time, Old Man Gillie knew. And he grieved in solidarity with us. We weren't the only ones who missed Hunter's light.

So bright, even death couldn't snuff it out. He was in every grain of sand on Crystal Beach. His hoot of victory rang through the air at the top of the bluffs. Our laughter rang out eternally in the wind. His place in my heart throbbed with life because here, in Sage Ridge, he was everywhere.

I pulled the end of my scarf out of my jacket and wiped my face.

Releasing a shuddering breath, I retraced my steps to the beach and walked through my old neighborhood where my dad lived. I thought about stopping but couldn't bear the unasked questions for which I had no answers.

My walk rivaled Hawk's strenuous escapes. I reasoned if I exhausted myself, I would sleep and put an end to this awful day.

My eyes filled anew remembering the anguish on Hawk's face. Telling his truth afforded him a modicum of peace. I fully understood his guilt now, a wound scraped raw by being with me. Would he ever get over it?

Once I reached the river, I understood the need that drove me there.

The bench set directly in my path, where my mother and I always sat, invited me to sit with her again.

Where I loved the beach and the bluffs, Mom loved the river.

"See, Noelle? It's always changing. It's never the same two days in a row. That's life, honey. If I miss my walk one day, I know I've missed something changing along the river. I can't wait to get back. It calls to me."

She read to me on this bench when I was small.

We picnicked on this bench.

She told me, much to my everlasting horror, about the birds and the bees on that bench.

Don't you know, you, yourself are made of love? You are love!

The things she said to me, the beauty she poured into our lives. She loved me. Loved Max. Adored my father. She didn't want to leave him, leave us. And when she neared the end, I held her on that bench as she cried for all she would miss.

I collapsed under the weight of my memories. "I can't do it, Mom. I can't take another loss."

Open your heart or you'll miss the magic.

Only one person I knew spoke of magic.

You, yourself, are made of magic.

My mother was magic. She taught me how to dream.

"My dreams didn't take me too far, Mom," I murmured.

The story isn't over yet.

How often she said that to us kids whenever something went wrong. Everything was coming back to me.

I pulled my ribbon from my pocket, weaved it through my frozen fingers. Remembered the day I got it.

The line of mourners stretched out the door and along the hall. I hated them and loved them in equal measure. They loved her. Were devastated by her loss. And all of them were secretly relieved the tragedy didn't befall their family.

Why did they get to live while she, who loved so well and appreciated every moment, had to die?

Then I spotted Hawk and Diane in the line. I excused myself to go to the bathroom. I would not shake that woman's hand. I would not look into his eyes for fear that he may see what would forever lie behind mine.

By the time I came back out, they had moved to the back of the room.

It was a small enough mercy.

When everyone finally left, I stole back inside the room. I sat in front of her casket, knowing she wasn't in there but hanging onto the final physical thread that held her to the earth.

My breath rattled in and out as I splayed my fingers across the wood. My heavy hair fell forward, sticking to the tears on my face. With a strangled cry, I ripped it back, holding it on top of my head before returning one hand to the casket.

A large hand covered mine, one I'd know anywhere.

He didn't speak. Neither did I. But I took the comfort he offered me.

Pulling a ribbon off the champagne roses that covered her casket, he moved behind me. Slowly, methodically, he gathered my hair back from my face, his palms smoothing over my temples, up the back of my neck, and behind my ears, until he held it all in his fist in a low ponytail. Wrapping the ribbon around and around, he secured it in place.

Stepping closer, he barely rested his palms on my shoulders and dropped his mouth to my hair. "I'm sorry, Noelle…"

I bowed my head.

And he left.

The next, and last, time I saw him was a few weeks later at what Harley christened The Great Gnome Slaughter of Sage Ridge. Did he think about that as much as I did? He comforted me then, too.

Needing a distraction from the painful memories, I opened the app on my phone. April had sent me a gift on the Pokemon app.

Was she enjoying her boys? Did she start her course? I sent her a gift on the app, knowing she'd get a kick out of it.

You are infinite. Your ability to give and receive love is infinite.

Deep inside, I knew it to be true. Even those I'd lost were still here. Our love, a celestial ribbon linking our hearts for all eternity. Everywhere I looked, I sensed their magic.

The magic that was love.

Connection.

Joy.

The ribbon served to remind me of one of the saddest days of my life. Did I still need it now that I felt and saw her everywhere? When the love she gave still lived in my heart?

Did I need it to remind me of Hawk's tenderness on that day? A tenderness he'd expressed over and over? He'd given me far happier memories since he gave me that ribbon.

That ribbon reminded me that to love was to lose.

And it was true.

But I would not fear it, because where love took root, you could never truly lose it.

I wanted to love the way she did. With abandon. Even knowing the pain that waited on the flipside.

I wanted to love him like that. As if I would lose him.

You are magic.

You are love.

You are infinite.

Three little words.

Walking to the edge of the river, taking great care not to slip with my precious cargo, I knelt down on the rocks and released the ribbon into the current my mother loved so well. I watched it spin and twirl until it danced away with the current.

"Mama, I'm sorry about the gnomes."

I swear I heard her laugh.

Chapter 32 – Christmas in July

You are infinite.

I tapped on his name and began to text.

Hi, baby. I walked out to Carousel Park today. Remember the pony we all carved our names in? Old Man Gillie fixed a plaque to its chest. 'For Hunter. Ride on, little buddy'. Hunter's not entirely gone. He lives on in the hearts of all who loved him. And a lot of people loved him, Hawk.

I love you.

He texted me back immediately.

I love you.

He texted me every day. Sometimes he told me what he was thinking or feeling. Other times he focused on me and my day and didn't want to share anything about his. For three weeks, we talked about everything. Got to know one another on a deeper level without the shadow of grief and guilt.

Every night, he asked me the same thing.

Can you give me another day?

And every night I answered the same way.

I can do that.

I missed him. Some days, desperately. But when I got him back, I wanted all of him.

I tucked my phone into my purse, swallowed my new vitamins, bundled up for the short walk to work, apologized to Bruce for leaving, and locked my door.

Hearing his plaintive meow from outside, I darted back in. "You're turning into a druggie, Mr. Willis."

Taking care to close the bathroom door behind me, I fished the catnip from the back of the cupboard and took a generous pinch before locking it away again.

This was the third hiding place. Damn cat could open cupboards and drawers. But he couldn't manage doorknobs.

Yet.

I sprinkled it over his scratch pad. He walked over nonchalantly, as if that wasn't what he'd been screaming for, then bumped his little head against my leg.

"Well. If you're going to be like that about it, I'll get you a treat as well."

Five minutes later, I left a silent cat and walked the 200 feet to work.

Lou waited for me in my office.

"Lou, hi! I didn't expect to see you. Is everything okay?" My words tumbled out in a rush, and I felt the blood drain from my face as I barreled toward her.

She pressed her lips together. "I am most upset with my son."

I leaned hard against my desk. This could not be happening. I knew he'd gone to their place to talk to them. I swore they'd been understanding.

"Lou, it was a tragic accident. It wasn't his fault."

Her mouth dropped open. "Of course, it wasn't his fault! I'm not mad at him for that. My heart breaks for him for that! I'm mad at him for leaving you in the state you're in. I'm mad at him for being gone so long. I'm furious he's left us all in the dark about what he's doing."

"The state I'm in?"

Lou's chin dropped to her chest, and she studied me over the rim of her glasses. "Yes. The state you're in."

Stalling for time, I walked around my desk to sit in my chair. "I've decided I want to stay on as the event planner if you'll have me."

"If I'll have you," she repeated.

"And, um, I'm going to start looking for a condo... so you can start renting the cabin. I, uh, know you haven't been taking anything from my pay."

She tilted her head to the side. "I think it's best you stay close to us for now. At least until the spring. Maybe even through the summer. What do you think?"

Probably better to be closer to family. With Dan and Lou on the premises so much of the time, and Dad five minutes away, it made sense to stay. I nodded my agreement.

She smiled. "I'm not mad at him anymore."

My eyes skittered up to meet hers, then darted away. If compartmentalizing was an Olympic sport, I'd be a gold medalist.

"Are you taking your vitamins?" she asked gently.

I met her eyes and admitted, "I picked some up last week."

She nodded. "Have you seen a doctor?"

"I have an appointment tomorrow," I felt my face flush. If she thought I was pregnant, I really must be. "How did you know?"

Walking around to perch on the edge of my desk, she stroked the dark patches that appeared on my face over the past week. "Your mother got these marks with both you and Max." She searched my face. "Do you want me to go with you?"

Tears came to my eyes. "Yes."

My pregnancy turned out to be the world's worst-kept secret.

Lou suspected a week before I told her, and she told Dan.

My dad approached Lou the day after that and asked her to talk to me woman to woman.

Harley went to her mom two days ago to tell her she suspected I was pregnant.

Max had called Dad just that morning.

And they all showed up in my office after my doctor's appointment.

My time as an ostrich had come to an end.

I stopped, shocked, when I saw all of them and then laughed. "Three months," I answered their unspoken question.

They all began talking at once. Asking their questions. Smiling. Laughing. Rejoicing.

"Three months?" Harley tilted her head to the side. Lifting her hand up, she counted back. Her mouth dropped open, and she whooped, "Why, you dirty whore!"

I covered my quickly reddening face with my hands, put my forehead down on my desk, and groaned. "Harley."

"Right," Dan clipped. "That's my cue to leave." He cleared his throat. "If you need anything, honey, just call me."

"For fuck's sake, Harley," Max whined as he stalked toward the door then stopped. "I'm happy for you, Noelle," he said, his voice tight.

I looked up, worried he was angry with Hawk again.

His glossy eyes met mine. "You're going to be a wonderful mother." Without waiting for a response, he slipped out the door.

My dad hung on a little longer, his eyes twinkling. "When's the baby due, Noelle?"

I let go of my rosy cheeks and looked at my dad. "July 27th."

His eyes lit up. "Christmas in July." He rounded my desk. "I love you, Christmas. You've made me very happy."

On his way out he kissed Harley on the nose. "Big mouth."

Other than Harley, Lou was the only one left. "Well, girl, you really know how to clear a room."

"They were taking up too much of her time," she replied nonchalantly, studying her manicure.

I laughed. "I can't believe you called me out like that in front of everybody."

"It would have come out eventually," she waved away my concerns. "Are you happy?"

"Yes. How can I not be? But I'm not sure how he'll feel."

"He'll be happy," Lou asserted. "Shocked, maybe. But happy." She smiled, her eyes far away. "He's always loved babies. How he doted over both of you when you were babies. He wasn't much more than a baby, himself." She patted my hand. "He'll be happy, lamb."

Turning her attention to Harley, she shook her head. "You need a spanking." Leaning over, she dropped a kiss on her head. Rounding my desk, she kissed me as well. "I'll leave you two to your shenanigans."

"Can I plan the shower?"

I slanted a sideways look at her. "What did you have in mind?"

Harley laughed and waved away my concerns. "Mom will supervise."

"I'll allow it," I feigned reluctance. "So long as Lou supervises."

Harley's smile faded.

I knew what was coming.

"You need to ask him to come home."

My fingers went to the ends of my hair. "I know.

Chapter 33 – Favor

Good morning, baby.

I have a favor to ask. I want to get my family together to celebrate Hunter. Will you help me?

I can do that.

Tell Harley I spoke to Andrea at Cake Me Away and she's ready for the specifics. She just has to call her.

Harley's legendary sweet tooth. The fact Hawk secured a cake before anything else attested to that.

He sent me the rest of his instructions and I followed them to the letter.

Today was the day. I paced back and forth, pretending to check on things in the kitchen to cover my nerves. On my fourth circuit of the house, I heard the roar of his truck coming up the driveway. Darting around a chair, I ran for the door.

A chorus of panicked, 'Carefuls!' followed me.

I spun and narrowed my eyes at them, pressing my finger over my lips. I wanted to be the one to tell him. At the right time.

I walked, sedately, to the door, then threw myself into his arms as soon as he opened it.

"Baby!" He wrapped me up and lifted me up against his chest. "Fuck, I've missed you." He pressed his mouth to mine. "I've missed you so much. Are you okay?"

I couldn't manage more than a nod. "Mhm!"

Leaning back an inch, he studied my eyes. "You okay?" His strong arms held me securely.

I relaxed in his hold. "Yes," I nodded. "Are you?" I searched his eyes for shadows and found none.

"I am," he asserted, kissing my nose. "This next part will be difficult, but I need to do it. All these years, I've never come to celebrate him, and I want to do that today. Will you cross your fingers for me?"

My greedy eyes caressed his face. "I can do that."

He smiled. "Of course, you can."

"Uh, son?" Dan interrupted. "We're all more than a little confused, more than a little concerned. You want to let us in on what's been going on?"

Dipping to put my feet back on the floor, Hawk tucked my hair behind my ear and kissed my forehead before nudging me in the direction of Max and my dad.

"Can we sit down in the living room? All together?" he asked.

Dad and Max led me to the couch and sandwiched me between them.

Dan sat in his usual chair, looking deceptively relaxed. Lou crossed to perch on the stool beside him, leaning hard against his legs. Dan placed his hand against her lower back, lending her his support.

Harley curled into the loveseat next to her brother.

Hawk cleared his throat and sought my eyes.

I nodded encouragement.

He took a deep breath and began. "Before I left, I told you the truth about what happened the day Hunter died. And my part in it."

Lou made to interrupt but Hawk held up his hand. "It's okay, Momma. I'm okay."

Lou made a strangled noise in her throat causing Dan to reach for her and guide her onto his lap.

Hawk smiled at his mom before continuing. "When I cleared out Hunter's room, I found a collection of old-school folders full of looseleaf paper. One folder for each year, and inside he had written his goals for that year. He," Hawk paused and cleared his throat, "had just finished that year's list. I kept it."

"Not only that, but I looked through the rest of them. At first, I felt guilty, but after a while, I realized this was his legacy. The best of him that he left with us. His sense of fun and adventure. His willingness to try new things, grab life by the horns. His love for his family. I can't tell you how many times all of our names showed up on his lists throughout the years. Things I thought were spontaneous or a lucky blessing, Hunter had planned to the nth degree.

"The car he found for me to restore? That was the exact make and model I wanted? He had that on his list."

"The angel investor that came through for the golf course renovation that stole half of Dad's hair?"

Everyone laughed. Except for Dan, who growled at his son before telling him his time was coming.

Hawk continued, "Hunter secured that. And those are just two examples. Two big ones. There are dozens of small ones. Each one of us is named."

"Dad, you asked me to do the eulogy at Hunter's funeral." Hawk's mouth twisted with sorrow. "I wanted to, I just couldn't. Not without you knowing the truth."

Dan's jaw cracked. He managed a brief nod as he wiped under his eyes.

"If I could go back, this is what I would say."

Lou sucked in a breath, her hand going to her chest.

Hawk unfolded a square of paper from his pocket and cleared his throat.

"Hunter was a dreamer...and a doer. I wish I could say he dragged us kicking and screaming into his madcap schemes, but that would be a lie. None of us tolerated boredom well. You'd think it would be an impossibility growing up here the way we did, but we had our moments. Lots of them if the following list is any indication."

Max began to chuckle beside me.

"Hunter was also a storyteller. He reveled in shocking and delighting us with the retelling of his escapades. If he was still with us, he would have told you by now, I'm sure. So, I'm going to take this opportunity to clear up a few mysteries. If he's looking down on us, he is rubbing his hands together and grinning, ready for the big reveal. And happy he is out of range of Mom's slippers."

"Yeah," Harley hooted, "but we're not."

"I'm not afraid," Hawk grinned at her. "I've already taken the punishment for almost all of these."

Max groaned beside me as Hawk continued.

"The Portal to Hell? That was Hunter."

"Fish in the swimming pool? Hunter. We should have thought that through a little more. The shock you saw on our faces that morning was real. We did not expect those poor fish to die. Hunter cried for weeks."

"He really did," Harley nodded with a smile.

"Do you remember the smell, Dan?" Lou asked.

"How could I forget? I swear I still smell it every time I go to the pool area."

Hawk smiled at me over their laughter. "The year the koi pond got overrun by frogs? That was Hunter's idea. We spent two days transferring tadpoles from the river. In our defense, we thought we were doing our bit for the environment."

"Bet you never knew before the great cotton ball mystery that a cotton ball dipped in water will freeze to anything. Hunter knew. We all agreed the momobile never looked better. The extra chores were well worth the look on your faces when you saw it the next morning."

Dad laughed out loud, probably remembering Lou's outrage over her baby covered in fluffy, frozen, polka dots.

"The amazing lawn tractor race that took over main street? Hunter's baby. We ran a betting pool for that. Made enough money to take us all to the movies. That was, uh, also the night of the not so amazing snowmobile heist in which Harley sprained her ankle and Dad nearly finished us all off."

Max, Harley, and I all groaned.

Hawk held up appeasing hands to his dad. "We are still sorry. Please, let's not talk about it again."

"Remember the keys to the carousel went missing for a few days? It's time Hunter got the credit for his brilliant mind. Hunter made copies before getting them back to Old Man Gilley. We rode those ponies every night after the island closed."

Lou clapped her hand over her mouth, her eyes wide.

"Our childhood was magical. We laughed. A lot. And we laughed more because of Hunter."

Harley sniffed.

"He was also a planner. He had these old school style folders, and every year before his birthday, he made his plans."

"Some of the items related to work, others definitely belonged in the play category and not all of those were PG. I'll save those to share when you old folks go home. Because he loved to make us laugh and I'd like to give that to him."

Tears ran down my face. Max handed me a tissue and curled his arm around the back of the couch.

"Life was never boring with Hunter around and I wish, with all my heart, that he was here because Hunter was the best brother a man could wish for. I loved him. I love him still. And I'll love and miss him always."

Hawk carefully folded the piece of paper into four. Nobody moved until Harley threw herself across his chest and clung to him.

He held her close and rocked her while she cried. Her quiet sobs loud in the silent room, and we all heard her clearly when she threatened, "If you ever speak of this, I'll slit your throat in your sleep."

He chuckled and released her. "I have no doubt."

When she drew back, he stood and faced his parents.

Lou beamed up at him, her heart forever fractured for the son she lost, and beginning to heal for the son she finally had back.

The potent mix of grief and gratitude reflected on her face pierced my heart, and I had to look away to gather myself.

Standing, she nestled under his arm and wrapped her arms around him, a hiccupping sob escaped followed by a slightly hysterical laugh. Harley snuck in under his other arm.

Hawk looked at his father, his heart plastered all over his face. Raw and exposed, he asked for absolution.

Dan uttered one word, 'Son', and could manage no more.

Lumbering to his feet, his head tipped down, he grabbed Hawkley by the back of his head and pressed their foreheads together before gathering what was left of his family in his massive arms.

I sat back, between my dad and my brother, while Hawk's family encircled him.

Max and my dad pressed against me from either side, and I reached for both their hands. I didn't even try to stop the tears that fell. How else would she know I loved her if I didn't send her these celestial emails?

Besides, I'd learned. Denying my grief led me to denying myself love.

When Lou and Harley released their hold on him, Dan took him outside to his workshop. When they came back in, they both looked all the better for it.

By that time, Harley and I were curled up on the couch together, cake plates all but licked clean, our fingers intertwined. I gave her a squeeze when he began making his way toward me.

She squeezed me back. "I'll give you guys some space."

Standing, she trailed her hand across his abdomen as she left.

He smiled down at her and briefly covered her hand with his.

Not generally demonstrative, I could tell she just needed to assure herself that he was back.

For real.

Hawk settled in beside me and nestled me under his arm. "Hi."

I sighed in contentment. "Hi."

He pulled me close. "I've missed you so much, Noelle. You look beautiful." His eyes skimmed over the darker marks on my cheeks. He touched one side with a gentle finger. "What happened here?"

"I have a little rash."

At his touch, the rest of the room melted away. I greedily drank him in.

He continued to study me. "Are you sure you're okay?"

"I'm perfect." *He looks ...rested? At peace?*

He smiled, his eyes roving over my face. "That you are."

"I'm glad you're back," I whispered.

The look he gave me touched my heart with an icy finger. "You are back, aren't you?"

He dipped his chin to come closer. "Can you give me one more day?" He smiled. "One more day and then I'm going to give you better."

"Give me better?"

"Don't you remember? I said you deserve better. You told me to give you better." He shrugged. "Going to give you better. Can you give me one more day?"

The panic in my heart stilled. I softened. "I can do that."

His eyes searched my face. "You'd do anything, wouldn't you?"

"For you, yes."

"I love you, sweetheart." A sense of urgency flashed in his eyes. "I'll meet you at my parents' anniversary dinner at Ayana's tomorrow night." He brushed the backs of his fingers over the dark mark on my cheek, his face tightening with concern. "This is the last time."

"Last time for what?"

He smiled and wagged his eyebrows. "I'll tell you tomorrow."

I furrowed my brows. "You're going to be the one to get punished."

Laughing, he bowed his head to mine. "I'm counting on it."

Chapter 34 - Checklist

I stuffed another pillow behind my back and made myself more comfortable on Harley's bed. "We need this after yesterday," I stated.

"Definitely." Harley sat at her make-up table and applied her third coat of mascara. She leaned back from the mirror to admire her eyelashes and held her hands out. "I love mascara. I mean," she tilted her head from side to side, "look at those eyelashes! If those don't catch me a good man, nothing can."

"I think you're overlooking your best asset," I teased. "Where is that red dress you wore to the Christmas party?"

She twisted her mouth to the side. "The one that makes me look like a cherry?"

I sat up straight on her bed and pointed at her. "Don't say that! He's gone and for good reasons, those comments included. Don't bring him back by speaking for him. The man is a royal ass."

"He is," she sighed, then stood up to look at her posterior in the mirror. "And I do have a nice ass."

"You do," I agreed. "It's all that kickboxing. Is your mom excited for tonight? How many years is this for them?"

"Forty! Isn't that incredible?"

"It's the stuff of dreams," I answered honestly.

"Are you looking forward to tonight?" She asked.

I picked an imaginary fluff off her comforter. "I just want him to come home. I'm worried, I guess, that he might not want me the way he did... I don't know what he's going to say about the baby. That worries me a bit." I huffed out a laugh. "A lot."

Harley sat down beside me and took my hand in hers. "Listen. I spoke to him this afternoon. He fully plans on taking you home with him tonight. I'm under strict instructions to make sure you have clothes for tomorrow, and I'm sleeping with the psycho cyclops tonight." She smiled cheekily. "He worried Bruce would be lonely without you."

I laughed and then the tears came. "Oh my gosh, these hormones!"

"Nah," Harley denied. "It's the bromance between your man and your cat that's got you tearing up."

I shouldn't have worried. Harley and I were last to arrive at the restaurant, and Hawk met us at the door.

He took my hand but spoke to his sister. "I was beginning to worry about you two. Everything okay?"

Harley saluted him smartly. "All good. She's got clean knickers and a new toothbrush in her purse. She's ready for whatever debauchery you have planned for her."

Hawk grinned at her.

I watched as the realization hit her that she was talking about her brother. "Oh, ew," she mewled. Covering her ears, she made a beeline to the table, Hawk's laughter ringing behind her.

Dipping his knees, he caught my eyes. "Hi, my beautiful girl."

I smiled. "Hi."

"You ready for your night of debauchery?"

"I wore out the batteries on my vibrator."

His eyebrows shot up. "You have a vibrator? Why don't I know about this? Do you have it with you? Can we pick up batteries on the way home?"

I laughed and punched him, then peeked up at him. "So, I am going home with you tonight?"

"Every night if I have it my way," he asserted, guiding me gently to our table.

Dinner was wonderful, as it always was at Ayana's. If I looked closely, I could see me and mom sitting at the table by the window on my thirteenth birthday. The table at the back hosted Mom, me, Harley, and Lou. We shared a dessert platter designed for a party of twelve on Harley's sixteenth birthday. And that romantic little alcove surrounded by greenery and tulle was where Hawk and I had our first date.

The toasts to the happy couple went around the table and ended with Hawkley.

He stood. "Mom, Dad, you are a living example of everything I want. Thank you for loving each other so well. You've taught me how to be a better man. You've all taught me so much. Harley has kept me in line. And Hunter taught me to grab life by the horns.

"I decided to take a page out of Hunter's book. Literally." He held up a piece of lined paper covered with writing. "As I went through and completed his list, at least those that didn't involve nudity, I wrote my own one-year plan.

"My first item was to complete Hunter's list in honor of him. All except the last one which will have to go unchecked. Even if we hadn't lost him, this item would have gone unchecked.

"By him.

"Because she was always meant to be mine, as I was only ever meant to be hers.

"So," he faced me and dropped to one knee, "next on my list is to engage one Noelle Brevard. The timeline is immediate." Smiling at me, he mouthed, "Eyes on me."

I bit the inside of my cheek to keep from crying and held his gaze. His beautiful, clear-eyed gaze.

"Noelle Brevard. God weaved you into my DNA the day you were born. There has not been a day that has passed that you were not on my mind. In my heart. Even when you weren't in my life."

I swallowed a sob. My fingers twirled together in my lap, itching to get to him.

The table behind me fell silent.

"Time is precious," he whispered, his heart in his eyes. "I don't want any more to pass without telling you what you mean to me. You are my life. My happiness. My purpose. My best friend. My soul's mate. My love. And hopefully, my wife."

I nodded frantically. "Yes."

He laughed. "I haven't asked yet."

"Hurry up," I circled my hand in front of me. "I need to kiss you."

"Oh, well then," he stood and drew me up into his arms, "why didn't you say so?"

I pushed my fingers into the hair at the back of his neck ready to meet his lips when emotion overcame me. Bowing my head, I pressed my forehead to his chest and looped my arms around his neck.

Cupping the back of my head with one hand, he turned his back to the table to shield me. "Sweetheart," he murmured. "Are you okay?"

"Mm-hm. Happy," I garbled.

His chest vibrated with his laughter. "Give me your finger."

"You better make it official and ask me. I want the words."

Laughing, he gave them to me, "Marry me, Noelle."

Three beautiful words.

Just three.

A mouthful of syllables.

Devin Sloane

Without moving my face out of his chest, I held my left hand in front of him with my fingers splayed. "It better fit," I mumbled. "I've waited a long time for this."

He slid it over my knuckle and dropped a kiss to my finger. "A perfect fit. Do you like it?"

Laying my palm over his chest, I lifted just enough to see a gorgeous emerald cut solitaire. "I love it."

"Truly?"

A sense of peace settled over me and I lifted my head to look into his face. "I can't imagine anything better."

"You said once that weddings are the ending, the happily ever after." He wiggled my ring finger. "This is the beginning of our happily ever after, the beginning of a new family, a new adventure."

Dipping his head, he smiled into my eyes, and captured my lips in the gentlest of kisses before wrapping his arms around my back and lifting me to his chest.

Turning back to the table, he teased, "For all you doubters, she said yes."

The next ten minutes passed in a blur of hugs and kisses, tears and congratulations. It wasn't until the evening wound down and I stood at the coat check that it all sank in.

It felt like a thousand suns had set since the last time we'd been there. So much had happened in such a short time, I was surprised to see the same coat check girl.

Hawk turned around to respond to Max as she grabbed our coats. Up close, she was not as young as I first thought.

She smiled at me and lifted her eyebrows in question, dipping her head toward Hawk.

In answer, I held up my ring finger and grinned.

Her answering smile lit up her entire face. "Nice," she drawled, then smiled saucily. "Was totes hoping you'd bag him."

Chapter 35 – Three Little Words

Tossing my purse on the table, I hung up my coat and held out my hand. "I want to see the rest of your list."

He raised his eyebrows as he shrugged off his coat. "Now?"

I shrugged, feigning a casualness I did not feel. "Yeah. I'd like to see it. Did you map out the whole year?"

He blushed. Blushed!

"Oh my gosh. You're shy about it!"

"I wouldn't say 'shy' exactly," he hedged. "I just don't want you to feel pressured."

I pointed to the pocket that held the paper. "And that might make me feel pressured?"

He shrugged, feigning a casualness I knew he did not feel. What a pair. "Hawkley, pretty please may I see your plan?"

"How about I take you to bed first? Remind you of my finer assets?"

He teased but his eyes betrayed more than a hint of vulnerability. Under all the pain and guilt and grief, he was the same sweet man I fell in love with. With a tendency to want to punish me in all the very best ways.

Stepping forward, I placed both of my palms on his chest and peered up into his face. "I need no reminders. I am yours. Wholly. Completely. Forever. Please, Hawkley. May I see the list?"

The wariness faded from his eyes, and he smiled into mine. "You're beautiful, do you know that?"

"So I've been told," I whispered teasingly, watching his eyes flash.

"Noelle," he warned.

"Please, Hawk. Let's sit down at the table with a cup of Peppermint tea and talk a bit. I need to connect with you before we go to bed."

Immediately, his entire demeanor changed. "Of course. Tea or wine cooler? If I remember correctly, and I remember everything, a wine cooler will get you into bed faster."

I laughed, thinking how horrified he would be when he realized he offered his pregnant fiancé, (FIANCE!), a drink. "How about both? We'll start with a tea and see if you still want to have a drink after our talk or if you want to head to bed."

"I'll want to head to bed," he assured me, his hand drifting down over my bum to give it a squeeze. "Go sit down. I'll make you a cup of tea."

While I waited, I assessed his home through new eyes. It would be easy to childproof. The bedrooms were all on the main floor and a heavy door barricaded the basement stairs. Three bedrooms were more than enough.

To start.

I laughed to myself. I don't even know how many children he wants. We never talked about that.

Friggity-frack.

I sat up straight in the chair. What if he doesn't want kids period? My palm went to my tiny bump, covering it protectively.

"You okay over there?" He walked toward me, a tray with my tea, his beer, and a wine cooler on it. "You look like you were getting into an argument. I'm hoping it wasn't with me." His eyes dropped to my hand. "Is your tummy sore? Is that why you wanted peppermint tea?"

"No, no," I waved away his concerns. "I'm good." I reached for the tea, my trembling hands betraying my nervousness.

"Hey," he called softly. "No need to be nervous." Reaching into his pocket, he took out the paper. "Here. You can see everything."

"Thank you," I whispered. Oh, boy. It was time. I dropped my eyes to the page in front of me.

He had drawn a line down the middle of the page and then sectioned it crosswise into six rows. Twelve squares all together, one for each month.

In January, he wrote:

Say goodbye to Hunter.

Make peace with the accident.

Propose to Noelle.

Move Noelle and Bruce into the cabin.

I looked up, my finger on the last item. "It's January 29th."

"I have two days. I want you here. I don't want to spend another night without you."

"Okay," I said.

"Okay?"

I smiled. "I can do that."

He relaxed back into his chair. "Go ahead and see the rest. That's the only part I was worried about."

Every single square had at least one item in it. Some were things he wanted to do with me, others had to do with planning for our future, still other things he wanted to plan with his family and mine.

"Are you flexible? Can I move things around?" This was how I would tell him.

"Of course. It's our plan. We do it together."

He scheduled a trip to his family's cottage up at Moose Lake in July. That would not do at all. I tapped it. "Why July?"

"Black flies aren't too active after June. I hate those nasty fuckers."

"Makes sense," I muttered. "How would you feel about going up there for Thanksgiving?"

"Put it in the October box as well." Rounding the table to the kitchen, he brought me back a pen. "Make whatever changes you want."

My heart skipped a beat. Maybe several. It was possible I was having a heart attack. I took a breath and pretended to think. Lowering my eyebrows, I scowled at him. "Don't look."

He immediately closed his eyes.

How smooth and peaceful his face was. I'd only ever seen him like that in sleep. Most times not even then.

His lips tipped up. "Are you writing or staring at me?"

"Staring at you," I admitted. "You're beautiful."

Without opening his eyes, he said, "Women are beautiful. You're beautiful. I'm a stud."

You have no idea. But you'll know in about a minute. "You are."

Beginning with July, I crossed out Moose Lake and moved it to October. Writing down the date of October 31st, I carefully wrote beside it, 'Baby's First Hallowe'en'. For December, I added 'Baby's First Christmas'. And in July, I simply wrote the date, July 27th, and drew a heart around it. After a moment, I went back up to April and wrote, 'Get Married'.

"Hurry up, beautiful girl or you're going to get punished."

"Will I?" I mused. I didn't think there would be any punishments in the near future. "Hm. We'll see." Placing the paper in front of him, I covered his hand with mine. "You can look."

His eyes went to July, and he pointed to the circled date. "You want to get married in July? Is that why you don't want to go to Moose Lake?"

"Keep looking, Hawk."

His eyes went back up to January and he skimmed through the months, stopping at April. His eyebrows shot up. "You want to get married in April? Isn't that too soon to pull it together?" He stopped abruptly. "What am I saying? April is fantastic. We can elope if we have to although I'd rather get married at the resort this time seeing as it's the way it always should have been."

My mind flashed back to the binder full of plans. "You didn't get married at the resort?"

He twisted his mouth to the side. "No. I couldn't do it in the end. We eloped."

"Why couldn't you do it?" My mind spun with plans. Harley and Lou and I were going to make it so beautiful!

"She complained incessantly and all I thought was that it should have been you." He shrugged. "Not very gentlemanly, I know, but I never claimed to be a gentleman. Speaking of which," he wagged his eyebrows, "can we go to bed now?"

I nodded toward the paper. "Just as soon as you see the rest of the changes."

He growled to himself and sat back in his chair, then regarded me with narrowed eyes as he drained his beer before picking up the paper. "I haven't seen your boobs in three weeks, Noelle. I really don't care what you add-"

He slapped the paper back down on the table. His eyes grew huge in his face as he struggled to take in what he read.

I reached for the pen and wrote under July 27th, 'Become a father.'

Finally, he raised his head to look at me, his eyes dropping to my hand that again rested protectively over my stomach. "Noelle…" His eyes skittered back and forth from my face to my hand to the note to the table and he leapt up. Snatching the wine cooler off the table, he informed me, "You can't have this!"

"I know. I wasn't going to drink it," I watched him carefully. He looked stunned.

Slowly he circled the table and dropped to his knee for the second time that night. "Noelle," he held his hands toward my stomach, "can I touch?"

"Of course." Yup. No punishment in my future.

Putting his other knee down, he edged closer and splayed his hands over my womb.

I placed my hands over his.

"You have the tiniest of bellies here," he whispered. "Our baby is growing in there." Realization hit him and he looked up at me. "July 27th. The baby is due July 27th."

I smiled. "Are you happy?"

"Happy?" He tilted his head to the side, a faraway look stealing into his eyes. His hands drifted around my hips, and he tugged me to the edge of the chair, bringing my chest flush with his. Touching his forehead gently to mine, he answered softly, "I am blessed."

He rolled his forehead gently against mine, touched my nose with his, and sighed. Standing up, he guided me to my feet before scooping me up like a bride.

"Eyes on me," he whispered.

Our eyes locked, and he gave me everything. All his joy, all his awe, all his gratitude.

"I am yours."

All of himself.

In our bedroom, he lay me down on our bed, stripped off my clothes, and lay his head over our baby.

"Hey, little guy. I'm your daddy." He stroked my stomach with his big hands. "You don't know this yet, but you have the best mommy in the world. She's beautiful. Kind. Smart. And so strong. She can do anything."

Tears sprang to my eyes. Happy ones.

Lifting his head, he pressed a kiss to my stomach, then slid up the bed to take my face in his hands. "I love you."

Dipping down, he pressed a kiss to my breast. "And I love you," he chuckled before moving to the other one. "And I love you, too."

"Oh my gosh. You talk to your little guy, now you're talking to my boobs?"

He raised an eyebrow. "Little? What did we talk about... oh, fuck... you're going to be a massive brat, aren't you?"

"I might," I teased.

Straddling my hips, he smiled into my eyes. "I'm a patient man, Noelle. I'll keep a running tally and dole out your punishments when you're not carrying our baby."

I smiled back. "I'm counting on it."

Laughing, he fused his mouth to mine and rolled to his back, taking me with him.

"Do you love me, Noelle?"

"Always have. Always will."

He gave me a gentle squeeze, content for the moment to hold us in his arms.

His sweet words repeated on a loop in my head.

I am blessed.

I am yours.

I love you.

Three little words.

A lifetime of afters.

Epilogue

April

The room measured barely larger than a walk-in closet. And with three of us in there, it felt a lot smaller.

"My sweet girl. You do me proud. You do your mother proud." With a final watery smile, Lou eased the door open and slipped through the narrow opening into the narthex.

My breath hitched.

Harley stepped in, ordering firmly, "Do not ruin your make-up." Grinning, she took hold of my hands. "You're my sister for real, now."

"Why do you think I'm marrying your stinky brother?" I teased.

"For all the good dicking-" She stopped abruptly and pressed her lips together. "Nope. Still can't joke about this."

Laughing like loons, we slung our arms around each other.

Then Harley went quiet, her arms tightening. "I love you, Noelle."

"I love you, too, Shrimpy."

She didn't let go.

"You okay?"

Patting my back, she cleared her throat. "Yup. I'm good." Stuttering, she added. "Just happy. To have my brother back."

I squeezed her tightly.

She drew in a deep breath and stepped back, her finger in my face. "We do not talk about this!"

I gave her big, innocent, eyes. "About what?"

"That's my girl." She winked then cocked her head as the music started. "There's my cue. See you on the flipside."

Leaving the door open for my dad, Harley began her journey down the aisle.

And then, it was finally my turn.

My dad stepped up and drew my fingers through the crook of his arm. "Are you ready, Christmas?"

I turned to my dad. "I was born ready."

He laughed. "You were. You were made for him. And he was made for you."

Remembering his earlier concerns, I asked, "Yeah?"

"Oh, yeah," he confirmed. His eyes glossed. "You know, you came home, and everything fell into place." He patted my hand at the crook of his elbow. "You love just like your mother."

I faltered. "I wish she was here."

He cleared his throat gruffly. "She is."

Patting my hand, he led me to the entrance of the sanctuary, where we turned to face my future.

Hawkley stood stock still, his heart flayed open. With his eyes locked onto mine, a brilliant smile lit up his face. Hopping down from the altar, he jogged down the aisle.

I stared at him bemused, then began to laugh.

Taking my hand from my dad, he said, "Excuse me, Pat. I've been waiting for this for a long time, and I just couldn't wait a minute longer. I'll be quick."

Pulling me close, he splayed his big palm over my belly and kissed me breathless while our friends and family laughed and clapped behind him.

Leaning back, he beamed at me and squeezed my hands in his before releasing me back to my dad.

Shaking his head, he walked backward and framed me with his fingers. "You look great. Just … great." Holding his hand in a stop sign, he winked at me. "Give me a few seconds to get back up there. I want the whole experience!"

Laughter and more than a few starry-eyed tears followed him as he jogged back up the aisle.

Dan held his hand out for a high five as Hawkley passed, and Max caught him up in a joyful hug when he hit the altar.

Harley clutched her bouquet and beamed at me from her place opposite Max.

My dad shook with laughter. "Nope. Not a doubt in the world, Christmas."

July

Hawkley looked wrecked.

The past few months were a whirlwind of activity.

True to his word, Hawk moved Bruce and me into his place in two days. Including picking up all the boxes my mother left for me from my dad's place. With my mother's dishes and all the tiny trinkets and notes she packed with them, I had a piece of her back. Sometimes things work out the way they should. Had I opened those boxes when she first passed... I shuddered to think what might have happened. I was not in a good place.

With my mother's things unpacked, Hawkley's house became mine as well. And I discovered another way I took after my mother. Gardening. Even when my belly stretched to the point I needed help getting back up, I loved to dig my hands into the earth and coax life and beauty from the dirt.

And as soon as I could, I planned to buy a gnome.

I laughed softly to myself.

"What are you laughing at, my beautiful girl?"

"You'd think you were the one who just pushed a ten-pound baby out your hoo-ha."

He winced at the thought and pulled his chair even closer to my bed. "You were amazing," he praised as he peered into the tiny face that captured our hearts not twenty minutes before.

They say not to have a baby shower too close to your due date as the excitement might induce labor.

Harley pish-poshed the whole idea as nothing but an old wives' tale. "How could we have it any earlier? We had a wedding to plan, and you just got back from your honeymoon at the end of May." She shrugged. "Perfection takes time, and my little niece or nephew deserves perfection."

"You better hope it doesn't induce her labor, Harley," Lou warned with a chuckle. "Hawkley will have your head."

Harley guffawed. "Speaking of heads, for Noelle's sake I hope it does induce labor. She's only got two weeks to go, and Bennett babies are known for their giant craniums."

Lou snorted with suppressed laughter and swatted at her daughter. "Don't say that to her!"

"I hardly think it matters at this point, Lou. Baby is coming out in two weeks no matter how big its head is," I commented drily.

Harley put a commiserating hand on my shoulder. "Your hoo-ha will never be the same."

Those old wives? They knew what they were talking about.

The pain began in the middle of the night.

"Hawk?" I stroked his shoulder, my fingers lightly caressing the dips and swells of the muscle.

His face was smooth and unlined in sleep.

Friggity-frack, he's beautiful.

I smoothed my thumb over his forehead down to his temple. How many nights had I done this? Still suffused with wonder that he was mine to touch. Mine to ease. Mine to comfort.

Mine to love.

I stroked across his forehead.

Was his head big? It was proportionate to the rest of his body. Harley's head was proportionate. So was Hunter's. Dan's was big but the man was enormous. Lou's head was normal sized. Maybe the baby would take after my side. Or Lou's. At least if our baby came out with a big head, I had the assurance of knowing they'd grow into it.

I withdrew my hand. It was a shame to wake him. All my tossing and turning the past few nights had kept him up as well. Maybe I could go back to sleep for a couple of hours. First babies were notoriously slow in coming.

Hawkley's soft snores lulled me back to that soft place between sleep and wake then sent me drifting into a dream.

A table set up in my parents' backyard. My dad and Dan manning the grill. Lou and my mom laughing as they set bowls of potato chips and potato salad down on the table. Mom heading back into the house, her hand gentle on my head as she passed.

I watched ten-year-old me smile.

Max was young here, too. So was Hawkley.

Harley stood with her hands on her hips, yelling at them about something, but I knew she wasn't mad. She was a distraction.

Hunter snuck up behind them with the hose.

A memory encapsulated in a dream.

My laughter broke the spell and catapulted me back to my bed.

Hawkley let out an obnoxious snort.

And another pain, this one more serious, ripped across my womb.

What the hell was I thinking? I didn't know the first thing about having a baby. Especially not a big-headed Bennett.

"Hawkley," I said louder, shaking his shoulder.

"Yes, baby?" he mumbled. "You want water? More ice cream?"

My eyebrows lowered as I pressed my lips together. I hadn't eaten that much ice cream.

"It's time, baby."

"Again?" He chuckled as he rolled to his back and opened his arms. "Hop up, baby."

It was a tempting offer. Any other time I would have taken him up on it. But with my luck, his dick would drill a hole right through my cervix to our baby's head. Nobody wants to explain that kind of dent to their kid.

"Time to go have our baby."

He laughed sleepily. "Okay, baby." Two seconds passed. And then my words hit home.

His sleepy eyes wide, hair adorably rumpled, he sat up and demanded, "What? It's time? Shit!"

Rolling back to his side of the bed, his feet tangled in the blankets. He tumbled out and landed on his ass on the floor.

I snorted with laughter, falling back on the bed. Rolling to my side, I pointed at him as he struggled to disentangle himself. "Pussy phobia!"

His face broke out in a broad grin. "I'm tallying, sweetheart. You're racking up quite a debt."

Another pain gripped my womb. "Hawk," I choked out. The cramps were coming quickly. Too quickly. "Holy moly!" I gasped.

The blood drained from Hawkley's face.

"Don't you dare pass out!" I ordered, then laughed at the insulted look on his face. My entire stomach hurt. Half from laughing. "I have to pee. Bad. Help me get to the bathroom."

In the bathroom, I freshened up for the hospital.

Hawkley gathered my bags and our supplies, cursing his sister and her baby shower games that had even him splitting his guts laughing when he crashed with Max.

Just like the old days.

Several hard pains gripped me on the way to the hospital and it was only twelve minutes away. Within minutes, the nursing staff transferred me to a room.

Hawkley leaned over me in the bed, his eyes locked on mine as he coached me through the longest pain yet.

Friggity-frack that hurt! "Mothertrucker!"

286

"You can say the whole thing," he murmured, his hand smoothing my hair off my sweaty forehead. "I won't tell."

Grunting, I began to bear down as another pain, a different kind, picked up steam. "I don't want the first word baby Bennett hears from me to be motherfucker," I explained.

"The head is out, Noelle. Don't push."

I gasped. "Ears, too?"

The doctor chuckled. "Yup."

"Friggity-frack," I breathed. I said 'motherfucker' in front of my baby. I was off to a brilliant start.

Hands moved between my thighs, a gentle tugging. "Okay. Nice and easy, Noelle. You ready? With the next pain, I want a long, slow push."

Looking into Hawkley's wildly stormy eyes, I nodded and smiled.

Hawkley looked at me intently. "You can do anything, my strong, beautiful, girl."

A blur of activity, laughter, a wet, squirmy, lovely, perfectly round-headed baby on my naked torso. Hawkley with tears streaming down his face, his teeth a broad flash of white in his beard.

His lips on my forehead. One hand on top of my head, the other on our baby's rump.

I sighed.

It was fast but it was beautiful.

And so was my husband. No matter how tired he looked, he had the look of a man in love two times over as he gazed down at our baby.

He swung his gaze up to mine. His face utterly serious, he murmured, "Thank you, Noelle."

"For what, Hawk?"

"For love, baby. So much love. You've filled my entire life with it."

Leaning over, his lips touched mine reverently.

A soft knock at the door broke us apart.

"You've got visitors," the nurse announced with a smile. "Lots of them."

I grinned. "Send them in."

She shook her head. "Five minutes only, then it's only a few at a time."

The room filled. Harley rushed in first, her eyes darting between the three of us. Seeming to get what she needed, her shoulders relaxed and she grinned at me. "Good job, babe."

Max, right behind her shook his head and laughed when he caught me grinning at Harley.

Dad, Lou, and Dan entered more sedately. Smiles all around.

My dad headed straight for me. His hand trembling, he cupped my head and bent to press a kiss to my forehead. "You okay, Christmas?"

"I'm great, dad," I whispered back.

"You are." His glossy eyes crinkled back at me.

"Well?" Dan boomed. "Who have we got here?"

Hawkley stood and stepped closer to my bed, our baby tucked snugly into his elbow. He reached for my hand and gave it a gentle squeeze.

Another thank you.

"Guys, this is Hunter."

Lou gasped, her hand going up to cover her mouth.

"Is that okay, Lou?"

She nodded frantically, smiling behind her hand. "I just hope he's better behaved."

Laughter rang out.

Hawkley nestled Hunter closer to his chest. "So do I."

Lou laughed and stepped forward, the first to claim a cuddle.

Her first grandchild.

When feeding time came, they all filtered out, promising to give us a few days before they descended on us en masse again. And within hours, we were headed home.

"And then there were three, baby." Hawk grinned as he slowly and carefully turned out of the parking lot. "You feeling okay?"

"A little tender," I admitted.

"I'm going to make you an ice pack when we get home," he promised. "Do you want to sleep?"

I looked out the car window. For the first time in weeks, I could breathe easily. "I could sleep," I agreed. "But, you know what I really want? I want to sit with Hunter in my garden. You think that would be okay?"

"We can do that," Hawkley promised. "I have the net to protect him from bugs and I'll put up the UV umbrella."

"You'll bring me an iced tea, too?" I cajoled.

Reaching over, he squeezed my thigh. "I'll bring you anything and everything you want."

Pulling up as close to the door as he could, Hawkley hooked Hunter's car seat over his arm and led me into the house. "Let me get everything ready outside for you first and then I'll come in and get you."

Two minutes later, he returned, his eyes wide. "Noelle? Come with me, baby."

"What is it?" I whispered, alarmed.

He held up his hands. "It's not bad." Bending over, he scooped Hunter's seat back onto his arm and took me by the hand.

Rounding the corner of the house, I scanned the backyard for whatever caused Hawkley's reaction as he led me forward.

Seeing nothing, I turned to my husband. "What is it?"

He stopped and placed Hunter's car seat down on the grass beside my garden. Drawing me close to his side, he nodded to my garden.

The first thing I saw was a garden stone made up of broken, brightly colored pieces. Written across it in wildly looping script, the words, 'The story isn't over yet'.

"It's beautiful! My mother used to say that to us all the time! Who do you think made it?"

Hawkley swallowed. "I'm guessing the same person who brought these little guys."

I gasped as I followed the line of Hawkley's finger and landed on the first of my mother's gnomes. "Hawk," I breathed in wonder. "Are these my mom's? Did you do this?"

"Yes. I believe they are your mom's. And no, I did not."

"Then, who?"

Kneeling on the grass, I pressed my hands onto the steppingstone. "These are the ones I broke." Tears rolled down my face. "Hawk, can you believe it?" I laughed as I found each of my mother's tiny gnomes. "Can you believe it?"

Leaning down, Hawk extended his hands and helped me stand, then pulled my back against his wide chest. Looping his arms loosely around my waist, he dropped a kiss to my neck. "Your chair is ready. I put an extra cushion on it. I'm going to go get your iced tea and the netting to cover Hunter."

Overwhelmed by gratitude, I sat down gingerly and pulled my cell phone out of my pocket.

It rang through to the answering machine just as I suspected it would.

"Thank you for holding onto them for me until I was ready. I love you."

The End

If you enjoyed *A Lifetime of Afters*, please consider leaving a review.

You can access Amazon here:

Turn the page for a sneak peak...

Thank you!

Thank you for reading A Lifetime of Afters. A Lifetime of Afters is the first book in the Sage Ridge Series, a spin-off from the Bridgewater Series. You can read all about the Bridgewater gang starting with Live Again.

Keep reading for a heartbreaking excerpt from Rebecca and Rhys' steamy and unforgettable second chance romance, Live Agai

Live Again –

Chapter One – Gilligan's Island

I studied myself in the mirror by the front door, trying to see myself as a stranger would. I'd changed a lot in the past seven years and not much of that time had I spent worrying overmuch about my appearance. I could kind of see how I looked before as a superimposed transparency over the mirror image of my present self.

My body, at forty-two, had not changed a great deal since I'd never had children and I'd been blessed with a decent metabolism. Still had a little extra on the thighs, a little less boobage in comparison, but all in all, I was well-proportioned.

Petite, but tall on the inside, somehow that got conveyed by my attitude...or so I'd been told. My straight black hair that once fell past my bra strap was now liberally highlighted with silver, mostly around my face, and cut short in a sleek, graduated bob.

I was still pretty, my face mostly unlined, but thank God, I had laugh lines to show for my years. My eyes were wide set and slightly tilted. They had been described as watercolor blue. I could see it. They looked as if blue watercolor paint spilled out from the pupil to paint the iris, and then another spill that didn't spread as deep, delineated by an almost white-blue wave, was marked by white-blue striations that burst from the pupil. I had a straight nose, small mouth, my upper lip, a small bow in my round face, and I had great cheekbones. My makeup was beautiful.

Still.

There seemed to be something missing in my face.

Flicking on my playlist it jumped to Chasing Cars by Snow Patrol, and I was tumbled back in time to a thousand and one memories of Jack. Larger than life, perpetually smiling, sexy as hell, love of my life, Jack. Ironic that one of the most romantic people, male or female, I'd ever met in my life, picked me up at Walmart.

It was after work, the Friday of the Labour Day weekend. I was grumpy. And hungry. And tired. With a weekend of dead air before me, I figured I'd get myself something to binge watch and headed to Walmart to check out their selection of old tv shows to make me laugh. I was endeavoring to make this all-important choice for my weekend entertainment when a man came up behind me.

"You like old tv shows?"

His voice, deep and mellow, came from over my right shoulder. I remained facing the wall of DVDs in the vintage tv section.

"Yup."

I didn't even turn my head. I was not in the mood. I'd just broken up with the second biggest dick I'd ever dated, and

I had decided to treat myself to the whole series of Gilligan's Island available on DVD. In some warped way I guess it made sense to round out a less than perfect summer by having to fend off some pickup artist at Walmart, with its seriously unromantic fluorescent lighting, piped in radio music, and blaring announcements voiced by a psychotically enthusiastic Walmart employee.

"I Dream of Jeannie or Bewitched?"

"Bewitched." I sighed, internally, I hoped.

My feet hurt. It was the end of the day, at the end of the week, at the end of summer, marked by the end of another failed relationship. I just wanted to go home to start my weekend and I did not want that start to include expending the energy to give this guy the brush off. I couldn't even rouse the charitable thought that at least he was giving me a compliment.

"Dick Van Dyck or Gilligan's Island?"

"Gilligan of course," I snappily replied. This guy could not take a hint.

"The Munsters or The Addams Family?"

"I'm definitely more Morticia than Lily."

He could take that how he pleased. He knew his shows at least and it wasn't just some lousy pickup line.

"The Flintstone's or The Jetson's?"

His voice held amusement now. I liked it that he remained unoffended by my failure to fall all over myself just because he noticed me.

"The Jetson's if I'm feeling sassy, otherwise the Flintstones."

I was starting to feel a bit sassy in fact. He had a nice voice. Even I could hear the smile in mine when I answered that time.

He chuckled. Nice voice and a great laugh that rumbled up from his chest.

"What about Leave it to Beaver?"

"No thank you," I clipped. "Wouldn't want to be a Cleaver."

At this he laughed outright. "You'd never want to be a Cleaver?"

I turned, chin tilted up. At five feet two inches there were not a lot of people I didn't have to look up to, but once turned to face him I found I had to look up and up and up. He was easily an entire foot taller than me.

My 'seeyalater' died in my throat. Long and lean, eyes lit with mischief and pleasure, he stood slightly slouched with his hands loosely tucked into his pants pockets, holding his suit jacket open.

It looked like he, too, was on his way home from work. Nice suit, tie loosened, short dark hair slightly mussed in the minute way that short hair can be, well defined lips tilting upwards at the corners, head tilted down towards me, and eyes so dark I could barely make out the pupil smiled down at me.

"Hello." He shifted his weight and stuck out his hand. "I'm Jack Cleaver."

"You are not." I did not shake his hand but instead crossed my arms over my chest and tilted my chin down, looking at him from under my brow.

"I am!" He laughed and withdrew his hand. He pulled out his wallet and handed me a business card.

At this proof that he was indeed a Cleaver, I laughed, too.

"I thought you were trying to pick me up with a lousy pickup line about old tv shows!"

"I am trying to pick you up with a lousy pickup line about old tv shows but I'm no longer sure it's worth it." He smiled.

"Oh? And why is that?" I challenged him, smiling. His words were dismissive, but his tone was friendly and amused.

"Well, if you've already decided you'd never want to be a Cleaver, I'm not sure I see the point in getting to know you."

"We're talking about marriage already? You move fast."

He grinned, and I was caught. "How about we start with a coffee."

I purchased my DVDs, we went out for coffee, and went on to spend every spare minute over the September Labour Day weekend watching Gilligan's Island. He didn't kiss me until Sunday night. Three weeks after our first kiss, on my birthday, he moved me into his place. Three months after our first kiss we were engaged, and a mere six weeks after that, we married.

Ten years after our first kiss, almost to the day, he left me.

The world belonged to us. He was my sunshine and I, every star in his sky. We were going to set this life on fire. *We* were on fire. Excited about our careers, full of plans for the future, so much hope, caught up in our love for each other and the dreams we were sure we would bring to life. And we had. We shone for ten perfect years, ten perfect years that came to a screeching halt seven years ago.

It hit me then what was wrong with my face.

It was my eyes.

They held no fire.

Chapter 2 – Whack-A-Mole

It was becoming apparent to me, for reasons unknown, that I was living more and more in the past, bombarded by painful memories over the past several weeks like I hadn't been since that first awful year. I thought I had been making progress, waking up and looking around a bit, seeing how everyone else had grown and changed.

My best friend, Mara, was probably over-stretched. Mara was writing full time, homeschooling full time, and raising her daughter Olivia, you guessed it, full time. Olivia turned eleven, already on the cusp of being a teen, God help us. Mara's younger sister, Willa, who became a close friend over the last few years, successfully ran her own graphic design business.

I opened my online business the same year Jack passed, but I'd generated little else new since. I had the same clients and produced much of the same designs. There was nowhere and nothing from which to draw inspiration because my ass had glued itself to my couch.

So, I took a look around and for the first time in a long while I actually saw, and understood, how stagnant I'd become. I resolved to make some changes, but my mind kept pulling me back into the past. Triggered by smells, triggered by weather, triggered by music, just frankly triggered.

On my way home from Mara's yesterday, I got stuck following a funeral procession. Time slipped away and it was late summer seven years ago. I could smell the barbeque in the air, hear the children squeal as they ran through sprinklers, feel the sun beating unrepentantly through the window of the limo that headed a long line of the same, a graceless black shadow slithering along the streets taking me to bury my husband.

The funeral home had been an absolute nightmare.

"Thank you, thank you for coming." *God, how many times am I going to have to say this.*

"He was a good man. He'll be missed."

"Yes." *Fuck you.*

"Anything you need, let us know."

"Thank you." *I need my fucking husband. Can you help me with that?*

"Bex." Mara slid up quietly behind me. "You going to blow?"

"Yup."

"Come, get some air."

We stepped outside the back door of the funeral home. The absence of all their fucking voices, murmuring bitter nothings, offered a welcome respite. My senses were overwhelmed: too much noise, too much sound, too much bright.

So much empty.

Today should have at least been grey, as the world should be without him, as I was without him.

"I love you, Bex." Mara hooked my pinky with hers.

Her touch, the glue to my grieving, fragmented self.

Her little finger, my tether to the world.

One I was pretty sure I wanted no part of.

I didn't know how to do life without him. It wasn't like we were joined at the hip, and certainly I didn't see myself as dependent on him as Mara was with Zale, no judgment, just her nature.

Jack was simply a huge presence, bursting with energy, honestly, he was the sun. His absence left a massive crater in my life. While we spent almost every available free minute together, we had separate lives as well.

Career-wise we had our own gigs going on and we were both busy. I worked for an older, successful jeweler who had his own business in town for years. He was looking to retire soon, which meant I worked more and more, slowly taking over his customers. I'd also been researching the merits of opening up my own online store. My work studio at home saw a lot of me in the evenings, which created no friction because Jack worked long hours as well. I worked when he did, as best I could, so I'd be free when he was.

Being in real estate, and damn successful at it, he worked odd hours and all hours. In the Spring and late summer, the hours were seemingly endless, and this past summer did not break the trend. However, he could not keep up as well as before. His energy flagged, he struggled to get his workouts in and couldn't keep his energy up. We were walking and spending time outside whenever we could, and he slept more, but he could not shake the fatigue. His appetite dipped, he developed pain in his abdomen, and he started losing weight. We were worried about an ulcer. That was also the doctor's initial thought.

We were wrong.

"You ready, baby?"

"Bex, you don't need to come with. I'm good honey."

Jack looked concerned. He never liked to worry me. Thankfully, he preferred me sassy and busting his balls. Lately, I couldn't help but hover over him a bit, and I laughed when he frowned and told me not to worry.

"I'm coming."

"You don't need..."

"I'm coming, babe," I cut him off, "Whatever it is, we'll deal together. And we'll start now."

He locked the house behind us and folded his long, lean body into the driver's seat. I climbed in on my side, not nearly so elegantly. My shorter stature did not allow for graceful folding into any seat.

The summer sun hit the windscreen, and we opted for windows rolled down. Between the many cold months and working inside, we got more than our share of recycled air.

It was a good drive. The air smelled sweet and warm, Daughtry on the radio telling us it's not over, good beats, my baby beside me, my hand tucked under his against his long, hard thigh, plans for dinner later with my best girl, Mara, and her husband, Zale, and Jack's busy season was finally coming to an end.

"What do you think about going to New York in a few weeks?" he asked.

We preferred to take holidays in the fall. That time of year was still warm enough to walk around comfortably, but cool enough to get dressed up in the evenings without the added accessory of pit stains.

Jack loved cities. Every year he'd pick a new one for us to explore. We'd done Paris, Athens, Fort Worth, Fort Lauderdale, Portland, Washington, and Miami. Living only an hour outside of Toronto, we spent many Saturdays exploring our city, too. He wanted New York, next, and I never cared where we went so long as we went together, so New York it would be.

I had no premonition while waiting for the doctor in the exam room. In fact, I refused to think anything could seriously be wrong, and when those thoughts popped up, I bashed them down like whack-a-mole.

We heard a brief knock and the door opened.

"Ah, good, glad you brought your wife with you."

"Hey, Dr. Sanders."

"Rebecca." He smiled faintly taking his seat. Something in his manner alarmed me and I began to feel faint. My face suffused with heat, and I heard the roar of my blood pumping in my ears.

He did not delay.

"Folks, it's not good."

He met Jack's eyes, those black eyes that never failed to smile at me, and Jack nodded for him to continue.

"It's cancer, it's aggressive, it's stage 4." He paused and his eyes flicked down to the floor before he again met Jack's eyes. "I'm so sorry. It's untreatable."

Jack swallowed hard, closed his beautiful black eyes, and nodded.

The world stopped.

I sat frozen, staring at the floor. I don't know how I got into position to be facing the floor. I heard this awful keening sound but couldn't figure out where it was coming from. I felt Jack's hands on my back, turning me, gathering me close to his chest. I tried to speak and realized the terrible moaning came from me.

"Oh God... oh God... oh God, no. Please, no..." My voice, stripped raw, abraded my ears. My hands clutched at Jack's shirt, and my fingers dug into his shoulders.

"Baby, baby, baby.... Bex.... Calm, baby..." Jack's deep voice whispered in my ear.

I gulped hard and arched my neck back trying to swallow some air. My tears streamed down my face, down my throat.

His face hit my neck, and his tears mingled with mine.

We went to New York.

Two and a half months later he slipped away even as I held him.

Which brought me to this fresh hell, trapped in a small room with recycled air that was recycling enough pity to choke me.

He was popular. People wanted to pay their respects. I understood this and part of me agreed he deserved it.

However, most of my spirit was in denial. This whole production, which suggested I could actually say goodbye to Jack-Jack, forced me to acknowledge that I'd have to go home and sleep without him a-fucking-gain and that I'd only ever see his sweet smile in photographs.

Adding to my disbelief were the people, so many people I didn't even know, who stood as witnesses to the combustion of all that was us, and they acted like the world would roll on. They stood around chatting and drinking fucking coffee and eating cheesecake of all things.

The contrast between how I was feeling and how I was expected to behave created a sort of cognitive dissonance that was rapidly deteriorating into the kind of pissed off that would have me saying all kinds of things that I'd later regret.

Maybe.

If I ever found it within myself to care about anything again.

Mara could see this. Mara with her soft touch, and her all-seeing heart. Mara whose little finger grounded me. Mara who fed me, and Jack when he was able to eat, for the past month. Mara, whose heart was also broken, my Mara who put others first always. My Mara, whose sensitivity made her at once so damn fragile yet so damn strong.

Mara drove me home in my car that day. Zale followed us in theirs. We pulled into the driveway of my sprawling white clapboard home. I wanted nothing more than to throw myself inside its welcoming walls and try to comprehend how it was possible I'd just laid Jack's beautiful body in the ground.

I convinced Mara that I needed to be alone, went inside, hung my purse on a hook, jacked up the A/C, grabbed Jack's t-shirt quilt off the ladder, curled up on what was now only my couch, pressed my face deep into the cushions and screamed myself to sleep.

Almost seven years later, and other than the fact that I slept in my new bed, I hadn't moved too far from that couch.

Acknowledgements

Oh, my gosh. Where to start!!!

This book was a joy to write from start to finish thanks to my ARC team. From the beginning, I wanted this experience to be different. Not just for me, but for my ARC readers as well.

Through much laughter, we brainstormed place names, people names, cat names, and even wardrobe! When I couldn't decide, my fearless PA, Crystal, set up a poll. Which was the equivalent of setting my soul on fire while I waited for the results.

I do not like waiting! Haha.

First of all, I need to thank Crystal Kaiser @crystals_book_blab. She is the best cheerleader a woman could ask for. She keeps me organized. And when my family went through a difficult time, she carried my social media.

Crystal, you are a blessing and a dear friend.

Sionna Trenz @sionnatrenzauthor and Rachel Childers @bookaddictblog, beta readers extraordinaire. Thank you for combing through my work. It's a tough job, but somebody must do it, and I'm so glad I have you.

Sionna, you have been a constant in this crazy book world. This year is the year we meet in person! Maybe you can make your way to Niagara Falls! Hope you like hugging because you're getting a big one.

Rachel. Where to begin. Your words bolster me. There's no other way to put it. I'm not sure if I'd be where I am if not for your words running through my head. Thank you.

Now for my ARC team who made writing this book so much fun. Thank you to everyone who brainstormed and participated in the polls! Specifically, I need to give credit to the geniuses who came up with the winning ideas or allowed me to bring them into the pages of the book.

April @aprilsbooknook_ was the first to step onto the page. She befriended Noelle when she lived in Bridgewater, and it was her words of wisdom that eventually led Noelle onto the path she needed to travel. Go Pokemon!

Amanda Glaeser, @the_retro_reader, aka swamp witch, aka sassy pants, came up with both names, Hawkley and Noelle, for the MCs. There were a few other good ones, but the team voted, and Hawkley and Noelle won. I love the names.

Bianca Duthie @bianca_reads_books, lobbied hard for Noelle's cat to be named Bruce, and she got it. How could I say no? I did give him a last name though. A tough guy like that needs a tough name.

Ayana Guerra @ayana.guerra_booklovers, volunteered her name for whatever I wanted. I immediately pictured a sign for a fancy restaurant. Ayana's was born. Ayana, herself, may make an appearance here and there!

Crystal Kaiser @crystals_book_blab gave up her name for the beach. She may have insisted on it but who's to say?

Shannon Hawkins @shannstar79, brainstormer extraordinaire, came up with Sage Ridge, Wildflower Bluff, and Novel-Tea.

I have Keza @keza.campbell to thank for Silver Lake and Hope Harbor. Love those names.

Jen 'Take that Woman's Camera Away' Theriault convinced me to adopt Little River. @jen_ner_reads.

Ashamed to admit my daughter came up with Hard Rod Café, but you have to admit, it's genius. Hello, apple, this is tree.

Andrea @books_fiction_desire graciously loaned me the real name for her cake shop, Cake Me Away. @cakemeawaybydrea. If you haven't checked out her site, do it now! The woman is an artist!

Thank you to Susanne Cloen, @susieq_reviews, for lending me her IG name for the diner. And of course, what would Susie Q's be without a Susie? Hope you love her alter ego!

Ashley @spinesbinds, you picked a killer dress for Noelle! (It was my favourite.)

Rachel @bookaddictblog stepped in to run Artitude, the artist co-op, and also came up with the name! Even her husband, Pete, made it in as her beleaguered assistant!

Anita @anita_thebookaddict suggested her mom's nickname, Mary Lou, and that became an old-fashioned candy store. Guess who the proprietor is?

Devin Sloane

Michelle Duncan @spilltheteawmichelle inspired the saucy bookclub, Spill the Tea. We'll be seeing more of Michelle and might even catch a glimpse of her firefighting hubby in book two! The crazy thing is that Michelle's hubba-hubba in real life is a volunteer firefighter! Who knew I was psychic? Not me! Also --- no perving over Michelle's husband. The man is taken.

Krippy's nickname inspired Krippy's Chippy, the fish and chip shop on the beach, and she was gracious enough to let me use it. Stuck her sister, aka partner in crime, in there with her to keep her company. @krippy.reads.books

I must mention a few others who have been with me from the beginning, some doing double duty on both ARC and Street teams. And huge thanks to those on both teams who have jumped in to help with the dreaded TT. I'm so very grateful for Madeeha Idrees @bibliophilewritrix, Terri @tlcbooktalk, Cali Mafiaa @blessedmommy_booklover, CK @mto32, Tina Alicea @tina_alicea69, Marla @marla_0519, Samina @krazyreader, and Cheryl @the_great_book_escape. You guys are solid gold.

Last, and most of all, I want to thank my research assistant. Love you always, mine Boo.

Also by Devin Sloane

Find me here:
https://linktr.ee/devinsloane

The Bridgewater Novels
Live Again

Breathe Again

Feel Again

The Milltown Novels
Broken Road

Chosen Road

Mountain Road

Sage Ridge
A Lifetime of Afters

Mulberry Place
Sweet Everythings

About the Author

As a reader and a storyteller, I am irresistibly drawn to more mature characters. Though they often carry the fears, insecurities, and traumas from their younger years, they tend to do so with humor and panache!

They bumble along until life forces them to deal with their brokenness in the midst of parenting, building a career, looking after aging parents, and starting or mending a romantic relationship.

Here is where I love to write my stories.

Stories where physical intimacy reflects emotional intimacy and healing. Stories of sisterhood that celebrate family and chosen family. Soul-stirring stories that take you on an emotional journey, one where you might easily recognize yourself or someone you love.

As in the real world, there are no easy answers. But their hard-won HEAs will make your heart happy.

At home, I am outnumbered by one husband, four kids, a dog, a cat, and plumbing issues that never quit. You can most often find me curled up on my front porch, earbuds in, music cranked up, with my nose stuck in a book.

Honestly, I'm most often hiding from my favorite people in the world who require far too many meals. When I'm really lucky, my husband, who is without a doubt the hero in my very own love story, is hiding with me.

Milton Keynes UK
Ingram Content Group UK Ltd.
UKHW042304180823
427026UK00018B/11